A BINDING CHANCE

MESSY BOOKSHOP MYSTERIES

BOOK ONE

JESSICA BRIMER

Published 2022 by Next Chapter

Edited by Megan Gaudino

Cover art by CoverMint

For my wonderful husband, Josh Brimer. Your support means more to me than being published and drinking coffee.

Acknowledgments

I have so many people I want to thank. First, my first writers' group, Deadline for Writers. Without them, especially Becky Crookham, critiquing my short stories, I know my writing journey would not have gotten this far. Cheryl Gilmore for understanding the struggles of a writer and being my friend. Ellie Alexander, you helped improve my manuscript and showed me what it means to be a cozy writer. Thank you Megan Gaudino for editing my story. You made it so much better. And a tremendous shout out to my husband. You read almost everything I'd written. You corrected my simple mistakes and then some. I appreciated your honesty because sometimes my ideas sounded better in my head than what I wrote. Another thanks to my two amazing kids. They remind me that I need breaks and it's fun. Lastly, thank you Next Chapter for taking a chance on me.

CHAPTER 1

JANE JACKSON, MY NEW BOSS, STOOD BEFORE ME. THE MOMENT SHE walked through Teresa's Bookstore, I knew Jane would be trouble. She wore a gray suit that was too hot for a Tennessee summer with a white shirt, snuggled tight against her neckline. Jane's brown hair wrapped into a tight bun, which made me wonder if it gave her headaches. Those high stilettos were a better match for women who sat in office chairs all day and attended swanky lunches, rather than spending a day opening heavy boxes or restocking bookshelves. My new boss looked as if she stepped out of Vogue magazine.

"Fired?" I asked.

"Fired is a strong word. But yes, Garnet," Jane said, nonchalantly. "After today, my aunt's bookstore will be permanently closed." Her bland brown eyes studied the sales floor. I knew Jane noticed the tower of books that needed a home on the shelf rather than being pushed against the wall to be dealt with later. The longer she absorbed the store's clutter, the worse her grimace became.

I wanted to say something. Anything to change her mind but, the shock of the store closing took my voice.

Finally, she turned her attention to me. "As I said in my email, I'll pay you for the work you've done." Jane paused, reading my face. "It's just a used bookshop. Nothing personal."

"Nothing personal?" I snapped. "The bookstore means everything to me. I've worked here for nine years and ran the store on my own for an entire month."

Jane gave me a blank stare. It felt like she was the school's principal listening to a trivial complaint from a student. While Jane believed closing the bookstore was strictly business, my heart shattered. Teresa's Bookstore was my life and passion.

My career.

Princess, a black and white cat who lives here, jumped onto the counter next to the boxy computer the store used as the register. Jane stepped back as if the tuxedo feline was a ferocious panther. Princess sat up straight, waiting to be acknowledged.

Jane gasped. "I didn't know Aunt Teresa kept animals inside her store."

I stroked Princess from her head to her back. She turned to me, purring. I admired the dotted black line along Princess's neckline, which entitled her to a name-bearing royalty.

How dare Jane call Princess a mere animal. Your Grace would have been more fitting.

"Your aunt loved cats." I debated if I should warn her about the other cat, Butterscotch, but quickly dismissed the thought. Jane would find out soon enough.

Jane sneered at Princess and turned her attention to her surroundings. "This place is a mess. You should have cleaned it before I arrived."

Stacks of books for online orders filled one side of the L-shaped counter while others were being held for customers.

Plastic bags remained inside a cardboard box rather than being hung on a hook near the register. Bookmarks rested in a large coffee mug free to anyone who wanted one. Thankfully, Jane couldn't see the mess in the cubbies under the counter. With one foot, I pushed the Windex and paper towels deeper inside the space. They didn't move far.

From the large bay window, the morning light peaked between the four rows of bookshelves. The smallest of the four at shoulder height held notebooks donated and were free to anyone. Most of the papers had been torn out, but locals knew Teresa was not one who threw things away because some, or half, of the pages were missing. They were perfect treasures for children who loved to doodle. The other three bookshelves were filled with fiction books from various authors that had been published in the last five years or maintained popularity. If I had the time and an extra set of hands, I would have reorganized novels by genre.

Boxes filled with extra copies that were already on the shelves, towered at the end of each row. I wanted to put them upstairs, but never got around to it since there were bigger things that needed done before Jane's arrival. The room to my right housed romance and horror books. Occasionally customers put an unwanted book in the wrong place, an ongoing battle that I refused to surrender. While in general fiction, the books were often crammed in sections. The novels needed to be spaced out better and alphabetized. Once I recycle the half-filled notebooks, I would have the space.

I cringed when Jane looked up. The globe string lights cast a magical glow even though some of the bulbs had burnt out. Time got away from me, and I hadn't had a chance to replace them, or better yet, asked someone who was over five-two to help me.

One employee could only do so much.

Jane failed to see what I had accomplished. Other than run the business, I donated children's books to churches and libraries, I operated a weekend-long sidewalk sale, which was a huge success, and I once stayed after hours, moving the ladder around the store with a Swiffer duster. Mentally, I patted myself on my back for all my hard work.

I probably needed to warn Jane about upstairs. If she thought the bookstore was in dire need of TLC, just wait until she saw the office. Teresa was known for many things, but tidiness wasn't one of them.

As I watched Jane brush cat hair away, I wished she had seen the place before I cleaned. If she had, then she would've appreciated the countless hours I had spent trying to get the bookshop in order. After stocking, re-organizing books, ringing up customers, answering the phone, office work, and tending to two cats, some days I didn't have the energy to do anything else.

"What are these spots on the carpet?" Jane glared at the green floor. She stepped away from the spot as if the stains were creeping up her legs to swallow her whole.

I meant to toss a rug over the stains but forgot to drag it out of my trunk this morning. "Coffee."

"Teresa served coffee here?" Jane's voice went up an octave as her eyes landed on Princess.

Princess purred louder. I gave her a good head rub.

"Only once." I recalled the memory. A curious cat didn't mesh well with hot beverages. Teresa set up a coffee station on a cold January morning, telling me. "This is going to be great. I've been wanting to do this for a long time." Unfortunately, when the first customer poured himself a cup, Princess jumped up and scared him half to death. Twelve cups of hot liquid dumped onto the floor. No matter how many times we shampooed the carpet, the stain refused to leave. Some days Teresa joked about changing Princess' name to Nosy-Rosy.

Jane collected herself by placing one hand near her neckline while the other wrapped around her waist. "This place is a pigpen. How did Aunt Teresa let it get so bad?" Her question sounded rhetorical. As Teresa's only niece, Jane must have witnessed her aunt's disorganized behavior.

"The pig is upstairs," I said, sarcastically. Jane's eyebrows shot up.

I kept petting Princess, enjoying her expression. It was the least I could do since all of my hard work resulted in being fired.

"There's an actual pig here?"

I debated for a moment before telling Jane no. By the look on her face, Jane didn't appreciate my humor.

Before anything else was said, the cowbells tied to the door handle clanged. Princess jumped from the counter to greet our first customer. I put on my best smile, hoping Jane would notice my work ethic and that Teresa's Bookstore was busy enough to stay open. At this moment, I knew I had to convince Jane to keep the store.

No better way than with a customer.

Jane called out, "Today is an extra thirty percent off."

My happy face fell at the sight of Sasha Whitlock. Instead of her usual bed hair, Sasha's blond locks were wavy. She wore a video game shirt that I knew she often slept in. At least her jeans didn't have any holes or rips, and her tennis shoes were spotless.

"Are you Teresa's niece? Jane Jackson?" Sasha asked after patting Princess's head. Jane nodded and started to answer when Sasha cut her off. "Actually, I'm here to get my job back. There was a misunderstanding and I want to redeem myself." Sasha flashed a smile.

“Job back?” Jane glanced at me before looking back at a beaming Sasha.

Silly Sasha, I thought. That cheesy smile never worked on Teresa. Or me.

“The store is closing permanently,” Jane said as a matter of fact.

Sasha's face fell “Oh. Why?”

“Actually,” I said before Jane had the chance to speak, “we haven’t confirmed that the store is closing. Jane hasn’t met—” I cursed myself for not thinking things through and said the first name that came to mind. “Peggy Sue. Jane hasn’t met her yet.”

“The mutt that kids read to on Saturdays?” Sasha sounded confused.

Perhaps I should have chosen a regular customer who spends money rather than Willie who brings his dog so children can practice their reading skills.

“Everyone loves Peggy Sue.” I turned to Jane, hoping the event impressed her.

Instead, my boss, or new owner, appeared as lost as Sasha, and not in an inspiring kind of way. She gathered herself. “I inherited the store after my aunt’s passing. I put a lot of thought into it and decided to close its doors.”

I needed to try harder, but I would wait until Sasha left. This was between Jane and me.

“That’s a shame.” Sasha shrugged. “Oh, well. It was worth a shot.”

I shook my head behind her back. Did she really expect to get her job with no effort? *Typical lazy-Sasha.*

Jane and I watched as Sasha headed for the front door. A short, dark-haired woman walked in front of the bay window. Inwardly I cringed. Why did Doris Hackett have to come today?

She had been here two days ago and bought three paperbacks. Had she read them already?

I trotted around the counter to whisper Jane a warning, but I was too late. She entered at the same time Sasha put her hand on the swinging door. The cowbells rang with instant tension. Doris narrowed her eyes as Sasha's body stiffened. Doris spoke first. "Here to beg for your job back?" she teased, half smiling.

"That's none of your business, along with everyone else in Sevier Oak." Sasha's temper took me by surprise. She had been snippy behind people's backs, but never to their face.

"Teresa fired you for a reason. Loafer. You played video games all day and was late for work too many times."

"Studies show that people who play video games are smarter than those who don't." Sasha's eyes shifted up and down.

Doris chuckled, but it sounded forced. "Did Google tell you that or a witch?"

"A Witcher," Sasha smarted back.

I wanted to bang my head against a bookshelf.

Doris looked puzzled. "A what?"

While Sasha described a character from a fantasy video game, Jane stepped forward. I shook my head, hoping she understood to not interfere. I'd learned it's best to let women, like Sasha and Doris, say what's on their minds. Once they have enough, they'll go about their day. Unfortunately, Jane didn't notice my hint.

"I believe Sasha is referring to the TV show with Henry Cavill," Jane said. "But, ladies—"

"The video game came out before it was a show," Sasha countered.

I rolled my eyes. As the real bookworm among this group, I decided to speak on behalf of the books. "Actually, it's a fantasy book series written by Andrzej Sapkowski."

The three of them faced me. Sasha sighed, annoyed. Doris snarled as if she smelled something bad while Jane gave me a hand signal to stop talking.

"Fun fact," I continued, "our cat here is really named Princess Ciri, after a character from the book." That was a lie. Princess was just plain Princess, but Teresa wasn't here to argue.

"What does that have to do with anything?" Sasha asked.

I suppressed another eye roll. Other than showing off my book knowledge and defending the Polish author, I suppose it meant nothing.

Jane repeated today's special, "The books are an extra thirty percent off."

Unlike Sasha, Doris looked like she might start crying. The day kept getting curiouser and curiouser.

"Looks like you're gonna have to spend your shiny pennies at the other bookstore in town." Sasha giggled.

I glared at my former co-worker. The last thing I wanted to hear about was our bookstore's rival.

Doris shared my passion. "Then you go there, loafer. Maybe Voss recycles trash."

"You're one to call, lazy." Sasha gave Doris a look that I couldn't understand. Something must have happened between them when Sasha was still working here. "One day somebody is going to hack you up with a jack of spades, and on that day, I'm going to laugh at it."

An expression crossed Doris's face. One that I had never seen in the years she shopped here. Fear. Jane looked as if she wanted to say something.

Time for me to step in.

"If you have something to say to each other, do it elsewhere. Not here." I used the authoritative tone that my family taught me.

Sasha parted her lips to say something, but then thought better of it and closed it. Doris went submissive.

Some days I loved my last name being Stone. "Well, make a choice."

Sasha shoved Doris aside, causing the forty-year-old woman to stumble back into the door. Doris opened her mouth. I expected a snarky comment from her, but nothing came out. She just watched as Sasha walked down the sidewalk.

They were acting strangely. From Sasha's laid-back nature to being snippy, and Doris's cold spirit going quiet. Today felt more like a Freaky Friday than a Monday. Something definitely had happened between the two of them.

"I don't need the discount, but I'll take it anyway." Doris made her way to the bargain room in the back as if nothing happened. Her reddening cheeks said otherwise.

Jane waited to speak until her footsteps faded deeper into the store. "Where's the office?"

The question brought me back to my troubles. Her tone reminded me why I disliked people who wore suits. All of them were money-hungry people, ignoring the feelings of others. I turned around and pointed to the romance/horror room. From our angle, we couldn't see the stairs leading up to the office. Without another word, Jane weaved around the bookshelves towards the main staircase. As Jane's heels clicked away, my shoulders dropped.

I looked around Teresa's Bookstore admiring it one last time. Some people, like Jane, saw clutter and piles of junk but I saw beauty and personality. Here, I could breathe in the heavy mustiness found by strolling through aisles of novels. This was a place where book lovers, like me, spent hours with their fingers, grazing against the spines as their shopping basket grew heavier.

Twenty years ago, Teresa Jackson opened the bookshop. She worked as hard as she read. All her "treasures" held a story. Teresa knew when and where she had bought each item and set them on top of the bookshelves as decoration. A handful of teacups sat along the top. She feared breaking them yet refused to give them away. Most of her treasures were miniature football helmets of the Tennessee Vols, one of the main colleges in the state. Peyton Manning signed one during his time at the University of Tennessee. I spotted it instantly because it was the only helmet in a plastic case. Teresa admired it so often that I think she had a secret crush on the former quarterback.

Teresa also had a sharp mind. She remembered all the books that came in and out of the store. If a customer asked for a certain title, Teresa would go right to its spot to retrieve it without checking the computer's database. Despite the clutter, Teresa knew her mess. After working here for six years, I did too.

We had plans to remodel the store, make the place bigger and less cluttered. Now, standing among the books, I felt alone as the cherished memories began fading away.

A cry interrupted the silence. I rolled my eyes hearing where it came from.

Upstairs. Jane must have found the second cat in the office. Or better yet, Butterscotch found Jane.

"Hey," Jane cried. "Garnet."

I rushed up the stairs knowing what had happened. Sure enough down the narrow hallway, Jane was pressed against the wall, staring into Teresa's office. I held back a laugh.

"Is something wrong?" I asked, coming up to her.

Jane glared daggers at me. "You failed to mention the owl."

I entered the office, laughing. Butterscotch sat on the desk with a grumpy face. Her bushy tail swooshed side to side. Her deep yellow eyes pierced into Jane.

I picked up the second cat. "Have you ever seen a four-legged owl?" I chuckled. "Her name is Butterscotch. Princess' sister."

Jane didn't move. "I thought it was a statue until I sat in the chair."

"Yeah, Butterscotch is good at sitting still and glaring." Probably her best trait. I couldn't count how many times Butterscotch had scared me when I sensed something watching me. I would turn around and find those big yellow eyes watching me from the top of the filing cabinet. From afar, Butterscotch could come across as an owl due to her brown patches of fur woven into the black.

"Butterscotch pretty much hates everyone," I added.

Once I set Butterscotch in another room upstairs, Jane towered over me, angrier than before. Perhaps I should have warned her about Butterscotch.

"It's messier up here," she complained, her arms slightly flailing.

"I didn't have time to clean up here. Teresa planned to remodel and was going to get rid of a lot of this stuff." Not for one second had I believed Teresa's words. The remodel would've only accumulated new stuff. Again, I didn't tell Jane that.

Jane took a moment to squeeze the bridge of her nose between her thumb and finger, before saying, "Where did Teresa keep the important stuff? Taxes? Rent?"

"The filing cabinet. It's in the office where Butterscotch sleeps." I said, then quickly scurried down the hallway toward the second set of stairs that led into the bargain room.

Doris walked down a narrow path behind a shelf. Not wanting to talk to her, I darted away. When I made it to the main area, it felt like fresh air. Princess laid on top of a bookshelf until she saw me and jumped down. She trotted up to me with a *please pet me* plea. I scooped her up in my arms. She nuzzled under my chin. Her fur smelled like books.

"What am I going to do?" I whispered. Princess meowed and headbutted me. *There must be a way to keep the store open.*

Then a second screech happened followed by something hitting the floor. I looked towards the bargain room. From here I couldn't see the entrance. What was Doris doing? Or did Butterscotch scare Boss-Lady again? *No,* I decided. The sound definitely came from the bargain room.

Just as I took a step in that direction, another crash reverberated through the store. I picked up my pace. I wondered if Doris was kicking the bookshelf? Princess leaped out of my arms, digging her back claws into me as she fled.

"Ouch," I cried. The kicking continued. "Doris?" I called out as I headed toward the back of the store. The sound grew louder. "Doris? What are you doing?"

"Garnet?" Jane's voice traveled down the staircase followed by the sound of her stomping feet. Or was someone else stomping?

I ignored her. When I entered the back, Jane crashed into me. We both fell on the floor. My head spun as more sounds echoed in my ears. I couldn't make out what was happening. Was someone screaming?

I tried to stand up, but Jane rolled over, pushing me down.

"Hey," I said to Jane. "Ouch. You're on me."

"You elbowed me," she cried as we squirmed out from each other's tangle.

"Why did you scream?" Jane demanded once we were free.

"It wasn't me," I said before wandering the aisles until I found Doris Hackett.

Jane trailed behind me, talking non-stop until she saw Doris too. We froze in place. Doris's eyes stared lifeless up at the ceiling. A small trail of blood flowed from her forehead.

Books from the bottom shelf scattered around her feet, along with a tea kettle.

I gasped in horror when I spotted a knife near Doris's hand and a small pillow with a gaping hole in the middle.

Jane whispered, "Is she dead?"

CHAPTER 2

I LEANED AGAINST THE BRICK BUILDING OF OLD TREASURES, WATCHING from under the awning's cover as I played with my necklace charm. A light wind and the shade helped cool me from the East Tennessee heat. Activity on Copper Street had come to a halt. Men and women in blue uniforms secured the scene with their vehicles and orange cones. Drivers diverted on side streets to avoid the blockage while store employees and familiar shoppers dotted the sidewalk, staring in disbelief.

Sevier Oak was a simple town tucked in a valley of the Smoky Mountains and named after the heavily forested habitat. People often overlooked the small town due to its lack of attractions, and miniscule population. Neighboring towns often describe Sevier Oak as "the middle of nowhere." Regardless of our size, it never stopped folks from grabbing a quick bite to eat before continuing to the nearest city, Bristol.

My hometown had a historical vibe, especially Copper Street and the roads leading off from it. The brick buildings surrounding the main strip were built in the early 1900s. This used to be the heart of Sevier Oak. There were once a drug, hardware, dry goods, general store, and a hotel where people stayed for two dollars a night. I knew that because the original owners had painted the price on the brick, which held up over the years. Those stores moved elsewhere in Sevier Oak while others moved into its place, yet the post office and courthouse remained in the same structure. The inside changed to meet the needs of modern-day, but not the framework. From where I stood, I saw the courthouse. The tall white columns, cupola, and flag poles were beautiful among the greenery planted nearby.

American Elm trees dotted Copper Street in between light posts. The facades of the stores had large bay windows while the upper level possessed three to five rectangular windows. Despite the heat, the landscaping looked stunning. I always thought bright green and faded red looked good together.

As a crowd grew on Copper Street, it reminded me of the town's most famous trait. Nosiness. I, on the other hand, knew how to maintain a balance. Growing up in a law enforcement family taught me to look out for my friends and neighbors. Yet I also knew gossip spread wild and thick, like butter melting on corn-on-the-cob. In my town, we don't look from the corner of our eyes, pretending we're not watching. In the south we stop and stare. Some people recorded the scene with their cell phones raised while others possessed the skill of watching and texting at the same time.

Megan, my best friend probably heard the news before I had a chance to tell her.

I rubbed my face, feeling sweat forming on my back. Fortunately, my platinum hair didn't hold onto heat, like it used to when I had embraced my natural black hair. For now, I sucked it up and continued waiting. I knew all too well that police procedures took time. Dad, Onyx Stone was a cop here before transferring to Nashville as a detective and my grandpa was the town's police chief.

At any moment, I expected to see Stone, my grandpa, emerging from the crowd. His bald head matched his no-nonsense demeanor. Last summer he retired as the police chief and became plain Sterling Stone. From an early age my family taught me to respect law enforcement, and to call my grandfather, Chief Stone or just Stone. Even Dad called his father, Stone. After twenty-two years, I couldn't call him anything else.

While keeping an eye out for Stone, I scanned the street, ignoring the looky-loos. In the corner of my eye, I spotted Jane Jackson. She paced while fanning herself. Looking at her gray suit made me feel sweatier. Despite the breeze and cloud cover, sweat ran down my neck. I was still bitter about the store closing, but I also didn't want her to pass out. When a cop looked in my direction, I would get their attention for Jane's sake.

While I watched the officers, my thoughts dwelling on what had happened. Doris Hackett was dead. Her lifeless body in the aisle flashed to mind. While calling for help, I had studied the blood on her forehead. I wouldn't have been surprised if the cause of death had been from a blow to the head. I heard plenty of stories from Dad and Stone to know that Doris's death was no accident. Someone hit her. *But who?* My eyes directed to the only other person in the bookstore.

Jane Jackson.

But how? She had been upstairs when Doris was killed. Jane couldn't run down a flight of stairs in stilettos, kill Doris, and rush back only to crash into me moments later.

Could she?

Or had more time passed when I first heard Doris's cry and ran to the bargain room?

Let the police handle this, I told myself while clutching my necklace.

To stop my mind from racing I stared into the distance. I spotted the top of a certain building. The tall concrete structure clashed against the bricks. I glared at it, fearing what the bookstore's rival would think. A celebration would be my guess.

Drake Voss owned Voss-of-Books. To me, the name sounded cheesy rather than being a clever play on the founder's last name. Voss-of-Books was a southern bookstore chain and quickly growing in numbers, mostly in Georgia, and the Carolinas. When Drake decided to build one in Sevier Oak two years ago, Teresa welcomed him with open arms. She believed the owner loved stories as much as she did. After their first encounter, it became clear that Drake Voss only loved money. I wasn't surprised by his greed because he wore fitted suits. Drake had offered to buy Teresa's Bookstore on several occasions. Thankfully, my beloved boss never surrendered.

I shifted to avoid seeing the building's roof. My eyes landed on Jane. *Could this day be any more stressful?*

Clara Hackett, Doris's sister, emerged from the crowd. Misfortune must have heard and struck. I groaned. She stormed towards the bookstore. Her face was beet red, either from the summer heat or from the devastating news. I had a feeling it was the latter. An officer met her halfway. With her hands firmly placed on her hips, Clara listened as the officer explained what had happened. She suddenly buried her face into her hands. My heart ached for her. I didn't believe the Hackett sisters were close, nevertheless, death wasn't a joyous occasion.

Then Clara marched around the officer before a second one blocked her path. "Give me my sister's keys," she demanded, holding out her hand. “All her stuff now belongs to me. Go find Doris’s purse. Her keys are inside.”

A third officer appeared. The other two officers stepped aside, letting him deal with Miss Hackett. If I hadn’t known Deputy Idris Underwood as one of Dad’s closest friends, I would be nervous about him too. Underwood’s deep voice alone could end bar fights according to Dad's stories.

“Doris’s belongings are evidence now,” Underwood boomed.

Clara took a step back, probably surprised at his tone. “Well, I,” she stumbled over her own words. After a few moments, she found her courage. “Doris was my sister, and as her only living relative, her stuff has to be mine now.” She stuck out her chin as if her words held more authority.

I rolled my eyes and slightly shook my head. Once Underwood put his foot down, there was no changing his decision. Dad’s stories didn’t have to teach me about his obstinateness. I had witnessed it when Underwood was the high school’s umpire. He didn’t take any crap from parents, fans, or anybody in that matter. Once his own wife heckled him over a called strike with their son up to bat. To this day, he still claims he made the right call.

Something moved beside me, causing me to jump. I looked over and saw Preston Powell standing next to me. He smelled like a mixture of sweat and sawdust, not a pleasant odor. A dirty, reddish rag was tied around one hand. His work boots had seen better days. Duct tape wrapped around the front section of one boot while the other looked faded. Paint splatter decorated his blue jeans. I couldn’t help noticing a hole in one of his back pockets. Quickly I looked away. Preston had to be around Dad’s age if not older.

Preston faced me. “What’s going on?” He pointed with his thumb. A subtle chuckle crept into his voice. “What’s

Clara-Bell so upset about that brought the entire police squad?"

I opened my mouth to answer and snapped it shut. I almost forgot that Preston was Doris's ex-husband.

Preston tilted his head, waiting for a response. I chose my next words carefully. "There was an accident. I had to call the police." I rather not break the news about Doris's death.

Before Preston could answer, Clara screaming and gesturing wildly at Underwood caught his attention.

Preston chuckled harder. "Trust Clara-Bell to stick her nose where it doesn't belong."

Between the police having their hands full and Preston finding humor in Clara's reason for being upset, I decided to tell him the truth.

"I'm sorry to tell you, but Doris is dead."

I studied his expression. Even though they have been divorced for some time, I would have expected him to show some remorse. Instead, Preston grunted before smirking.

"Good riddance."

Guess I worried for nothing.

While Preston watched Clara argue with Underwood, I counted the years since their divorce. Four. I remembered the timeline because Teresa invited me to a private business party during their ugly divorce. Other than standard business chit-chat, nearly every conversation at the party had steered toward the Powells. Most people took Preston's side, including me. The evening was nearly ruined because Drake Voss and his grandson crashed the event. Teresa sent the Voss men out, causing more tension between the bookstore owners. Thankfully, people quickly forgot about the spat because someone got a text about Doris having an affair. The rest of the evening became an endless game of guess who.

Finally, Clara walked away from Underwood. Her eyes

landed on Preston. I had a bad feeling when she marched toward us. Underwood came closer and stopped. He crossed his arms over his chest, watching.

"You killed her," Clara accused Preston.

Preston looked as taken back as me. *Killed Doris? How?* Clara must have misheard something. I glanced at Underwood. His face gave nothing away.

Doris's ex-husband quickly collected himself. He replied, "Only a crazy woman would think that. I didn't know Doris was here. I was working next door." Preston pointed behind him with his bandaged hand.

"Still?" I mumbled under my breath. Karl, the owner next to the bookstore and Old Treasures, had hired Preston two months ago to repair the upstairs bathroom. Thankfully neither of them heard. I didn't want to be a part of their quarrel.

"It's always the husband," Clara claimed.

"*Ex*-husband," he corrected. "If your case is based on her latest lover, then you actually mean Mateo. The boy-toy."

That shut Clara up. Her eyes searched around as if she was mentally struggling for a comeback. Preston wasn't wrong. Mateo was the main reason the Powells divorced.

"Murderer. Don't come anywhere near me!" Clara screamed.

Preston laughed.

I glanced back at the deputy. Underwood shook his head, clearly seeing the drama ahead of him.

The officer, who first spoke to Clara minutes ago, escorted her near some parked squad cars while another took Preston aside. The former in-laws bickered as they went their separate ways. It reminded me of an episode of The Jerry Springer Show. Except, the guests didn't care about the main concern. Doris was dead. Clara believed she would inherit everything. Maybe that was the real reason Preston didn't care. He knew neither of them would see a penny of Doris's lottery winnings.

"Garnet, are you alright?" a deep voice asked.

Deputy Underwood now stood next to me. My head came to the baseline of his neck. I felt like a penguin standing next to a robust ostrich.

I turned away from Clara and Preston. "I'm fine."

"You sure?"

Behind his sunglasses, I knew Underwood was giving me a look. The same one Dad always gave when he suspected something was bothering me. For a moment, I wondered if Underwood learned it from Dad or, if it was the other way around.

"Just shaken up. What happened?" I nodded toward the bookstore.

A woman, who I assumed to be the medical examiner, walked out of the store. Behind her, workers in uniform rolled a stretcher. I focused my attention on Underwood. I didn't want to see the body bag.

The deputy pressed his lips before saying, "Doris Hackett was murdered."

I suspected as much. "How?"

He lowered his voice. "Am I correct in saying that you had a good look at the scene?" I nodded yes, eagerly wanting to help with the investigation. "Then you noticed the strange manner surrounding her death?"

"Strange?" I felt less confident at what I had seen.

"We think the killer struck Doris in the back of her head with the tea kettle. A knife was found, but there's no blood on it. Despite the objects on the scene, the coroner believes Doris was suffocated."

"From the pillow?" I questioned, mentally recalling the small pillow next to the body.

"Correct."

I soaked in the information. This was indeed *strangeness* as Underwood claimed. A tea kettle, a knife, and a pillow. It sounded like the start of a joke when random items or different people walked into a bar. But this wasn't funny.

Sevier Oak hadn't had a murder in years. Drama, yes. Rumors, yes. But not murder. The reason why Dad transferred to Nashville was to help in the homicide department.

Underwood pulled out his cellphone, tapped a few times, and looked at me. Back to being a deputy. First, he asked me the standard questions about my day, starting when I first arrived at Teresa's Bookstore. I answered them truthfully, including the part about being fired.

Then he moved onto more specific questions. "Did the bookstore own a tea kettle?"

I liked how he asked if the *bookstore* did, rather than saying, Teresa. "Yes. Four of them. Well, five if you count the one in the storage room upstairs. That one has a cracked bottom. It leaks. One stayed in the break room. Teresa used it when she got in the mood for tea. The others were for decoration. Two sat on the bookshelves near the entrance and the last one..." A knot hardened itself in my throat. "It used to be in the front part of the store. At certain times of the day, it was blinding. I moved it to the bargain room after Teresa passed away." I wished I threw it away instead of putting it in a windowless room.

"What does it look like?" he repeated the question.

"Bright yellow."

More questions followed. I confirmed the pillow was one of Teresa's projects. She liked fixing things. Most of the time she could, however, the number of projects far outnumbered the things she did repair. Stitching the ripped pillow was on her to do list. I'd last seen it in the receiving room where deliveries come through. Yes, I found it odd how the pillow made its way onto the sales floor, and no, Princess didn't carry things. Teresa never kept weapons in her store, not even against shoplifters. She once said, if someone stole a book, then they probably needed it more than we needed the sale.

"Who's the new gal?" Underwood nodded in Jane's direction.

I glanced to our left. Jane stood in the same spot, staring at us. She didn't look frightened anymore. She looked angry with her narrowed eyes.

"That's the new boss, Teresa's niece. Or my former boss, I should say. Her name is Jane Jackson."

Underwood's lips pressed harder. I could tell that he didn't like Jane.

"Here she comes," I warned seconds before Jane joined us. As she approached, I studied her outfit for any sign of blood spatters. I only saw a perfectly gray suit. But that didn't rule her out as a suspect. She could have worn gloves and disposed of them while I called for help. Yet given the time frame, that seemed unlikely.

"What's taking so long?" she demanded. "It was an accident. We witnessed it." Her finger moved vigorously between herself and me. "The woman hit her head. Probably from all the clutter." Jane glared at me as if Doris's death had been my fault.

Did she not see the knife and blood on the tea kettle?

Underwood put his phone on his belt clip. "Evidence says otherwise."

"What are you saying? Did the woman commit suicide?"

"I'm going to need to see your hands and arms."

Jane's eyes widened. "Excuse me? You think that woman was murdered, and I did it?" she said, half smiling. She looked at me, probably thinking I would come to her defense. Her humor disappeared when she realized I wasn't. Those brown eyes shifted between Underwood and me before staying on

Underwood. "You have no right to accuse me of any wrongdoing," Jane continued. "I demand to know what happened in my bookstore."

My jaw tightened hearing Jane say, "my bookstore." I know she never stepped foot inside her aunt's business until today. I didn't recall a time when Teresa's family visited. She always traveled to see them.

"This is a murder investigation," Deputy Underwood said. "By not showing me your hands and arms, you're giving me a reason to think that you're hiding something."

Jane removed her gray jacket, revealing her arms all the way up to her shoulders. No marks of any kind. Her French tip nails looked professionally done. If she killed Doris, she must have worn gloves. I struggled to recall if Teresa kept any upstairs.

"I don't know that woman. Ask her." Jane pointed at me.

Underwood tensed. "*Her* is your employee." He scowled. "Her name is Garnet Stone. Respect the Stone."

Jane looked unsure how to respond.

Another man in uniform joined our huddle. He dressed differently compared to the others. Instead of a navy uniform, like Underwood, he had on shades of green and tan. The sunglasses covered half of his face, making it impossible to read him. I assumed he was the new sheriff.

"This way." The man grabbed Jane's upper arm and escorted her away.

"Sheriff Estep," Underwood muttered once they were out of earshot.

"He's the new sheriff?" I watched them walk inside the bookstore. Sheriff Estep barked orders as they went. I didn't like him. My father would agree, and he used to be a sheriff before he moved to the middle of the state.

I scanned the street. Clara and Preston were nowhere to be

found. The crowd seemed to be smaller yet the number of law enforcement remained the same.

"How is Estep as a sheriff?" I asked before Underwood slipped away.

Again, Underwood pressed his lips, thinking. "Has your father mentioned anything about coming back?"

"That bad?" I asked.

"This is his first big case. Sheriff Estep wants to prove himself. There's no better way than by solving a murder."

"Tell me all the details," I said, half-jokingly. "Maybe I can help you solve it."

For the first time, he smirked. I waited for him to tell me something, even if it was to mind my own business. Once the silence became too much, I asked, "Nothing? Not even one teeny tiny clue?"

"I can't go into details."

"Because I'm a girl?" I placed my hands on my hips, hoping my stink eye came across as fierce rather than looking like a bug flew in my eye.

"No," he said as a matter of fact, "your father and former Chief Stone wouldn't appreciate me telling you gory details." I eased my fierce face. I understood that logic. "And you're also not on the task force."

Before I could roll my eyes, a woman's cry interrupted us. I looked up. Sheriff Estep was escorting Jane Jackson into the backseat of a police cruiser.

"I didn't," Jane protested.

Sheriff Estep slammed the door shut, silencing her.

CHAPTER 3

After Jane Jackson was taken to the station, the police reopened Copper Street. Most of them left soon after. Onlookers dismissed themselves as they went about their day, probably spreading the word about Doris Hackett's death as they went. I was sure by dinner time every person and child would have heard the news.

Underwood and a few officers stayed behind, finishing their last tasks. My dad's friend informed me that Teresa's Bookstore was a crime scene and would remain closed until the sheriff cleared it. I couldn't get an answer on when that might be. From what I knew from Dad and Stone and novels, it could take days.

I worried about the cats. If my roommate wasn't allergic to them they would've been coming home with me. Grandma and Stone could watch Princess, but after Butterscotch hissed at Grandma once they were too nervous about taking her under their care, even temporarily.

"What can I do with the cats?" I asked Underwood after explaining they didn't have anywhere to go.

He pondered for a moment. "Is there a room they can stay in? Preferably upstairs."

A burden lifted off my chest. "Yes."

Underwood made a quick phone call and allowed me inside to tend to their needs, under his supervision. Two remaining officers were packing up what I thought was a fingerprint kit. The case closed before I could see for sure. They looked relieved to see me. Right away, I knew why.

"We did our best," one of the officers said to Underwood. "Last I saw, it was over there." He pointed toward the back part of the store.

It had to be Princess, the black and white cat. She didn't respect bubble space. According to the two police officer's conversation with Underwood, they had struggled to keep her away from the crime scene. One claimed Princess had jumped on Doris's body before scurrying upstairs, only to return a minute later. Thankfully, after that point, she had stayed out of reach, hovering on top of the bookshelves.

"That damn cat is messing up my crime scene," Sheriff Estep bellowed behind me.

I jumped at his sudden voice. It wasn't as deep as Underwood's, but the sharpness behind it startled me. I thought he left to take Jane to the station. Clearly, he must have ordered someone else to do the job.

"Get moving." He snapped his fingers. The officers quickly grabbed their kits and scurried out, leaving me with the sheriff and deputy. Then he snapped in front of my face. "That includes you too, missy."

"Don't call me missy," I said. Part of Southern Charm was to use nicknames, but I could tell the sheriff was using it as a slight.

Sheriff Estep snapped his fingers again to get moving.

I had an urge to say something but held back. Movement

caught my eye. I spotted Princess walking along a bookshelf. Too bad she stepped around the small figurines rather than knocking them onto Estep's head

"Princess," I called. She stopped and cast her big yellow eyes down on us. Her back half started wiggling. "Come on." Then, like a typical cat, she changed her mind by rubbing her head on the shelf.

The sheriff huffed.

I reached both hands out. "Come on, Princess," I cooed.

"Just grab her," Sheriff Estep ordered.

I inhaled a deep breath, restraining myself from speaking my mind. There wasn't much a five-two-foot woman could do against an eight-foot bookshelf. If Estep wasn't already upset and a sheriff, then I might have explained the simple math problem.

I kindly raised my tone. "Princess." The cat got into a pounce position. I was about to call for her again when the sheriff hollered at Underwood for assistance. Princess jumped and the ten-pound cat landed in my arms. She nearly leaped out of my grasp. I tightened my arms around her while making sure that I didn't hurt her. Princess started purring.

"Let's get you upstairs," I said to her.

"Where are you going?" Sheriff Estep barked.

Since the back staircase was closer, I naturally headed there. Otherwise, I would have to weave through the front area, into the romance/horror room, and up the main staircase. By the time I registered what Estep was saying, I was standing in the bargain room's entrance.

The area had always felt constricted. Books squeezed on the shelves. Chairs sat at the end of two of the narrow aisles. Tucked in the corner was a fake plant that needed to be tossed out since Princess had clawed most of its leaves. The large room often made customers feel claustrophobic, one of many reasons for the remodel. By removing part of the second floor, the store would be spacious.

Now the bargain room looked as if a tornado touched down. Books scattered in one aisle, as if someone ran their hand down the shelves knocking all the books onto the floor. Hardcover novels crushed paperbacks, bending their spines, while others flapped open with newly bent pages. Only Princess was small enough to weave around this mess. The sight made me cringe. All my hard work to make it tidy had gone out the window. It would take a solid week to clean and reorganize this room. Time I no longer had.

"How did this happen?" I demanded, facing Sheriff Estep. When I had found Doris, there had been about ten books around her feet. Now there were three times as many.

"That cat," Sheriff Estep pointed at Princess. "Officers were trying to catch her. That *rodent* destroyed my crime scene."

Thankfully, they didn't catch Princess, I thought. "If you had gotten me none of this would have happened."

Sheriff Estep finally removed his sunglasses. He had smooth, rounded cheeks and bright blue eyes that narrowed at me. It took a lot of willpower to not smile at his baby face. He almost looked too adorable to be taken seriously. Or to be a sheriff.

"I know who you are, missy," he said, crossing his arms over his chest.

Ugh, I hate that nickname.

"Just because you're a Stone doesn't give you power or authority to speak to me like that."

I didn't know how to respond, other than a snarky remark. Words would definitely get me into trouble. Too bad Underwood didn't tell him about respecting a Stone. I considered stealing Underwood's motto when the sheriff continued.

"As a Stone I expected better from you."

"I just want to help," I said, easing my tone.

Sheriff Estep studied me. His head tilted. I felt him zeroing on my wrist tattoo— an open book with teal and purple smoke floating upward. Teresa said the colors matched my platinum hair. Based on Estep's narrowed expression, I probably looked like a silly bookworm, who loves cats and knows nothing about the real world.

"If I want your help, then I'll ask," he said, slowly. "Right now, I want that cat upstairs and locked up."

I looked away, biting back words. Just when I was about to head for the main staircase, I noticed a speck of pink against the faded green carpet. I stared at it, trying to figure out what I was seeing.

"Is that a pill?" I asked aloud.

Sheriff Estep and Deputy Underwood leaned over for a closer look. While Underwood lingered on it, the sheriff shrugged, and then looked back at me as if he wondered why I wasn't moving.

"That wasn't here this morning," I said. "I vacuumed."

"With that vacuum?" Sheriff Estep pointed toward the front of the store.

I nodded.

He scoffed. "That thing is older than my granny. That thing probably can't even pick up a dust bunny."

I couldn't disagree. The vacuum cleaner had outlived its glory days. However, if Teresa was here, she would argue that it still got the job done. Sometimes.

"That pill wasn't here before," I said.

"Teresa owned a lot of junk. It's probably been here for months. If not years," he muttered the last part, glancing into the bargain room.

"I know Teresa's mess and that isn't part of it."

His face turned hard. Baby-face wasn't funny anymore.

"Right now, missy, I want that cat out of my sight," he yelled into my face.

Princess hissed and swatted at him. Too bad she missed.

Underwood stepped in before a real catfight broke out. The deputy kindly led me by my elbow toward the front of the store and upstairs. While Dad's friend and former co-worker escorted me away, I took in some deep breaths. This was a murder investigation, I reminded myself. I couldn't get mad at the police for mistreating books and being in a grumpy mood, but I wouldn't forget how Sheriff Estep treated everyone.

I turned my focus to the cats. They needed me now more than ever. For now, they had to stay in a designated room upstairs. Butterscotch never minded being in the Cat's Lounge, as Teresa called it. The tortie cat would jump in her window bed, and curl up for a long nap, perfectly content being in there all day. Princess, on the other hand, might struggle. The nosy cat loved roaming freely and going wherever the action led her. Teresa spoiled the cats rotten. She bought them more toys and beds than two felines need. Novels that were too damaged to sell, she stacked them in towers for them to play. "Cats love books too," Teresa had said when I saw her making the stacks. In other words, "I don't have the heart to throw them away, so the cats can have them."

It took me a few minutes to fill their food and water dishes, clean the litter box, and most importantly, make sure Princess was in Cat's Lounge. Before leaving, I gave them a big pile of treats. Princess must have known this was a trick. While Butterscotch scarfed the chicken flavored bites, Princess's big yellow eyes gazed up at me.

"You'll be okay. I'll be back tomorrow," I promised. I peeked over my shoulder, hoping the police would let me back inside in the morning. When Underwood nodded, I felt relief.

I closed the door behind me before Princess could dart out.

I told myself she would be fine. After all, Princess had her sister and they normally slept together in the Cat's Lounge at night.

A depressing thought hit me. Since Jane planned to sell the bookstore, the cats couldn't live here anymore. Quickly, I shook this thought away. I needed to convince Jane to keep the store. How to accomplish that was the million-dollar question.

"Your grandpa is here," Underwood said.

Right on cue, I heard footsteps walking down the narrow hallway as Stone approached us. Today he wore sandals, a gray T-shirt, and what people call old man shorts. He was bald by choice, giving into his age rather than fighting it with hair growth remedies. The tips of his fingers were dotted with shades of green and light brown. Smudges of green stained the bottom of his shorts as if he had tried to rub the paint off his fingers. Despite his bland clothing style, Stone's face looked sharp as if he never retired.

"Deputy Underwood," Stone addressed. Underwood nodded back before Stone turned his attention on me. "How are you holding up, Garnet?"

I wished Stone hadn't left the force. He would've overseen Doris's murder, and made sure Estep respected people. The current police chief, from what I've heard, was touring Europe for the remaining month of June. Too bad Stone couldn't sub for him until he returned.

"I'm fine," I answered.

Satisfied with my response, Stone turned his focus back onto Underwood. They started to discuss the case. Hearing about crimes wasn't new. While some households talked about sports or upcoming vacation plans, the Stone household talked about criminals. Growing up with two law enforcement personnel, it became second nature to overhear ongoing cases. Now, living on my own, and the men no longer on the task force, I realized how much I missed hearing the conversations.

Underwood went over Doris's death. He skipped over gory details, nodding in my direction. I rolled my eyes while Stone nodded for him to continue. When he concluded the story with Jane Jackson being taken to the station, Stone frowned.

For almost a full minute neither man said anything. From experience, I knew Stone was soaking in all the information, trying to see the entire picture from puzzle pieces. Stone was known for his listening skills and pondering for long lengths of time. He could teach the new sheriff a thing or two.

Then Stone held out his hand, staring at me. I sighed and concealed a whiny groan. "I promise, I'm fine. No harm came to me."

"This is a murder investigation." His eyes were still fixed on me. His fingers moved in a give-me gesture.

"You know, you can text or call me. I promise I'll let you know that *I'm fine.*"

Stone's expression didn't change. One look at Underwood told me that he agreed with my grandpa.

I sighed before reaching in my back pocket and handed Stone my cell phone. We stood in silence as Stone tapped away. I knew there was no point in arguing. He would track my whereabouts one way or another. Plus, I really didn't want to rehear stories as to why he wanted to track me. Some battles were not worth the fight. Once Stone was done, he handed back my phone.

"You can go Miss Stone," said Underwood, "but, don't wander too far in case we have further questions."

While Stone approved of Underwood's logic, I glared at them. *Once a policeman, always a policeman.*

"I can take you home," offered Stone, "or get a bite to eat."

I waved my hand and walked around them. "No thanks. I'll be at the bar."

I left knowing Underwood would go into detail about the

murder investigation. I crossed my fingers hoping Stone would tell me exclusive information later— like how the killer got in the store. And why did a pillow become a murder weapon rather than a knife?

CHAPTER 4

THE HEART OF SEVIER OAK WAS TWO BLOCKS FROM COPPER STREET. The grocery store, the hardware store, Dollar General, and two gas stations competed for the town's businesses. Big-name stores were a good hour away in Bristol. Instead of Dunkin Donuts, Sevier Oak had a locally owned coffee shop. There was no Red Lobster, but Smack Fish had the best river food in the area. Spaghetti Tree served the best Italian food in East Tennessee. As I drove past the restaurants, the various food aromas found their way inside my car. My stomach growled. Stress always stirred up a hunger.

One of the best attractions in my hometown was the old movie theater from 1930. It used to be on Copper Street, but after a fire it had been rebuilt. I never knew it wasn't the original until Grandma told me. The notorious marquee survived, shining brightly at night with its multiple light bulbs. Underneath it stood the ticket booth. When standing behind the booth, it felt like stepping back in time. The theater didn't play big shows like on Broadway, it hosted dance or band recitals and school skit performances. It was a treat when a musician from Bristol visited and performed, often attracting the entire town.

While waiting at a red light, my eyes drifted toward Crockett Park. Tall trees surrounded the large park, giving a peaceful vibe. Deer and turkey often wandered across the baseball fields during the winter months. A walking path surrounded the area with smaller ones weaving throughout. My family brought me there as a kid to play on the playground and for family picnics. I often came here on emotional days, sitting alone, to untangle my worrying thoughts.

Kids of all ages enjoyed their summer break by racing down slides, playing tag, and swinging as high as they could. Water balloons and Frisbees flew on the same patch of grass. The sight brightened my day just a little.

An old cottage from the 1700s rested in the park's center. Some say Davy Crockett lived there for a time, while others claim that the famous frontiersman never traveled through this area. No one knows the truth. Either way, the park has been named after him.

The light turned green, and I made it to my destination without stopping at any more traffic signals. I smiled at the sign with red cherries painted on the top corners. Dessert Bar. This was the perfect place to cure a rough day, or simply satisfy a sweet tooth.

When I entered, the cold air hit me, slightly blowing my hair. Dessert Bar always had a chill. On hot summer days, like today, it felt wonderful. Three customers stood in line. A summer hire worked the register while my best friend and roommate, Megan, and her mom, hustled behind the long counter.

Dessert Bar used to be a regular bar, owned by Megan's

father. Sixteen years ago, he vanished. Dad, Stone, and the rest of the police had searched for him. It didn't take long to learn that Megan's father hadn't disappeared; he left. The bank account had been drained, and some of his personal belongings were missing. Molly, Megan's mother, discovered that the bar was also in debt. Dad found out there had been some shady drug business after hours. As time went on, Dad and other law enforcement officers believed Megan's father had fled and was currently living under an alias.

Instead of self-wallowing, Molly turned her husband's bar into something great. She painted the walls bright teal, changed all the light fixtures, remodeled the storage room into a kitchen, and voila, the place was brand new.

Dessert Bar had high tables with barstools, except for two spots reserved for people with disabilities or small children. Pictures of their most famous desserts hung on the walls. Pies were a popular choice, especially during autumn. Personally, the triple chocolate cake with a large cherry on top was my favorite, the banana sundae was a close second. Or possibly fudge walnut brownies. My stomach started sinking into itself.

While walking to the counter debating which dessert to eat, I spotted Sasha. She sat at a table eating a monster-size chocolate muffin. No doubt drowning her sorrows in sweets after she failed to get her old job back. But that was hours ago. After a closer look, Sasha looked happy in between bites and her feet swung like a little kid. This was a celebration, rather than a pick me up. Her words to Doris came back to me.

"One day somebody is going to hack you up with a jack of spades, and on that day, I'm going to laugh at it."

At the time I thought Sasha was just being rude since she no longer worked at the bookstore. Now I wondered if her comments had a darker meaning. I studied her body language, searching for any clues tying her to the crime. Sasha kept eating, oblivious that I was watching her.

Was eating something sweet Sasha's way of laughing at Doris's death? The jack-of-spades comment sounded like something a poker player would say. To my knowledge though, Sasha played video games, not Texas Hold'em.

"Hey, Garnet," a voice called out.

Megan worked behind the main counter. Strands of curly blond hair had slipped from her messy bun. She waved at me while grabbing a brownie from one of the domes that lined the bar. I greeted her with a wave before she handed the brownie to the customer paying at the register. At the far end of the counter, Molly, Megan's mom, called out an order. She had more gray hair than blonde and smiling wrinkles.

Before heading up to the counter, I studied the cold desserts. Instead of the typical solid slab under the bar counter, there was a display of refrigerated desserts. Slices were missing in cakes and pies while the cookies were being restocked by another summer worker. Some days it was nearly impossible to pick just one dessert.

Today was going to be a double dessert day.

"Garnet, over here." Megan waved from the far end of the bar where customers waited for their desserts. Instead of being her bubbly self she looked concerned. "What happened at the bookstore?" she lowered her voice when I came up. "People are saying someone died at Teresa's Bookstore. Is that true?"

I debated how much I should say. I'd learned that the police often withheld some information from the public in order to find the killer. I wondered if murder was on that list or the way Doris had died. For all I knew, people thought Doris choked on a grape. Megan flicked my hand, growing impatient.

"Someone did die at the store," I confirmed. Megan slightly

narrowed her big green eyes. She knew me too well. "That's all I can say," I quickly added.

She snarled at me. "Gosh, you sound like your dad. No, your grandpa."

I couldn't disagree, even though I really wanted to. Then again I suppose there were worse comparisons. I should be grateful that I didn't look like the woman-version of Dad or Stone.

Before Megan peppered me with more questions, I told her I wanted a brownie sundae. "Make it a double and an extra shot of sprinkles," I said sweetly.

I watched Megan work. She grabbed a wide bowl and put two brownies inside. Next, she measured out vanilla ice cream and sprayed a healthy amount of whipped cream. Megan got a shot glass, filled it to the brim with rainbow sprinkles, and dumped it over the ice cream, then repeated the process. After adding a cherry on top, she placed the dish on the pick-up section. She poured milk into a beer mug. I simply adored how every customer was entitled to milk with their dessert. If a group shared a dessert, they got a half-gallon milking bucket on the table to help themselves.

"It's on the house," Megan said before I could hand the cashier my debit card. "Mom would kill me if I made you pay." She slapped her hand over her mouth. "Sorry I—"

"It's okay." I flashed a smile to reassure her that the killing idiom phrase didn't bother me, especially when a brownie sundae was involved.

I found an empty table, away from Sasha and dug into my dessert. Before taking the second bite, I froze with my spoon mid-air. Drake Voss sat at a table to my left. He ate a slice of cherry pie with no Cool Whip. His martini glass contained water. When he looked down at his food, I glared at him. For a moment, I considered switching to a new spot, but feared he might notice me. I stayed in place and pretended he wasn't here.

A soft moan escaped while I chewed. The rich brownies with extra sprinkles were my favorite. This was just what I needed after dealing with Sheriff Estep and being fired. I pushed away the image of Doris's lifeless body. I didn't want to get sick.

Jane's words from this morning came to mind. The thought of the store forever closing its doors ruined my appetite. I stared at my food, wishing I could stop these thoughts.

Fired. The word alone made me clutch my spoon. I'd worked at the bookstore since I was sixteen and had never been written up. I reminded myself the store closing wasn't the same thing as Sasha's case. Teresa let Sasha go because of her constant tardiness and laziness. I'd done nothing wrong.

While frowning at the delicious sundae, I realized being fired wasn't what bothered me the most. I felt I had been used. Jane had emailed me shortly after Teresa's passing, telling me why she couldn't attend her aunt's funeral and asking if I could run the store until she arrived. I never got the impression she wanted to close the store. All my hard work to impress my new boss had flown out the window. Then again, I may not have stood a chance. Even if I had succeeded in making the store spotless, Jane seemed adamant about her choice.

She was always planning to sell the bookstore.

The thought made me want to cry and scream at the same time. I took too big of a bite and had to chew slowly. I placed my napkin over my lips, hoping to hide my struggle.

"Garnet," a warm and familiar voice said.

I chewed faster before swallowing a huge chunk of brownie. Bad move. I coughed and my eyes began to water. A strong hand pounded on my back. Embarrassment heated my face. I held up a finger, trying to take a drink of milk. Thankfully, I was able to wash down the food.

"Bit off more than you can chew?" I heard the humor in his tone.

Karl stood next to me. His blue jean overalls, stained T-shirt, and well-worn baseball hat screamed country. He flashed a wide smile, one that made people smile back. "How are you doing, given the circumstances?" he lowered his head and softened his tone at the last part.

This was proof word traveled fast. Karl was normally one of the last people to hear gossip, but even he couldn't have missed news of Doris's murder. He owned the antique shop next to Teresa's Bookstore. Either he had watched from the store's window or Preston told him the news.

I took a long drink to wash down the last of my embarrassment. Thankfully, my accident hadn't drawn anyone's attention.

"It's sad," I said, fishing to see what Karl heard. Like with Megan, I wasn't about to give out information.

Karl took the empty chair next to me, thankfully blocking my view of Drake Voss. Karl shrugged without a care. "I suppose if one had feelings for that woman then it would be sad."

That confirmed Karl knew the victim was Doris Hackett. Preston must have told him. "Was Preston upset? I talked to him for a few minutes before the police pulled him aside for questioning."

Karl shook his head. "Nah, they divorced, what three? Four years ago?"

"Four."

"That's right. Doris won the lottery two years ago. She was divorced by then," Karl's voice turned bitter. "It's a shame Preston never got a penny from that. He should have gotten something since he built that nice cabin for them. I still can't believe Doris destroyed it and built a fancy house in its place. If you ask me, she should have sold it and move elsewhere."

I agreed. Most people in town shared the sentiment as well.

"Yeah, I don't reckon anyone will mourn over Doris," he continued. "Including her li'l sissy."

Clara Hackett had looked shaken up. Then again, it was only a minute until her demeanor changed.

"I wonder who will get all that money now Doris is dead." His words caught the attention of nearby customers. Voices ceased; only soft piano music played through the speakers. Dessert Bar fell into an eerie silence as if Karl had announced that we were playing the quiet game and the winner got the money. Even Megan, Molly, and their employees stopped working to listened.

Karl yawned, unaware his question carried the weight of a bombshell. Doris had won the lottery two years after her separation. This kept Doris and Preston in the town's gossip mill. Everyone, including my family and me, thought she would move elsewhere. She had stayed.

When Karl finished his long yawn, he hollered, "Hey, Molly. You got any of that espresso cake?"

Molly came up to our table. "Sure, honey. You want a small or big slice?"

"The biggest you got. I'm exhausted."

Molly leaned on a prompt elbow, looking like a concerned bartender. Megan and I swear she enjoys this pose too much. "You want coffee instead of milk? I can make one with an espresso shot."

Karl stifled a yawn by bringing his fist to his mouth. He nodded his answer. Molly winked at us before walking behind the counter.

"Darn diet drinks," Karl complained. "Ever since I switched from regular Coke to diet, I've been so gosh-darn tired. It doesn't bother my wife, but for some reason it makes me sleepy."

I glanced at my dessert. My once fluffy Cool Whip was now melted. I scoop a normal bite.

"I say good riddance," Sasha said aloud. Heads bobbled around her. "I'm glad Doris Hackett is gone."

"Greedy woman," snarled a man near Sasha's table.

"She revs her BMW and races up and down my street at two am," someone else added. "She does it just to show off. Ya'll know that I need sleep to function."

"Preston also lives on your street," snarled the first man.

"No need to bash Doris," I said loud enough for everyone to hear without yelling. "Let the dead rest."

I was not a fan of Doris. She blared her horn at drivers who switched lanes too slow. Doris bashed Teresa's Bookstore in front of Teresa. Why she kept coming back instead of shopping at Voss-of-Books was a mystery. Clara told everyone how Doris had always been selfish and greedy while Preston blamed Doris for destroying his 1965 mustang. After she won the lottery, she became a nuisance to her neighbors. Not only did she rev her engine at night too, she also left her garbage in the yard for weeks, forcing neighbors to sell their homes. Yes, a lot of people had a right to be mad at Doris Hackett. Now she was dead, I didn't feel entitled to openly dislike her or point out her flaws.

By the looks of everyone's faces, I stood alone.

"Doris was awful," Sasha ranted. "Sevier Oak is better off without her."

"She was," Karl added, after another yawn. "Doris was nothing but trouble. She came into my store last week, demanding free delivery." He scoffed while shaking his head. "Preston told me she was murdered."

Customers gave Karl their full attention

"Don't you be going shy on us, Karl," a woman eating a pie said. She pointed her fork in his direction.

"Tell us," The man sitting next to my table added.

Heads nodded around us.

While they listened to Karl's story, which he heard from Preston, I ate my brownie sundae. There was no stopping the gossip wildfire, and I had no desire to fan the flames. I came here for something sweet, not to spread rumors or recall what Doris had done to me, which mainly consisted of complaining about book prices and cat fur on her pants.

As I took another bite, I thought of Drake Voss. I pictured him with a wicked grin while rubbing his hands together. He wasn't hearing *how* a woman died, but *where* the murder took place. I leaned over and spotted him. To my surprise, Drake was frowning.

"Who killed Doris?" someone asked.

Once again, the restaurant fell quiet. One by one, I noticed all eyes drifted towards me. The sight creeped me out. Everyone stared at me, waiting for an answer. Guess this could be a downside of being a Stone.

Before I could say something, Karl broke the silence. "Did that new girl in town kill her?"

Sasha gasped. "The woman who inherited Teresa's Bookstore?" Her eyes widened from shock. She half sat up as if she was going to bolt. "And to think, I wanted to go back there."

Oh no, I thought, *how can I stop this?*

"Teresa's niece owns the store now. Her name is—" Karl snapped his fingers, struggling to remember. "Oh, darn what's her name?"

"Jane Jackson," Megan said. She came to the table carrying

Karl's dessert and a steaming mug of coffee. She hovered over my shoulder, making herself part of the conversation.

Karl breathed in the steam before taking a sip. The scent of the strong brew even woke me up. As he gave his thanks, Drake Voss stood up and made a hasty exit, deserting his half-eaten pie.

The crowd began recalling stories of how Doris did them wrong. Megan took my plate and nodded for me to follow. Gladly, I slithered away.

I followed Megan through the swinging door and into the massive kitchen. The sugary aroma hit me first. Molly baked while another staff member boxed cookies for an order. I waved at the familiar faces while being led to the breakroom. We sat at a table with my dessert. The AC blew directly on us, causing me to shiver. Megan wrapped her arms around herself.

"You saw it didn't you?" Megan sounded sad rather than curious.

I played with my food. At the moment, I didn't want to go into details, especially with her nosy coworkers possibly overhearing us. "Drake left quickly. I'm surprised he wasn't smiling like the villain he is."

"Forget about old Drake. Is everything they're saying true?"

Since Megan was my roommate and best friend since second grade, I knew she could keep a secret. I whispered everything I'd learned. Starting with Jane closing the store, to crashing into her just before we found Doris. After I told her a summary of the day's events, Megan took my spoon and stole a huge bite of my dessert.

"I hate myself for saying this, but," Megan's voice turned serious, "we have to solve the murder."

I laughed until I noticed she wasn't joining. "Oh. You're serious?"

"Yes." She stole another bite.

I pondered as she chewed. Despite Sheriff Estep being new, I didn't see why we needed to poke our noses into police business. I imagined Dad and Stone sitting around the kitchen, retelling stories. The time Dad was nearly thrown off a bridge because the drunk driver he was trying to arrest didn't want to go to jail. Then Stone would remind me of what had happened when he chased three robbers through the woods at night. He told me it felt like a cat and mouse game, and later admitted it was one of the scariest moments of his career.

"First thing first, do you really think Jane killed Doris?" Megan questioned.

"I don't think so," I said, reflecting on the morning's events. When Doris arrived, I didn't recall Jane sneering or making any rude comments, unlike Sasha. Jane and Doris seemed to be strangers to one another. I saw no motive for Jane wanting her dead.

"Are you doubting the possibility because Jane wore a suit?" Megan asked.

"How do you know she was wearing one?" Was she reading my thoughts?

Megan gave me a knowing look. "You don't like anyone who wears suits. Or tuxedos. Besides, according to one of the summer hires, Jane looks hot."

I couldn't argue about the suit thing. Thanks to Mom, I never trusted anyone dressed in business attire.

"You need to solve the case. One—" Megan ticked off a finger— "you come from a police family. Two—" she raised another finger— "what will happen to the bookstore if Jane is behind bars?"

My body tensed. The thought never occurred to me. Jane couldn't sell a building when she was trapped inside of another, right? Then again, I could see Drake Voss visiting the prison to make her an offer. I didn't know Jane well enough to know if she would accept a deal. The saying, prison changes people, came from somewhere. Jane might take any proposal just to be done with Sevier Oak. If she got out and took Drake's deal, she would leave town, and Teresa's Bookstore would close forever. The thought made me sick. I pushed the sundae aside.

"I know you can't buy the store," Megan continued.

My body lowered into itself. I had some money saved, but enough to pay the monthly bills and buy new tires if my car demanded. If I had a better credit score, and took out a small loan, then I could make Jane an offer. But I didn't.

"There is a way to save the bookstore." Megan drummed her fingers on the table before perking up. "I know. Tell Jane how wonderful the store's history is. That will convince her to let you run it, or at least not sell it."

I ran my necklace's charm up and down the chain. "Sure. Such an easy fix, just tell her."

Megan flicked my hand. "And along with other stuff obviously. Show her pictures of Peggy Sue with the kids and Teresa working. The good pictures so Jane can see the bookstore has a magical vibe. Don't use the ones when Teresa was in a cleaning mood." The images stirred happy memories. Teresa made more of a mess during her cleaning moods. I took pictures of her to prove it. "I know there are some cute Christmas photos from last year. Oh," she gasped, "I can bake my famous apple pie. Bring it into work tomorrow and show that Yankee why her aunt loved the south."

I sucked in my lips. Megan's plan sounded delicious.

I could ask Stone's advice without him knowing what I was doing. It had to be subtle, or I would find him and Dad standing at my doorstep reminding me of the bridge story. I pushed aside what my family might say and thought about how I could solve the case. Megan worked at Dessert Bar. The restaurant was a hot spot for gossip. I had always lived here. Surely people trusted me enough to spill some information. Maybe all those dinner talks and reading books had given me enough wits to solve a real murder. I found myself sitting taller.

"Yeah," I said, feeling empowered. "We can do this. Let's solve a murder."

CHAPTER 5

It felt good to be home. Some days, there's no better place than home. The scent of sweet BBQ chicken greeted me when I opened the door, a perfect smell on a scorching summer day. I forgot I had tossed all the ingredients into the crock pot before heading to the bookstore.

I wandered into the one-level cottage, admiring the cleanliness. No clutter tucked in corners to be dealt with later. On my off days, I vacuumed the carpet, Swifered the linoleum floors, and dusted all the rooms. Shoes were kept in our closets. Dishes went into the dishwasher rather than pile high in the sink.

It had taken some time to accept Teresa's mess at the bookstore. She enjoyed buying treasures with the goal in mind to add onto the store's cozy atmosphere. Sometimes she needed help controlling it. At home, it was a different story. Growing up, Dad was a stickler for organization and cleaning after oneself. Beds had to be made, shoes went in the closet, and toys picked up before bedtime. I hated doing chores as a child.

Now, I've come to enjoy it. Megan shared my neat lifestyle, making us living together a piece of cake.

Megan and I moved in together soon after graduating high school. Between a terrible breakup and Dad moving, I had to find a new place. The transition helped me be happily single and it worked out that Megan wanted to leave her childhood home. Timing couldn't have been better. An elderly man wanted to travel across America in an RV, but didn't want his home to be empty. Stone, a good friend of his, suggested he rent the cottage to us. He agreed and we'd been content here ever since.

The cottage house was built in 1938. Its small yard was great because it took twenty minutes to mow. Afterwards I would sit on the porch swing, drinking ice-cold lemonade.

Our home was simple and made for a small family. One bathroom had a shower and the other was just big enough for a person to squeeze inside and close the door. There were three bedrooms. In order to get to the master room at the back of the cottage, we had to walk through a room. That room was designated for books. We each had our own shelves. Megan's consisted of cookbooks and mine were fictional novels. Overall, the place was perfect for two single ladies.

I had a feeling our bachelorette days were coming to an end soon. Megan and her boyfriend, Austin, had started dating when he moved to Sevier Oak months ago. Lately, most of her time was spent at his place rather than here, a sign things were getting serious. I was happy for my best friend. He was a great guy. Most young people moved out of Sevier Oak before returning home if they did. Megan got lucky, while I remained on the single menu. I was fine being single until I turned twenty-nine last month. The big day hit a feeling that I never knew existed. Lonely. Meanwhile, everyone my age moved onto the next phase. One that I wanted to be a part of.

"Stop it," I told myself. I had read enough books to know that love would one day smack me in the face. Secretly, I hoped it would happen sooner than later.

I went into the kitchen, and shredded the chicken. The smell made my stomach growl. After tasting a small sample, I added another half-cup of BBQ sauce. It needed to soak for fifteen minutes.

To pass the time, I stood in front of my bookshelf. I traced my fingers over the books, trying to figure which to pick up. *Re-read one of my favorites, or choose one that I bought, but haven't read?* Last I counted, there were one hundred twenty-seven books. All organized by genre and then by the author's last name. Mystery novels far outnumbered the romance, women's fiction, and certain paranormal authors I only read during the month of October. I wasn't in the mood for a murder mystery or a character searching for love. After reading all the titles, I discovered I needed new books.

What I really needed were answers to my real-life mystery. Who killed Doris Hackett? Why did the police take Jane to the station? Did she really do it? And the most nagging question, what will happen to the bookstore?

I grabbed a notebook we used as our grocery list and found a pen. On the top of the sheet, I wrote 'suspects' and jotted down people who might have wanted Doris dead.

Jane Jackson had to be first. Despite not having a motive— none that I was aware— the police took her to the station for a reason. And she was the only other person in the store. Unless...

Sasha Whitlock, my former co-worker. Teresa had given her a key to the bookstore when Teresa lost hers. It turned out Butterscotch was laying on them. On my days off, Sasha opened the store. Teresa also noticed Sasha playing on her phone rather than helping customers and ignored the store's incoming calls, and caught her lying about opening the store late. Once Teresa had enough of Sasha's behavior, she let her go. It wasn't until a week later that we realized Sasha still had a key. To avoid chasing her down, I suggested changing the locks. Teresa agreed. But when Teresa died unexpectedly, seeking a key from a former co-worker and calling the locksmith never crossed my mind. Until now.

"Teresa," Doris yelled. Teresa and I were dusting the top of the bookshelves. If Princess didn't play with the Swiffer, it wouldn't be a two-person job.

Princess and I watched while Doris complained. "What's wrong with your employee?" She pointed a stubby finger at Sasha. Before Teresa could say anything, Doris continued. "This girl is extremely rude."

"I'm not a girl," Sasha smarted back.

Doris's eyes widened. "See? I should get a discount for the way she's treating me."

Sasha's mouth dropped when Teresa agreed. After that encounter, the two women nearly came to blows when Doris returned.

Like everyone in Sevier Oak, I assumed Sasha was also jealous of Miss Hackett. Between the encounters at the bookstore and Doris's history, it made sense why Sasha threatened her.

Her motive seemed far fetched and opportunity remained unknown, but means checked the box. When I saw Underwood tomorrow, I would pass on this information. I ignored thoughts of possibly having worked alongside a killer, and continued the list.

The next suspect was Preston Powell, Doris's ex-husband. He claimed to be working at Old Treasures during the murder. Although he had an alibi, it didn't dismiss the fact that he hated

Doris, and rightfully so. His wife had an affair with Preston's biggest competitor. I sucked in my lips, struggling to remember the guy's name. I'd recalled it earlier today. After a few moments, I gave up and wrote *Competitor Lover*. Then pondered more about Preston. I didn't personally know him, only what I'd heard from others. We made small talk when he came into the store to discuss the remodel with Teresa and me. He seemed okay, but I did detect a vibe. The only way I could describe it was that he sounded like a bitter man. It was no secret that Preston had asked Doris for money after she won eight million dollars. Doris said no and flaunted her new wealth.

I drew a star by his name. Out of everyone in Sevier Oak, Preston had the biggest motive despite their divorce happening four years ago. I also added a question mark. His means and opportunity weren't as strong as his motive.

Clara Hackett was also at the scene, making her a necessary addition to my list. The Hackett sisters had their share of arguments too, both before and after Doris won the lottery. They remained civil until their parents passed away. Clara inherited the house while Doris told Preston that he needed to build her a home.

Sevier Oak was known for looking out for one another, but Clara took that concept too far. Her neighbors often reported seeing her on their property, peeking into their windows, or watching them from within her car, holding a pair of binoculars. Dad and Stone groaned after hearing Clara's address when a call came in. Growing up, it seemed Clara caused more trouble than minding her own business.

Like Preston, Clara hadn't received a dime from Doris. If Clara inherited everything from her sister's death, that gave her eight million motives. How she had sneaked inside the bookstore without me knowing and committed murder, remained a mystery. I made a note beside Clara's name to ask Underwood about Doris's will.

The last person on my list was Doris's ex-lover. Again, I made a note to ask Underwood about his name. I couldn't call him *Competitor Lover* forever. If I remembered correctly, they had dated while he built her mansion. Once the job was done, Doris kicked him to the curb. Rumors claimed that Doris had only stayed with him to get a discount. If that was true or not, was another story. Like Preston, *Competitor Lover* had a motive that happened years ago. How he committed the crime was a bigger mystery than Clara's means and opportunity.

After pondering a little bit longer, I couldn't think of any more suspects or recall any more information about them. I closed the notebook. A BBQ sandwich was calling my name.

I was on my way to the crock pot when someone banged on the door. I recognized those quick rapping knocks. Before he broke the door, I rushed to answer it. Just as I suspected, Roland Bingham. He stood on my porch wearing his post office uniform with the white postal truck parked in front of my home. Roland shoved a box into my chest without saying a word.

Roland looked the same since first grade, short black hair, high cheekbones, and long eyelashes that women would kill for. The only thing that changed since school was his height and a stubble beard. If he outgrew his foul mood, he might be married by now.

"What is it?" I wondered aloud. Based on the box's weight, I knew it wasn't a new appliance, or a book won from an unexpected Goodreads giveaway.

"It's for Megan," he said.

I read the label. Surely enough it was addressed to my best friend. "Are these the potholders?" I asked myself and was surprised when Roland answered.

"There are four potholders. They look like they came from *Jaws*."

"They're pockets." I eyed him. "How did you know they're sharks?" And potholders?

Roland shrugged and quickly looked away. "Delivery guys just know stuff."

"Did you open this?" I asked. Roland was overall a decent guy, but I didn't like how he knew the package's details.

"The box was dented when it got to the post office, so I did Megan a favor and repackaged it. Happy? How about a thank you?"

That was thoughtful, though his attitude didn't make me want to thank him. "These were supposed to be here weeks ago. And speaking of late shipments, the bookstore is still missing three orders." Not that it mattered anymore, but our customers had already paid for the books. The least I could do was hand-deliver them.

Roland looked back at me with a defensive glare. "I brought them this morning."

I chose my next words carefully. "When?"

"Before Doris croaked."

"Are the orders in the receiving room?" I asked, referring to the small area in back of the building. Teresa added a door to make it easier for the post office to pick up and drop packages, rather than them squeezing a dolly through the rows of bookshelves. I just remembered I had chucked trash bags in there when I heard of Jane's arrival.

"Work has been busy," Roland snapped. "Be happy it got here."

With that, Roland turned, and power walked to his truck. The tires squealed loudly as he sped off. I shook my head, watching the postal truck disappear.

Before I went inside, a terrible thought hit me. I stared

down the street, knowing Roland was probably a mile away now. He was at Teresa's Bookstore that morning. Like Sasha, he had a key to the store— and most businesses on Copper Street.

Did Doris hear Roland and pestered him about something? Roland has always had a short temper that ruined friendships, and caused family drama. His fights started at the middle school's gym and worked their way up to bars. Mostly over minor stuff that Roland couldn't let go such as spilled beer or losing in a game of pool. Again, I shook my head. Maybe, I was overthinking this investigation.

Maybe.

CHAPTER 6

After burning my tongue, I let my sandwich cool. I checked my email, hoping Dad had written. Since he worked crazy hours, we mainly communicated through email. I missed him. Talking through words on a screen wasn't the same as our chats over dinner at Grandma's and Stone's house, waving at each other when our paths crossed on the road, or him popping in at Teresa's Bookstore just to say hi.

I was bummed when I didn't see a new message from him. Nashville kept him busy. My gaze brushed over Jane's messages about running the bookstore and zeroed in on the second message. No matter how hard I tried avoiding the "*Hey Garnet*" subject line, I never could. The words were burned into my memory, as they had changed everything I thought I knew about my mom.

Hello Garnet Stone,

My name is Regan, and there's no easy way to say this but we have the same mother, Aoife Suillivan. Sorry to be blunt, but I was afraid you would delete the message if I rambled about, please "read me!" I found out last month. (Long story how I did and a bigger one on how I found your email) It took me this long to work up the courage to write. Again, I apologize for the awkward message. I have so much I want to say and ask. I haven't told Mom about finding out about you. I want to get to know you first. Please write or call me.

The email concluded with Regan's phone number.

"What should I do?" I had phoned Dad after reading Regan's message for the first time.

"I didn't know Aoife had another child," Dad said. He sounded as shocked as I had been. "Or if she was married," he mumbled the last part. "Just sleep on it for a few nights."

A few nights turned into two months.

I haven't mentioned Regan to Dad since getting the email. I got the sense he didn't want to talk about it. Learning about Regan probably hurt him more than he let on.

He once told me how he met Mom. Dad went on a cruise before becoming a full-time cop. Mom worked as a bartender. They spent every possible moment together that week at sea. Once the vacation was over, so was their relationship. He tried reaching out to her, but silence echoed back, leaving him heartbroken. Then, out of the blue, Mom showed up on Dad's doorstep with three-month old me. Dad tried to convince her to stay. But my mother left as quickly as she came; jumping on the chance to work on a private yacht. According to Grandma, Mom ended any hopes of Dad marrying, fearing he would get hurt again. While Mom sailed the seven seas tending to wealthy guests, the Stone family raised me.

Mom had visited America one week during every summer break. Grandma always drove me to Florida for our visits. Mom always came bearing gifts. As a little girl, I loved getting expensive clothes that no other kids had in school, yummy treats, sunglasses, and jewelry. As the years rolled on, my desire shifted to wanting to spend one-on-one time with her rather than receiving gifts. I yearned for mother and daughter bonding time, like Megan did with hers. I wanted Mom to see me for who I was, for her to ask me questions about myself. Unfortunately, that day never came. After my eighteenth birthday, Mom mailed me packages and the Florida visits stopped. The only positive thing I could say about her was that she gave me the Stone name.

Mom was the reason I distrusted people who wore suits. As a chief stewardess, her uniform resembled expensive clothing; a white blouse and black pencil skirt. When off duty, she wore similar apparel as the guests she served. Mom chose her career over me, making sure clients received first-class service at all times. Deep down, I knew not everyone dressed in tuxedos, skirts, or blazers were money chasers, yet I struggled not to judge.

I pictured Mom. Right now, she was probably smiling into the distance as the wind touches face. Her hair clipped in a night bun. Regan stood next to her, wearing the yacht's uniform.

So many times I wanted to ask Teresa's opinion on what I should do: write back, message Mom, or ignore it all together? Teresa was a wise woman. I wanted an opinion from a non-family member. Before I found my courage, Karl and I found her at the bottom of the stairs. A tragic accident from carrying too many books. I've pushed the thought of Teresa, Regan, and Mom away.

"Enough of memory lane," I said to myself.

When I took a bite, my dinner was cold. My heart sank. Instead of making a new sandwich, I found myself thinking about Regan again. Perhaps murder and death made me think these thoughts. The unknown.

It wasn't as if I hadn't tried to find Regan on social media. I wanted to see Regan first before I wrote back. Unfortunately, there wasn't anything I could do since Regan didn't give a last name. After Googling the name, I learned that Regan was considered a gender-neutral name. Not knowing if I had a brother or sister drove me crazy. This and not knowing a last name, it was impossible to find my sibling on social media.

Thankfully, the front door opened, forcing me out of memory lane. I closed my email.

"That smells uh-mazing," Megan said, tossing her purse on the table. She made a beeline for the crock pot.

I took a bite of my cold BBQ sandwich. It still tasted good.

Her eyes sparkled. "Oh, is that my package?"

She grabbed the box before I could answer. Seconds later, and tape torn, Megan squealed with joy. As Roland claimed, there were four sets of shark potholders. A beaming smile crossed Megan's face. She giggled while sliding her hands inside the pocket of fabric teeth as though a shark was chopping on her.

"What do you think?"

"Cute, like the other million ones you have," I teased thinking about some of her potholders: avocados, happy ghosts, t-rex hands, and my personal favorite, white ball gown gloves.

"One can never have too many."

Megan pretended to be screaming while dramatically, easing her way onto the floor.

I sang the notes of the *Jaws* theme. Megan jumped up, in an attempt to scare me. It didn't work.

"Whatever," she said, tossing the potholders onto the table. "So, have you solved the case yet?"

"I have four suspects," I answered a little too cheerfully.

Megan gave me a strange look while I went to the living room to retrieve my list.

"Are you sure Jane didn't do it?" Megan asked once I finished going over the suspect list. During that time, she made herself a sandwich, and ate half of it.

"No, I mean, yes. I'm positive that Jane didn't kill Doris." I finished my sandwich in two bites and went for seconds. "Unless Jane has Sonic speed, killed Doris, and ran up the stairs to crash into me a minute later."

Megan smiled. "Hey, you solved the mystery."

I half smirked. "Jane did not kill Doris. It was physically impossible."

"Then why did she get taken to the station?"

"It's procedure."

Megan waved a hand at me. "Yeah, yeah."

We ate in a comfortable silence. Regan snuck back into my thoughts. I needed to make a decision soon if I was going to write back. The longer I push him or her off, the harder it would be to form a relationship.

Focus on the case, I mentally scolded myself. The bookstore's future depended on me. It had to be my top priority. Not Mom, or her other child. The reply could wait a little longer.

"Did you hear any more gossip at Dessert Bar?" I asked, leaning back in my chair with a full stomach.

"The real question is who isn't talking about Doris's death. From what I've overheard it's nothing that we don't already know." Megan went to take her last bite and stopped. "Clara Hackett came in for a little bit. She bounced from table to table, listening to everyone's conversations. She only ordered water." She hummed a chuckle as she finished her sandwich.

"Did Clara say anything? It's not like her to keep quiet."

She nodded while chewing. "She thinks she's getting Doris's money."

"Thinks?" I asked. She nodded again. "Did she say when she'll know for certain?"

When Megan shook her head, I added another question for Underwood tomorrow.

Megan continued, "When Clara finds out, everyone in Sevier Oak will know."

I agreed. Clara liked to gossip. She gladly told everyone about Doris being greedy. Many people in town believed Clara was the reason why Doris installed a tall fence around her property. Clara found another way to spy on her sister. She parked her car in the street, stood on top of the hood with a pair of binoculars. The image used to make me smile. Now it was creepy.

"We have a clever killer," said Megan. "We need to have our eyes and ears peeled."

She had a point. The killer must have known Doris would be at the bookstore and found a way inside without anyone knowing, that is if Jane wasn't the killer.

Great, now I'm starting to second guess myself.

"I hope the cats are okay," I said, changing subject.

Megan rolled her eyes. "They're fine. They've lived there for what? At least two years now. And it's not the first time they had to be put up."

I didn't want to think about the last time Princess and Butterscotch had to be locked in the Cat's Lounge. I knew they were fine for tonight. But what if Teresa's Bookstore closed for good? It wouldn't just break my heart, but the cats would be homeless.

"We need to solve this fast," I said.

"That's the spirit." Megan flashed a smile. "Sooner you solve it, the sooner you can make Jane feel bad and run the bookstore yourself."

I smirked, not fully liking the idea of guilt tripping the new owner. Thankfully, Megan moved onto a new topic. She was in the middle of telling me about her plans with Austin tomorrow, when someone banged on the front door.

Megan stood up, "I'll get it."

I had a feeling who was at the door. I dug through my purse and saw I had several missed calls. *Shoot.*

I heard Megan said, "she's in the kitchen."

Deputy Underwood entered, still wearing his police uniform. He took a deep breath while keeping his focus on me.

I spoke before he did. "My phone was on silent. I'll call Stone back." I held my phone, staring at the screen. Stone was going to lecture me about answering all his calls because a killer was on the loose. Which was true. Once I considered seeing things from a cop's perspective, I wasn't as annoyed. Knowing my whereabouts alone didn't necessarily mean that I was safe. Underwood left once Stone's voice came through the speaker.

CHAPTER 7

I GOT UP EARLY THE FOLLOWING MORNING TO MEET UNDERWOOD AT the bookstore. It was going to be a scorcher. At eight o'clock in the morning, the inside of my car was already blazing hot. No clouds floated in the sky, just a massive ball of sunshine. I cranked the air conditioner while racing to Teresa's Bookstore. I wasn't used to getting out of bed before nine, since the bookstore didn't open until ten.

When I stopped for a red light, I checked the volume on my cell phone. After Stone banged on my front door last night, concerned about my well-being, I made sure it was fully charged and not on silent. I wouldn't make that mistake twice.

When I pulled onto Copper Street, I instantly spotted a cop car parked along the busy road. I didn't have to see the vehicle number to know it belonged to Underwood. The deputy leaned against the store's bay window, watching me park.

"Hey. How's it going?" I asked, walking up to him. Underwood didn't crack a smile. "Sorry about last night. I didn't realize my phone was on silent." Or that Stone had called seven times.

"Do you have your cellphone on you?"

I pulled it out of my purse. He gave an approving nod checking to see that the battery life was at its fullest, and the volume was set on high.

"Now is not the time to lose your phone or have it on silent," he said. "A murder occurred in the same building as you."

I didn't have to see his eyes to know Underwood was giving me a firm look behind his sunglasses. Sarcasm got the best of me as I saluted him like a good soldier.

Underwood finally broke a smile. "Better safe than sorry. And to answer your question, no. I was just leaving the station when Sterling called."

"Sterling?" I questioned as Underwood unlocked Teresa's Bookstore. "No one calls him that." Not even Grandma.

"I can't call him Chief anymore, so it has to be Sterling."

The cowbells clanged as Underwood opened the door. I welcomed the familiarity: the musty smell, the crowded bookshelves, a random cat toy on the floor, and even the ugly green carpet. And yet, something felt off. My nose detected new smells. A hint of men's cologne and laundry detergent. It clashed with the common scents. I didn't like it. It reminded me of Teresa's accident when medical personnel were here. Once the crime scene investigation was complete, I could open the front doors to air out the place.

"Sheriff Estep has not released the place to be open," Underwood said, as if he heard my thoughts. "I'm asking on his behalf for you to look around the store and tell me if anything is out of the ordinary."

A loud and long meow yowled above us.

"You are also allowed to check on the cats," Underwood replied

"Not a problem," I said, glad to help with the case without Estep barking out orders.

Once I opened the Cat's Lounge door, Princess bolted out as if she had been trapped in the tower for years. I stared at Underwood, fearing he would be upset.

"She's fine." Underwood grinned. "Princess's fur is everywhere."

Butterscotch was lying on the floor, slowly blinking at me, as if she had just awoken from her beauty sleep. The tortie cat sprawled out in the middle of the room, a foot away from three cat beds. I gave her a good pet and inspected the room. Everything seemed to be the same: clumps of fur, book towers, cat beds, and an arrangement of toys. After I refilled their food and water dishes, Butterscotch fell back to sleep.

"Ready to get started?" Underwood asked, scanning the office from the hallway. He didn't sound hopeful.

"I know Teresa's stuff better than anyone," I reassured him. He nodded but remained doubtful.

As we lingered in the hallway, I recalled my notes from the night before. If I wasn't in a rush to get here, I would've grabbed my notebook. Rookie mistake. I started with the most burning question. "Did Jane kill Doris?"

"It's too early to tell."

In other words, he was not allowed to say anything.

"You gotta tell me something," I begged. "This place means so much to me. You know I can help."

Underwood inhaled a deep breath before gazing into the office. "We've uncovered prints from the knife."

My heart raced, already thinking of more questions.

"And the answer to your next question, the prints belonged to Doris Hackett. Except for one."

"Jane?"

Underwood shook his head no. "No ID yet."

This case was getting weird. Why were Doris's fingerprints on the knife? She didn't come across as a person who carried one. In her defense, people pestered her for free handouts. Doris once grumbled how someone grabbed her arm, wanting money. I'd never heard who touched her, but Doris often overreacted to things. Perhaps after that incident, she felt the need to carry a knife. But that still didn't make sense. Doris had pepper spray on her keychain, a pink fancy case, one she gladly showed me while ringing up her purchase. If Doris owned both weapons, I would think she would use the one made for a quick getaway rather than stab a person to flee. Based on the lack of powerful odor, I assumed Doris didn't use the pepper during her attack. Sad that neither weapon helped Doris in the end.

A new thought occurred to me.

"Do you think the unknown print belonged to Teresa?"

"We're working on it." Underwood clapped as if we were breaking a huddle. "Alright, we got a lot of ground to cover; let's get moving."

Before we could start, the cowbells clanged. Deputy Underwood sprang into action. He ran toward the staircase and down the steps, all while telling me to stay put. I darted to the back staircase. If I hurried, I could see who's here without Underwood knowing.

A line of yellow tape stopped me halfway down the stairs. I pressed my hands against the wall for support. Not wanting to contaminate any evidence, I backtracked and went the way Underwood had.

By the time I reached the main staircase, I could hear voices from below. I bolted down so fast I nearly tripped over the last three steps.

"The store is closed off," Underwood said sternly.

I zipped around the bookshelves, not caring about the

hardwood floor creaking. It was impossible to avoid this section unannounced. When I came around a bookshelf, my tennis shoes screeched to a stop for a second time today.

"Jane?" I said.

Jane dressed in the same gray suit as yesterday, yet there were some clear differences. It reminded me of the game with two pictures side by side, prompting the viewer to spot the irregularities. Her outfit was now wrinkled and once tight bun disheveled, leading me to believe she had slept at the jail.

"What is she doing here?" Jane demanded, turning her attention back on him.

"Respect the Stone," Deputy Underwood bellowed, making Jane's brown eyes widen. "Garnet Stone is assisting the police."

While Jane collected herself, I harbored a laugh. Underwood was having too much fun with this made-up motto. This was going into Dad's next email.

"The sheriff released you," I said, seeing Jane's presence as good news. Boss lady wasn't a suspect.

Dang it, I just remembered Megan's apple pie sitting on the kitchen table. Once we were done searching the bookstore, I would race home to bring it here.

Jane shifted her attention between us. "Sheriff Estep has no reason to hold me any longer than he had. I came here to clear my name and clean this mess." Jane waved her hand in the air, referring to the bookstore's clutter.

"This is a homicide investigation. You can't remove anything," said Underwood.

"I was referring to when the case is closed, then I can clear out the store to put it on the market.

My heart filled with sadness. Selling the store was Jane's biggest concern? If Underwood wasn't here, I would have told Jane all the great stuff about her aunt's bookstore and Sevier Oak. Teresa's Bookstore was more than just a pay day.

Underwood must have sensed my feelings and suggested that we work as a team. Jane seemed more than happy to help. They faced me. It took me a moment to realize they were waiting for me. I made the first move before Jane decided to take over. I had to show Boss Lady how well I worked.

I headed to the far right of the store into the romance/horror room. Underwood and Jane followed while Princess walked along the bookshelves until she had to jump down to enter the next room.

"This is going to take forever," Jane muttered under her breath.

These bookshelves were the most unorganized in the store. Customers were most to blame, misplacing their unwanted books in the wrong place. Fortunately, I'd been straightening this mess for years and knew the difference between clutter and a possible clue.

I wasn't a huge fan of romance or horror, but I adored this room. Teresa installed a sheet of glass over the bookshelves and added books. When gazing up, it appeared as if books floated overhead. The hovering books were overstock from ones on the sales floor. Stephen King and Nora Roberts mostly dominated the space until I noticed mystery novels by Vicki Delany, Dean James, Lucy Foley, and Harlan Coben creeping in. When I asked Teresa how those books got up there, she admitted that its her secret stash and would buy them later. I joked with her about how her TBR list became literal. Teresa and I wanted to keep the floating book idea for the remodel. We never decided if this room would be romance or horror. If I had wire lights, the room could've been super lovely or super spooky. I made a mental note to tell Jane about this idea after we searched the store.

"Why did my aunt put two genres in one room?" Jane stared at a row of books stacked horizontally and vertically.

Underwood reminded us about the task before I answered Jane. Boss Lady and I glanced at each other, silently agreeing to postpone this conversation. We both shared an urgency to solve the case. Unfortunately, our reasons didn't match.

We worked in silence until I couldn't keep quiet. While studying every spot and bookshelf, I told Jane about the floating book idea for the remodel. My story got interrupted often because Underwood pointed out anything that wasn't a book, and Jane complained about the overcrowded shelves. She didn't admit it, but I knew she liked the idea. I caught Jane admiring the sight above her before searching the bookshelves for clues.

After an hour of searching, and gently pushing Princess aside, the romance/horror and front area of the store was done, clear of any foul play. Which I suspected since the murdered happened in the bargain room.

I frowned when Underwood escorted us upstairs. I was itching to snoop in the bargain room. All the stuff I removed from the sales floor went upstairs, into one of Teresa's storage rooms. This area would take the longest.

"What in the world is this?" Jane gasped. She stood in the Cat's Lounge doorway with her mouth wide open.

"Teresa gave the cat's their own room."

Her griping about the mess started to get on my nerves. The internal struggle of not voicing my opinion got hard. I zipped my lips and kept working. Snapping at Jane might hurt my case to save the bookstore.

Butterscotch looked annoyed. We probably disturbed her slumber. She left as soon as the three of us entered the room. Princess strolled between us, ignoring her sister's foul mood. Less than five minutes later, Cat's Lounge was done.

When I walked past the office to search the other rooms, Underwood stopped me. "We need to look here too."

I doubted clues hid in the office. Sure, Jane had been in here during Doris's attack, but I struggled to see Jane as a killer.

"I didn't do anything suspicious," Jane said defensively.

"All rooms must be searched," he said, facing her. "Including the office."

Jane crossed her arms, waiting in the hallway because Teresa's office couldn't fit more than two people. I scanned the desk, opened drawers, and flipped through scattered papers. Book orders were taped on the wall behind the boxy computer. The receipts reminded me of Roland. According to him, they were waiting in the receiving room.

"I was looking for tax documents," Jane continued. "Teresa owned the building."

Underwood had to have heard her, but made no comment.

"Do the police need to check the computer?" I asked. Behind Underwood, Jane gave me a -how-dare-you look.

"Did you use the computer?" Underwood asked Jane.

She replied, "No, I haven't had the chance to use it."

Underwood glanced at me, unconvinced.

"The computer is password protected, and I haven't told her it yet," I said.

He nodded before moving on.

Besides, if Jane had hacked onto the store's computer, I doubt she researched how to get away with murder while Doris shopped downstairs. That sounded far stretched.

Once finished in the office, we went through the other rooms upstairs. The upper level used to be an apartment. After Teresa bought the place, she lived here until she decided that living and working in the same building wasn't as enjoyable as she thought. Since then, the apartment became a "storage area," as Teresa liked to call it. Extra copies of books, store decorations for the holidays, and odds and ends had found their permanent home.

"Did Teresa mention remodeling the store?" I asked Jane, trying to break up some of the awkward silence. Secretly, I hoped Jane would go on a rant and spill the beans about her plans on Teresa's house because she inherited that, too.

Jane didn't respond. I was about to say something else when Jane finally said, "Aunt Teresa emailed me your plans." Her tone sounded proper. I couldn't tell if she liked the idea or was just answering the question.

"When?" I asked, keeping the conversation going.

Jane kept her hands to herself like a germaphobe as she peeked in a tall cardboard box that stored Christmas wrapping paper.

"A few months ago." She faced me. "You have a good eye, but remodeling is costly."

"Teresa has been saving money for years. It should cover everything."

"Unexpected repairs and surprises always come with updating old buildings."

Her steadfast resolve to sell sickened me to continue the conversation any further.

Why did Teresa leave her with everything and not me?

Soon we found ourselves downstairs, in the receiving room. The concrete room was added after Teresa bought it, making it the coldest room in the building. Even on the hottest days, there was a coolness.

As Roland said last night, a large box sat near the exit. I stared at it. The orders were for three different customers and placed on different days. There should've been three small boxes.

Strange, but not connected to the murder.

While Underwood and Teresa wandered inside the rectangular area, I spotted another strange thing. Inside one of Teresa's project boxes was a white teddy bear cradling a red heart. Embroidery on the shape read, *I Love You*. It looked like a Valentine's Day gift. Teresa never had a lover to my knowledge and more importantly, the bear wasn't there two days ago when I took out the trash, the night before Jane's arrival.

I pointed to the toy. "This didn't belong to Teresa."

"How do you know?" Jane asked as Underwood marched over.

He froze in place before reaching into his pocket, retrieving his phone. "Don't move."

Jane and I made eye contact.

Underwood held up his phone, snapping pictures before instructing me to put it back exactly where I found it. When I placed the bear back inside the box, I saw the name Doris written on its foot. It looked to be with an ink pen rather than a marker. Then my eyes shifted towards a red spot on the bear's ear, the reason for Underwood's sudden urgency. Blood.

CHAPTER 8

Once again, Jane and I were escorted outside. After Underwood put the stuffed teddy-bear in an evidence bag, he marched us to the front door while making a phone call. I didn't understand why we couldn't stay inside. It wasn't like the bear was a bomb. When I voiced the question, Underwood wouldn't answer.

I stood in the same spot as yesterday. Jane looked like she wanted to stand by me, but changed her mind and waited near the bookstore's entrance. Old Treasure's awning did nothing against the sun's heat. I felt bad for Jane standing in direct sunlight. She had to be sweaty— again— in that suit. I felt hotter just by looking at her.

Tires squealing pulled my attention to Copper Street. A cop car came to a halt behind Underwood's police cruiser. Sheriff Estep hopped out. He marched up to Underwood without acknowledging Jane or me, as if we hadn't been invited to help with the case. I found his lack of acknowledging people rude and even ruder when the sheriff interrupted Underwood by gesturing for them to talk inside. Perhaps the reason why we were kicked out of the store was more of the sheriff's doing than Dad's friend.

I fanned myself, hoping this wouldn't take long. Meanwhile, Jane fiddled with her nails and constantly rubbed her eyes. She tried stifling yawns but failed miserably. She needed a shower and sleep. A part of me wanted to reassure her that the Sevier Oak Police were good people, and she should go home.

Before I walked over to Jane, a boxy post office vehicle raced down the street. I recognized Roland from his grumpy face and jet-black hair. I waved for him to stop. Roland's focus didn't stray. He rolled past me and turned onto a back street, probably making his deliveries for the stores on Copper Street. My question about what was inside the box would have to wait until Sheriff Estep gave the okay. Bummer, I wanted to know now.

Clara Hackett's red car piqued my curiosity. Her sedan was parked across the street. I sighed deeply when a pair of binoculars appeared over her eyes. All the windows were rolled down. Clara had to be the worst spy in history. If she came into the bookstore, I would have recommended Graham Greene or Lee Child novels. I chuckled when I remembered a book by Louise Fitzhugh, *Harriet the Spy*.

The cowbells clanged, pulling me towards the bookshop. Sheriff Estep marched up to me with Underwood closely behind. He jabbed a finger near my face. "I thought you told us everything."

I wanted to say, *you should have let me help yesterday, and I did tell you everything*. Instead, I replied, "Deputy Underwood was with me when I found the evidence." I gave Dad's friend a look that hopefully came across as stern, and a plea to back me up.

"As was I," Jane said, power walking towards us. "Perhaps

you should allow us to continue searching for more evidence, rather than shoving us out the door."

Sheriff Estep's frown deepened at Jane's last words. His lips swayed, upset. "Did you find the evidence?"

"No," Jane replied.

"Have you ever been inside the place before yesterday morning?"

"You already asked that question."

My eyes shifted between them as the tension escalated. As I watched them go back and forth, I found myself uncertain who I wanted to win this battle of wits. My boss, who sounded like she had some common sense, or the sheriff, the person out of the two who had authority to find and put murders away?

After a long moment, Sheriff Estep won by saying, "Get off the property."

Jane crossed her arms over her chest. "I'm the owner."

"Leave or I'll book you for obstruction of an investigation. I can hold you another night if that's what you want."

Jane's lips pursed. She wanted to argue. A part of me wished she did. Estep was a jerk. After she reminded Sheriff Estep that he had to inform her about the store's condition, Jane stormed to a black sports car parked nearby.

I walked toward Underwood, not sure what would happen next.

"Where do you think you're going?"

"I wasn't—"

"Wrong," he interrupted. "You're going through that pile of crap, find anything else that was overlooked."

I hated how he spoke to me, but now wasn't the time to fight back. A handful of shoppers stopped and stared. Clara's binoculars were fixed on us. I held my head up and walked inside.

For the next few hours, Sheriff Estep made me look

through the entire bookstore, including the areas we already searched. Poor Princess. I had to put the cats back in Cat's Lounge. I wished I could've switched Estep barking orders for Jane's complaining. *At least I have Underwood,* I thought.

When I got to the bargain room, it looked the same as yesterday. Books were still scattered on the floor, but now resonated a creepy vibe. The only thing missing was Doris herself. I pushed the feeling aside to focus. Carefully, I scanned the shelves and the green carpet. I found the half crushed pink pill. Again, I told Sheriff Estep, and he ignored me by blaming it on the store's clutter.

Thankfully, the sheriff's cell phone rang and he stepped away.

Underwood stood over me. "Benadryl," he lowered his voice.

Duh Garnet, the color should have been a giveaway.

"Teresa never took Benadryl, and I swear it wasn't here before the murder. I came early yesterday to clean before Jane got here. I know Teresa's mess." I emphasized the last sentence.

Underwood stared into the distance, pondering. Then Sheriff Estep returned. His piercing blue eyes and unhappy baby face ordered us to get back to work.

I spent over an hour searching under every fallen book, nook, and corner of the bargain room. After all of my hard work, only the stuffed bear and Benadryl were out of place. I tended to the cats before I was practically thrown out of Teresa's Bookstore. The sheriff told me to stay in town.

While Sheriff Estep hovered over Underwood, locking the store, I headed to my car. I wanted to talk to Dad's friend, but couldn't with Estep around. Like with Roland, my burning questions would have to wait. The cranky sheriff wouldn't allow me to take a quick peek inside the box Roland delivered.

According to him, customer orders were not part of the case. I agreed, but had to try.

I checked my phone and was shocked at the time. I worked an entire shift. My stomach growled, fussing at me for missing lunch. The scent of food made my mouth water.

I walked away from my car and headed down the street. Dessert Bar wasn't going to satisfy a starving stomach. I needed a meal with calories. One place came to mind.

While walking, I searched for Clara. Her little red car hadn't moved, but there was no sign of its owner. I took that as an indication that Clara was either roaming the streets or was eating at a restaurant, eavesdropping on the local gossip. Eating or roaming around town, I was glad not to see Doris's sister.

Retail stores were closing. I watched a worker at Vintage Disguise, a costume shop, flip the sign from open to close. The owner of the music store waved at me while locking the door. Normally, I lingered and talked to my fellow work neighbors, but I really wanted food, and I had a feeling people might ask about Doris's murder. *Another time*, I thought.

The air smelled delicious as I neared Kountry Wings. The restaurant was known for their salty chicken and waffle fries, just the sustenance I needed. I felt relieved at the sight of empty tables. Before I entered, I spotted a certain individual. I stopped walking and stared, making sure my eyes weren't playing tricks on me. Jane Jackson sat at a table with two men dressed in dark suits. I recognized them. Drake Voss, the owner of Voss-of-Books, and his youngest grandson, Leo Voss. My heart dropped. I didn't have to be a genius to know what they were discussing.

Teresa's Bookstore.

If Jane had already signed an agreement with Drake, then saving the bookstore was already over. Old Drake looked serious, like he always did when trying to convince Teresa of selling. Jane looked like she was doing most of the talking, probably voicing her terms. It seemed Drake would get what he wanted.

I stared at Leo. Drake's grandson was five years older than me at twenty-seven. For a Voss, he was handsome. According to Teresa's rants and rumors around Sevier Oak, Leo wasn't uptight like the other Voss men. A single memory with Leo confirmed it to be true. I pushed it aside.

Leo stared at his cell phone as if he was bored. Then he gazed around the restaurant until his eyes caught mine. He smiled. My face warmed. He really was handsome. I quickly turned away, feeling like I turned into Clara, spying on my boss with Teresa's two nemeses.

There were other restaurants, even though the chicken and fries smelled amazing. At the second bay window I saw Sasha Whitlock. I froze in place. She sat alone at the table, running her fingers through her blond hair before applying more red lipstick to her already ruby lips. I glanced up and down the street debating. *Go inside to question Sasha and risk being spotted by Jane and the guys, or avoid all drama by going elsewhere?* But the latter wouldn't get me any closer to solving this case. There could still be time to find Doris's killer and save the store. For all I knew, they were just talking. I didn't notice any papers on their table.

I tapped my foot, hating my options.

"For the bookstore and the cats," I mumbled. I held my head up high and entered the restaurant.

CHAPTER 9

THE WELCOMING SMELL OF HOT FOOD HIT ME HARD. IT WAS SO strong that I practically tasted the tender meat. I went straight to Sasha's table before a server stopped me. Up close she looked nice. No gamer or graphic T-shirt or super short shorts, but a nice summer dress.

"Hi," I said sitting in the empty chair across from her. Her citrus perfume nearly overpowered the restaurant's smell. Sasha looked taken back and checked out the window. "How have you been?" I started, hoping she wouldn't chase me off. "I've been worried about you."

Her face brightened. "You have?"

No. "Yes," I lied. "The police have been struggling to solve the case. I wondered if they've been pestering you as they have with me."

Sasha shrugged nonchalantly. "Doris had it coming. You knew that."

No remorse, I noted. "Did you see anything unusual?" I asked as casually as I could manage. When Sasha shook her head, I continued. "Clara has been hovering around Copper Street more than usual. Have you seen anything?"

Sasha rolled her eyes. "That woman is crazy. She's been following me around. So annoying. She's almost as bad as Doris." She ran her fingers through her hair. "But I haven't seen anything. After the bookstore, I went..." her words faded away.

"Where did you go?"

Sasha gave me a shy smile. "Please don't be mad, but I need a job. My parents threatened to kick me out of the house if I don't."

"O-kay."

"I work at Voss-of-Books."

She maintained being timid as if she expected me to blow up. Sasha couldn't know that I was internally struggling to conceal a laugh. It was no secret that Drake Voss was a difficult man. He liked things done his way, and if anyone questioned it, Drake sent them out the door. If a task took too long to finish, I'd heard he let them go for being "too lazy." Teenagers who started working at Voss-of-Books never made it through the summer break. The rumors painted Drake as being a strict businessman and having zero patience.

Teresa gave Sasha several warnings before sending her out the door. Something told me that Sasha wouldn't last long.

"Leo asked about you." Sasha smirked. "Since Jane is closing the store, I can recommend you—"

"No, no, no."

"—since I work there now. But you don't need my personal recommendation. Leo asked about you during my interview. In passing of course." She winked.

After the first meeting Teresa had with Drake, I vowed to never step foot in that store. I wouldn't break that promise because Teresa's Bookstore closed. I would drive an hour to Bristol before buying books there.

I changed the subject to avoid Sasha talking more about Voss-of-Books. Or Leo. "You were being interviewed by Leo when Doris died?"

Her face blushed and she quickly took a sip of her lemon water. "Actually, I was with Mateo."

I mentally snapped my fingers. That was the name of Doris's ex-boyfriend and Preston's biggest competitor. My heart raced with excitement.

"Why?" I asked.

"You really are clueless when it comes to dating." Sasha giggled.

I wanted to deny it, but Teresa also pointed out the fact. And Megan. And Grandma. Maybe Molly, too.

I never could figure out when I was being hit on or when a guy was just being nice. Thinking back, I remembered Mateo visiting the store while Sasha still worked for Teresa. I assumed he was there to chat with Teresa about the remodel. Perhaps Mateo had an ulterior motive.

"We started talking a while back. He finally asked me out and well..." she beamed. "We haven't stopped seeing each other."

It just dawned on me. Sasha's nice dress. Her red lips. The strong perfume. She was on a date with Mateo.

"Isn't he a little old?" I didn't know Mateo's age, but he had specs of white creeping his black hair. If I recalled correctly, Sasha graduated high school a year after me.

Sasha took a long drink. I assumed the age gap was more than ten years. She placed the glass on the table, borderline slamming it down. When she leaned over, I stared at Sasha's nose to avoid staring down her dress.

"It was fun chatting with ya, but I'm a little busy."

"Sasha," a male voice said next to us.

I looked up. Mateo stood over me. His hair was slicked back, revealing his receding hairline. He wore a nice dress shirt and dark jeans. Sasha squealed with joy when she spotted the large bouquet of flowers. His smile lessened when he noticed me. I jumped out of Mateo's spot.

"Oh, one last question," I said, remembering a mental note. "Do you still have the store's key?"

Sasha huffed and narrowed her eyes. I knew that look too well. It was the same face she gave when a customer interrupted her gameplay. "I told Teresa a million times. I lost it."

"Lost it?" How convenient.

Sasha's tone turned cold yet friendly enough to escape the hidden meaning from her date. "I was late because I lost the key and Teresa had to come down and open the store. Doris made things worse by showing up. If Teresa knew what Doris did, then she would have banished her from the store and not fired me."

Teresa told me when she arrived Sasha and Doris were having a nasty spat, but she never went into details. I wanted to ask what Doris did when Mateo cleared his throat.

Time was up.

After saying goodbye, I left. I kept my eyes on the exit, hoping Jane or her guests didn't see me.

Once outside, my mind raced. Sasha and Mateo being an item bothered me. Not because of the age gap, but because Mateo was Doris's ex-boyfriend. I wouldn't have wanted to date any of Doris's flings. Then again, everyone dated and had an ex. Including me. But still, something about it nagged me like a mosquito bite.

I headed toward my vehicle, deciding to settle on last night's leftovers for dinner. I stood next to my car with keys in hand when something shoved into me, hard. My forehead smacked the window with such force my vision blurred. Seconds later heavy footsteps raced away as I found myself staring up at the evening sky.

CHAPTER 10

Deputy Underwood took my statement. No smile or jokes. Strictly cop mode. He wrote my statement on his smartphone while another officer questioned bystanders, which there weren't many. The neighboring stores around Teresa's Bookstore were closed. The food places were located further down, and most people on the opposite end of Copper Street were leaving. A good Samaritan saw me and called for help. It was a shame he didn't see who attacked me.

My head pounded while answering Underwood's questions. Whoever attacked me came fast and fierce. A goose egg would be visible by morning. I felt embarrassed. Dad put me in self-defense classes during my teenage years. He and Stone constantly told me how I needed to be aware of my surroundings at all times. If I were, then I wouldn't be in this situation.

"This is getting serious," Deputy Underwood said after I gave him my statement.

I didn't disagree. The person who ambushed me could've also been Doris's killer. If that was true, why?

"I can't catch a break today, huh?" I said sarcastically,

trying to add some humor to the situation. Underwood gave me a disapproving eyebrow raise. "Sorry," I added. "It's been a long day."

"Have you talked to your father yet?"

I knew where this was heading. "Yes," I lied, but promised myself to send him an email when I got home. Underwood seemed to buy my story.

We both looked up hearing a familiar engine. I smiled. Stone parked in the nearest spot. We met him halfway as he hurried out of the driver seat. Instead of old man clothes, Stone wore solid dark pants and a wrinkled gray shirt he kept in his truck for emergencies. He embraced me for a moment and pulled away, studying my face. The wrinkles around his mouth hardened, and hands gripped tighter on my shoulders. Those steel blues shifted toward Underwood.

"I have the address," Stone said to Underwood.

I almost forgot my phone was still in my purse. For once, being tracked benefited me. I hoped this would be the only time.

The deputy called over the other officer. The men whispered to one another. I had yet to master keen hearing. I crept closer, and heard an address.

Then I caught Underwood tell Stone, "We appreciate your help. We can handle the rest from here, Sterling."

The look on Stone's face said he wished he could accompany them. He thanked them and turned to me. "I'll drive you home." He guided me toward his truck while Underwood and the other officer headed to their squad cars.

"I'm good enough to drive," I assured him.

"Do you have your driver's license, young lady?"

I frowned. "My house is five miles away."

Stone gave me a knowing look. Even as a retired cop, he wouldn't bend the rules.

"Fine," I grumbled as two police cars zoomed away.

"Hungry? Your grandmother made some soup at the house. We'll head there instead."

No complaints from me. I was starving and could take medicine at their house.

Stone's truck smelled of cigarettes. I never saw him smoke though the interior confirmed that he did. He once claimed to be a stress smoker, when cases or people became too much. The stench reminded me of his days as the police chief. It also made me feel good. I'd rather he didn't smoke cancer sticks, but knowing one was lit up because he worried about me was flattering.

While Stone waited to merge into traffic, I snooped around. Everything looked the same as if he never retired. A small toiletry bag and clip-on ties were still inside the glove box. On the door's compartment were three pepper sprays. Dress shoes rolled on the back floorboard when Stone pushed on the gas pedal. The only thing missing was a duffle bag. *Wait.* No, that sat on the backseat with a wrinkled shirt half hanging out.

We rode in silence until I couldn't take it anymore. "It was Clara," I said. I overheard Stone reading the address to Underwood. While the good Samaritan called for help, I noticed Clara's red car was gone.

Stone's mouth twitched, but said nothing. That twitch answered my question.

"Why did she attack me and take my purse? It doesn't make sense." His tone came out sharp. "Law enforcement will sort it out. Always check your—"

"Surroundings," I mumbled.

"Do you need a refresher? I can get you a personal—"

"No," I interrupted. I didn't mind taking self-defense classes, but spending my free time with an instructor, who enjoyed putting fear in his students more than he should, wasn't ideal. Besides, I remembered the moves. Clara just took me off guard.

"It will be a good reminder," Stone continued. "Your first instinct is to protect yourself, not panic."

"I didn't panic," I scowled, but I saw his point. I didn't want Stone to think that I couldn't take care of myself. "My instincts just failed me at the moment. You know with all the stuff going on. It won't happen again."

Stone opened his mouth as if he was going to speak, but then closed it again. We both knew it could have been worse; it was the town's spy rather than a man of Underwood's size.

We rode in silence as Stone drove. My grandparents lived on the outskirts of Sevier Oak on a windy country road. He obeyed the speed limit of twenty-five. I used to cringe at the turtle pace. After getting my driver license, I learned why. Their road narrowed down to only one vehicle. The sharp turns and hills demanded a slow speed. It wasn't uncommon to see tire tracks in the grass due to two cars on the road at the same time. Animals far outnumbered the residents. Deer often darted out, while squirrels took their sweet time before making a split decision to get out of the way. Turkeys and neighborhood dogs often paraded through people's lawn.

My grandparents's farmhouse appeared two miles down the road. The white house had darkened over the years from weather and pollen. The Stone house was my second home. During my school days, Grandma picked me up and brought me to their home until Dad finished his shift. On summer breaks, I spent more time there than at my own home. Grandma and I baked, worked in the yard, went to garage sales on the weekends, and visited some of her friends on her side of the family. One of my favorite memories was when I was thirteen and Grandma taught me how to drive. The horseshoe driveway and two acres of grass surrounding the property was perfect. By the time I got my driver's permit, I knew how to navigate the roads with ease.

At seven o'clock, the Tennessee sun slowly made its way behind the Smoky Mountains, painting the sky a pinkish orange. The fluffy clouds absorbed their color, making it look like cotton candy.

Grandma was rocking in her chair when we pulled up. She waved as Stone parked his truck in the usual spot under the maple tree. The moment I stepped out, my troubles faded away; something that could only be done at a grandparent's house.

"Howdy," Grandma said, raising out of her rocker. She hugged me tight. Her hair smelled like a mixture of rosemary and coconut. She put rosemary essential oils in her shampoo, swearing that it helped hair growth. I couldn't tell if it worked or not since Grandma usually wore a sunhat. She wore a floral dress, short curly gray hair, red lipstick, and laughing wrinkles around her eyes and mouth. A tiny nose stud made her stand out.

"Are you hurt?" Her chocolate brown eyes studied my face. When she saw my forehead, she grimaced.

Stone walked past us. "Let's get inside, away from the mosquitoes."

He led the way inside the house. The dining room opened up after walking down a short hallway. My grandfather disappeared to the staircase behind a closed door, leading up to the master bedroom. I sat the table, taking in the heavenly smell. Creamy chicken soup, my favorite.

"Have a seat," Grandma said, strolling by me. "I'll fix us a bowl."

I sat at the table, admiring the kitchen. It looked like something out of a country magazine with all the apple décor. Apple picture frames lined the wall above the coffee station and mugs shaped as the fruit dotted the counter. The walls had been painted Granny Smith green for as long as I could remember. The dark cabinets gave the kitchen a cozy country vibe.

"How are you feeling?" Grandma asked. She carried two bowls and a container of nutmeg between two fingers.

"I'm fine," I reassured her.

She placed the bowls down, giving me a worried look. If it wasn't for my rumbling stomach, I would have gone in the bathroom and looked in the mirror. My forehead must've looked worse than I thought.

Grandma sprinkled an earthy spice on top. "I have some whiskey stashed away, if you need a shot."

I declined. I knew if I had one drink on an empty stomach, I would've been snoring on the couch before the rerun of *Everybody Loves Raymond* aired. I wanted to be alert when Underwood called. I knew from experience he'd stop by before going home.

I inhaled the steam. The nutmeg smelled wonderful. Some people loved cinnamon or cumin, but nutmeg was my true love.

"You should spend the night, sweetheart," Grandma suggested.

I spooned a bite of soup and then blew. "And leave my roommate all alone? In an empty house?" I said before eating. I closed my eyes, savoring the taste. If there were leftovers, I would bring Megan a bowl.

"She is more than welcome to stay here. There's plenty of space."

I shook my head and dipped the spoon for more. While chewing, my fingers played with the charm on my necklace. A man gave me a teardrop garnet when I was seven after he survived a bad car accident. The accident was caused by a driver who sped through an intersection, trying to beat a yellow light. Two drivers made it out fine, but the third one got trapped. Dad was one of the first officers on the scene, and pulled him out before the car went up in flames. The man owned a jewelry store, and offered Dad a treasure for saving his life. Dad refused a tip, but the man couldn't settle on a simple thank you. Instead, he gave me a garnet necklace. I cherished the story behind the necklace. Even though Dad worked a dangerous job, crazy hours, and sometimes missed out on special events, I was okay with his career choice. Unlike Mom's job, sailing the ocean kept her away from me. I released the teardrop charm. Now was not the time to reminisce on childhood stories.

"Is Stone still enjoying retirement?" I asked, changing subjects. Grandma gave a tight smile. I knew this look. Stone had been a pain in her neck.

"Stone decided that fishing isn't for him. He's taken up a new hobby." Grandma blew on her soup.

"A new one? I swear it changes every month."

Grandma hummed her agreement. "Rock painting."

"Seriously?" I laughed, trying to picture tough Chief Stone sitting at a desk, rock painting with a delicate paintbrush. The next time I emailed Dad, I would tell him. He would get a kick out of this. Better yet, I would take a picture of him in action before he found a new hobby.

"Sterling painted some nice pieces." Grandma's tone sounded off. The art pieces must be terrible. I was dying to go to the basement to check out his finished work.

The doorbell chimed. Before the tone died out, Stone's footsteps rumbled down the stairs. I ate while my grandparents rushed toward the front door, as if this was a game to see who got there first.

I heard men speaking. They were too far away and spoke in soft tones to understand what was said. At my angle I could see the entrance, but only the back of my grandparents's heads. I continued eating while running the garnet charm up and down the chain. No need to let my soup get cold when I knew they would tell me once they got the news first.

Minutes passed when the front door closed and my grandparents returned to the table. Stone placed my purse on the table. I grabbed it and searched inside.

"Everything is there," he said.

Wallet. Chapstick. Pens. Cellphone. Extra hair ties. Mints. Yep, everything was there. I looked up at Stone. "What did Clara have to say for herself?"

"Clara claims she didn't attack you or take your purse. She let Underwood into her home, and he found your purse inside. You can press charges. The choice is yours."

Grandma and Stone's eyes focused on me, waiting. A part of me wanted to teach Clara a lesson. She couldn't attack people to gain information, but another voice whispered how she lost her sister yesterday. Clara could be Doris's killer. If so, being charged for murder will be a harsher sentence than theft and assault. I went with my heart.

"Have Deputy Underwood give Miss Hackett a firm warning. Oh, and tell him to give her the saying." Stone narrowed his eyes in confusion. "He knows what I'm talking about."

"Are you sure this is what you want?" Stone asked slowly.

After I gave my answer again, Grandma looked like she wanted to say something. Instead, she picked up my empty bowl. Her feet stomped into the kitchen. Stone, on the other hand, seemed pleased with my answer, or he hid his disappointment well.

"Why did Clara do it?" I asked.

Instead of answering, he got up and helped himself to a bowl of soup. This was his way of not wanting to respond. Tomorrow, I intended to find out why.

CHAPTER 11

My alarm went off at eight am, only an hour earlier than normal, but it felt like more. Today's agenda pulled me out of bed, along with the beeping sound down the hallway. I loved the delayed brew setting on the coffee maker and wandered toward the kitchen as the smell grew. The rich scent perked my senses, but only a cup-of-joe would fully awaken me. First thing first, I put creamer and a dash of sugar into a to-go mug, just the way Megan liked it. Then I grabbed a second mug for myself, just black, and two blueberry muffins.

Megan, being an early bird, was awake and sitting in bed with phone in hand. She eyed me when I handed the tray with a blueberry muffin and the coffee. I flashed my best smile.

"What do you want?" Megan asked.

I sat at the edge of her bed. "Hear me out," I started. Megan groaned. "I need you to drive me to Clara's house."

Her green eyes narrowed over the mug's rim. "Why?" she asked before taking another sip.

"Because my grandpa is tracking me. I need to know why

Clara attacked me and I don't want him to know that I'm sleuthing."

When Grandma drove me back to Copper Street last night, she didn't know why Clara attacked me either. She believes Stone and Underwood had a theory, though. *Why wouldn't they say?* I assumed they wanted to protect me. "Must be a cop thing," Grandma told me. I hated that answer. She said the same thing when Dad wouldn't let me travel with Mom during a spring break. "Too dangerous," he said, "it's a cop thing." I was twenty-two years old, not a child. I wanted answers, not protection. They knew something, and I was going to find out.

And ask Clara questions about her sister's murder.

Megan didn't ease her stare. I had the feeling she was weighing out her options. One: drive to Clara's house, risk getting scolded by Stone, and confront Sevier Oak's spy. Two: call Austin for an emergency date. Three: chuck the mug at me and go back to playing on her cellphone.

"You said *we* needed to solve Doris's murder. Her sister is a suspect, and—" I pointed to the goose egg on my forehead.

Megan frowned as she set her mug on the nightstand. "What if Clara is the killer? Do you really think it's a good idea to confront her at her own home?" She gave me a look that Molly often gave when Megan was about to do something stupid.

I scoffed. "The worst spy in history? What can Clara do?" *Other than give me another headache and steal my purse.*

"I think you forgot that Clara hated Doris."

"And so does everyone else in Sevier Oak."

"What if Clara is putting on an act? She wants everyone to think that she's terrible, but she's actually really *good*?" Megan emphasized last word. "After last night—" Megan gave a shy smile— "not bad for the world's worst spy."

"We'll be in broad daylight," I said. "We need to investigate to save the bookstore."

Megan's head moved during her dramatic eye roll. "Alright, fine. Let me drink my coffee and eat my muffin first."

I shook my head while sliding off the bed. "I have to meet Underwood at the store in—" I checked the time on Megan's alarm clock— "less than two hours. We need to move."

In the following minutes, we pulled ourselves together. I sprayed dry shampoo, promising myself a shower later. I skimmed through my clothes for a tough look. Not an easy task when my wardrobe abided by a dress code. Several outfit changes later that resulted in me putting on a gray t-shirt and skinny jeans, we were ready to go. Upon leaving my bedroom, I pulled out a pair of Ray-Ban sunglasses. Mom bought them years ago. They would finally be put to use instead of safe-guarded in my closet. The glasses were worth more than my paychecks. Today seemed like a good day to risk my luck. I put on the dark glasses and studied myself in the mirror. Tom Cruise would've nodded his approval. I gave my reflection a fist bump and walked out.

Megan stood by the door stuffing the last of the muffin into her mouth. Unlike me, Megan applied makeup and wore bright yellow shorts with a white tank top and cute flip flops. For having blonde hair, she rocked the lemon color.

"What?" she asked with her mouth full.

"We matched perfectly. Good cop—" I pointed at her— "and bad cop." I pointed two thumbs at myself.

Megan rolled her eyes.

When I opened the door, Jane Jackson stood there with her fist up as if she was about to knock.

Quickly, she dropped her arm. "Good morning," she greeted.

Adding more contrast between us, Jane dressed like a

model. Her business attire consisted of a coral top, an off-white jacket, and white capris. The baguette purse was the same color as her shirt. Instead of a tight bun, her brown hair clipped back.

"May I come in?" asked Jane.

"No," Megan and I said at the same time.

Jane didn't appear as taken aback as I had hoped. "We need to talk about the bookstore's future."

"I'm not going to help you sell the store." I put my hands on my hips. "If you want to clean up the store, then hire some-one. I'll take the cats."

Megan's foot tapped my heel. I would reassure her later that I haven't forgotten about her cat allergy.

"Miss Stone—"

"Call me Garnet."

Jane gave a quick sigh. "Alright, Garnet. I could use your help regarding the bookstore."

Excitement rose. Did this mean she reconsidered selling, or did she want my help to clean? Megan kicked my heel. As much as I wanted to explore her motives, we had to leave now. I had to chat with Clara before meeting Underwood.

I checked the time on my phone. "How about I meet you at Teresa's Bookstore in two hours?" That gave me enough time to question Clara, come back home to grab Megan's apple pie, and talk to Underwood before she arrived. I closed the door, not giving Jane a chance to counter, and walked to Megan's vehicle.

"May I accompany you?"

Megan and I stopped. We looked at each other, thinking the same thing. *Now what do we do?*

CHAPTER 12

JANE RIDING IN THE BACKSEAT MADE THINGS AWKWARD. WE WANTED to say no, but how could we? Refusing made me look bad. I cringed on the inside and forced a happy face.

While Megan drove her hatchback, Jane chatted non-stop. "What's that on your wrist?" She leaned forward from the backseat with a pointed finger.

"My tattoo." I held up my arm for Jane to get a better view.

"Did Teresa approve or did you have to cover it?"

Megan side-eyed me, annoyed. Unlike me, my best friend struggled with being nice to people she disliked. It gave me pleasure telling Jane that Teresa loved my tattoo, to the point that I secretly wondered if she wanted one, too. Since I sat in the front seat, I couldn't read Jane's expressions.

"People tell me that you come from the Stone family," Jane continued, "but I want to hear about your family from you. What are they like?"

I answered, but left out my mother and Regan. After giving the rundown of the Stone Family, Jane went quiet for a few moments before firing another round of questions. This time about Sevier Oak's weather.

Every now and then, Megan and I glanced at each other. Jane was more talkative than I expected. Or nosy like everyone else in town.

When Jane peppered Megan with questions about Dessert Bar, I found myself eager to know more about Jane's personal life. I knew little in comparison to Teresa's. Teresa had spoken little of her family other than she was from Vermont and chose a simpler career rather than following her family's footsteps of lawyers or paralegals. Teresa found her passion in East Tennessee as well as the love of her life, until he passed away ten years ago. Teresa left her home state and never looked back.

The only times Teresa spoke of her family was in December. She clearly cherished her three nephews and a niece, Jane. One nephew enjoyed science fiction books, while the other two were into non-fiction. Teresa mailed Jane historical fiction novels. I knew because Teresa used to ask for my suggestions as she pulled books from store shelves. I didn't believe Teresa disliked her family but loved them more from afar.

It came as a huge shock when I didn't inherit the bookstore, or anything for that matter. We were so close that I felt as though we were family more so than her relatives up north. My heart broke when I learned Teresa favored her niece, who never came to Tennessee. Or at least during the six years I worked at the bookstore.

Teresa and I had shared countless fond memories. We always talked about our latest read, especially the ones we disliked. I remembered coming into work one day and there were two little kittens playing in the office. Then the time Teresa purchased a couch, thinking it would fit in the bargain room for customers to sit and read. After four hours of rearranging the store, Stone came over and delivered it to Teresa's house instead. Teresa also vented to me about customers, book orders, and of course Drake Voss. Unlike her family, I remembered her birthday— two days after Christmas. I gave her space on the anniversary of her husband passing. I also knew what dessert she needed after a sad or rough day.

In some ways, Teresa was more like a mom to me than a boss.

Now listening to Jane's tourist-like questions made my heart sour. I couldn't understand why Teresa's niece had inherited everything while I got nothing. It was a question I needed to ask Jane, but not in a moving car with Megan.

The fifteen-minute drive felt like hours. Jane went quiet when Megan turned onto Clara's street. Tiny houses cluttered the area, too tight for my comfort. The homes were a simple design and built during my grandparent's youth, if not longer ago.

"Who are we visiting?" Jane asked. She poked her head between the front seats, startling Megan. I found her question humorous. This moment reminded me of Pippin Took from Lord of the Rings when he asked Elrond where they were going after volunteering to join the perilous quest to Mordor.

"What's so funny?" Megan asked.

"Clara Hackett," I answered Jane's question.

Jane turned toward me. "Who's Clara?"

Megan's jaw dropped. "Doris's sister. The one who—"

"We need to ask Clara some questions," I kindly interrupted. Despite Jane inviting herself, we didn't need to be mean. Then again, Gandalf had his moments with Pippin, too.

"What kind of questions?" asked Jane.

Megan pulled up to the address. Clara's cottage was similar to the one Megan and I rented, but wider built and painted sky blue. It looked well maintained with its mowed lawn and clipped bushes, yet Clara's personality rubbed onto the house. There were no blinds or curtains on any of the windows and a chair faced the front window rather than inward. Her car was backed into the driveway, ready to speed off at a moment's notice. I knew she owned a police scanner, or she did when Dad and Stone were on the force.

Megan pointed. "Is that a for-sale sign?"

Surely enough, there was a blue and white FOR-SALE sign near the mailbox. Megan and I exchanged another look. Perhaps Clara inherited Doris's home along with everything else. It seemed premature, considering that her sister passed away two days ago. We unbuckled our seatbelts, and I straightened my sunglasses. *Tough mode time.*

"Wait in the car," Megan told Jane, before opening her door.

"Clara might get upset seeing you. She thinks you killed her sister," I explained while studying myself in the side mirror. I fixed my sunglasses and stepped out.

Megan and I walked up to the house, spotting movement from a window. The door opened before we had a chance to knock.

"Why are you here?" Clara demanded as one eye peered behind the chain that hung from the door.

I did my best to look intimidating by crossing my arms over my chest. "Why did you attack me and take my purse?"

The door started to close. I used Dad's trick by sticking my foot in the closing gap. My toes ached as they caught in the door. I hoped my cringe reflected attitude rather than pain.

"I'm debating about pressing charges." I leaned a little closer and removed my foot. "You're not off to a good start."

I stared at her letting the information sink in, hoping she didn't see through my lie. I'd rather not cause further heartache. After all, her sister had just been murdered.

A sense of victory overcame me when Clara unchained the lock and opened the door wider. She kept one hand in place, ready to slam it shut if needed. I avoided looking at her super short pajama shorts by studying her face. The Hackett sisters shared a round chin. The biggest difference between them was Clara had more wrinkles around her eyes. I assumed she got them from years of spying. Clara repeated her question about why we were here.

"I just said why," I replied, growing annoyed.

"Stupid move if you ask me," Megan added. She crossed her arms over her chest, mirroring my stance. Instead, my best friend looked like a cute honeybee.

Clara's lips snarled as if she smelled something bad. "Did Doris leave you anything?"

It took me a few seconds to respond. "What? No. Didn't Doris have a will?" *And why would Doris leave me a dime of her fortune? She barely spoke to me.*

"My sister didn't put me in her will," Clara snapped. "Her lawyer won't tell me anything. I don't know who gets the house or the one in Myrtle Beach. Her BMW. Bank account. Clothes. I don't know what will happen to any of her stuff. As her only sibling and living relative, I should get everything."

A part of me understood why Doris didn't leave her sister with anything. According to the stories, Clara pestered her sister about the lottery winnings more than Preston did. Clara had always been super nosy. Doris sometimes vented to me when buying books. On another note, I pitied Clara. I knew too well how it felt to think you were getting something, only to end up with zilch.

"Why is your house for sale?" Megan gestured toward the sign.

Clara ignored our question by ranting about Doris. Her stories on how she treated people was old news. While she rambled, I struggled to find an opening to steer the conversation back to our reason for coming. *My gosh*, Clara kept talking. I felt my body tense from being annoyed.

Thankfully, Megan managed to squeeze in a comment. "I don't know if Doris said anything like that at the bookstore?"

Megan nudged my heel as Clara stared at me. She was such a good cop.

"No," I concurred. "Doris never talked about her personal life." Which was true. Other than complaining, Doris kept to herself. What I already knew came from the rumor mill.

"Really?" Clara sounded baffled. "That was the only place she went. Doris got everything else through the mail. I thought she talked to you and Teresa."

"The mail?" I said, ignoring the part about Teresa.

Clara nodded fast. "Oh, yeah. Doris bought her groceries online and had them delivered. But most stuff came through Amazon. I recognize that smirk on the box. You know what I'm talking about?"

Geez, someone been snooping.

"Do you think Preston Powell inherited everything?" I asked. Since Doris had never remarried, had no children, or nephews and nieces then he could be the sole beneficiary of her estate.

"Preston?" Clara sounded disbelief. "Nah, he wouldn't get a rusty hammer from her if he tried. She took everything when she left him for Mateo. Even the dishes Preston's parents gave them as a wedding present. Doris took just about everything. Vases. Picture frames. The dining set. Rugs."

"We get it," Megan interrupted.

"When Mateo was building Doris's fancy mansion, Preston broke in and stole a bunch of stuff. Doris called the cops, but there was no proof and Preston's place was clean. But my sister and I knew it was him."

Clara ventured off the topic again, this time about Preston hating Mateo. I wondered if she had witnessed Preston creeping into Doris's home, but that probably would've been a silly question to ask a spy. And more importantly, I didn't care about a love triangle that had happened years ago.

"Preston is still bitter," Clara continued. "Soon after she won that money, he slashed her tires. He done it on several occasions, when he thought no one was looking. But I saw him do it once. I said nothing. She won't help me, so I won't help her." Clara's lips pressed for a moment. "Damn, I wish I had balls like him."

Megan nearly choked. "What?"

"She's referring to Preston being brave," I explained, knowing that Megan was actually laughing at Clara's comment. "Even though you attacked me." I narrowed my eyes before realizing my Ray-Ban sunglasses covered them.

Clara was about to close the door when I trapped my foot in its path again. This time with my other foot.

"Tell me, why did you do it?" I demanded.

"You won't believe me."

"Try me."

"I didn't attack you or take your purse. I was home for five minutes when Deputy Underwood pounded on the door. I allowed him inside, proving that I didn't do it. But there it was in my laundry room. I swear someone put it there." Her voice went up an octave. "Someone broke into my home and planted it. Someone was spying on Doris's house. Has been for weeks. I saw the figure. I know it was a guy because he wore a baseball hat."

"I don't believe you. You're the biggest spy and you attacked me. Why?"

"See? I told ya that you wouldn't believe me."

I felt my blood pressure raising.

"Why were you spying on Doris?" Megan changed subjects.

Clara opened her mouth to answer, but snapped it shut. She was hiding something.

When I asked Clara what she knew about Mateo, other than being her sister's ex-boyfriend, Clara's face changed. Her head perked up, staring at something behind us. Without warning she pushed us aside and marched a few feet away.

I felt my jaw dropping as Megan groaned. Jane was across the street, talking to the owner of the house. *Why couldn't Jane stay in the car?*

To make matters worse, a mail truck pulled up, blocking our view. Roland appeared with a small cardboard box in his hands. He made no eye contact as he powerwalked, then practically threw the box into Clara's bosom.

"Is this damaged too?" she yelled at the fleeing postman. "I got my eyes on you, too," she added when Roland hopped in his vehicle and sped off.

When the white truck moved, Jane reappeared still talking to the neighbors. Based on their body language, Jane seemed to be on good terms with them.

Clara half turned around, pointing at Jane. "Ain't that the girl who murdered my sister? Did she inherit her stuff?"

Megan mouthed, "Time to go."

I agreed. We walked towards Megan's car.

"Why is that killer pestering my neighbors?" she called behind us.

After the way our conversation went, I couldn't resist a smart remark. "Like you haven't pestered them before."

Clara looked shocked, then said, "I'm calling the cops."

Seconds later, I heard a door slam shut. Megan and I bolted.

"Get the car started," I said. "I'll grab Jane."

CHAPTER 13

Everything happened quickly. Jane and I jumped in the hatchback. Megan drove well over the speed limit. After we arrived at my place, Megan and I rushed inside, leaving Jane to see herself home. We had spent more time at Clara's than expected. I scrambled to find my purse, which was hidden under my pillow. Then I grabbed my car keys, phone and Megan's apple pie before running out the door. Megan hollered behind me, telling me she had been called into work because an employee called in sick.

It was no surprise finding Deputy Idris Underwood waiting under Teresa's Bookstore awning when I pulled up. I braced myself for an interrogation. I hadn't come up with a lame answer as to why Megan and I were a murder suspect house. My spur of the moment wits would have to do.

Instead, Underwood gave his usual hello. He held the pie box as I unlocked the door. Once inside, I expected him to unleash a lecture, but it didn't come. Princess meowed after the cowbells stopped ringing. While Underwood wandered around the sales floor, I put the pie on Teresa's desk and tended to the cats. The moment I opened the door, Princess sprinted out and into the unknown. Butterscotch, on the other hand, trotted to the office and laid on Teresa's chair. It seemed both felines had enough of the Cat's Lounge.

"Did you find anything on the stuffed bear?" I asked Underwood when I returned downstairs.

He closed a book he was reading and placed it back on the shelf. The motion was too quick to read the title, but it was from the fantasy section. I almost told him to keep it when he said, "Blood samples take a few days. Sheriff Estep gave the green light to reopen the bookshop. Good luck cleaning up the place," he eyed the back area.

"That's great," I said, feeling excited. I could finally open the boxes Roland delivered and call the customers before they demanded a refund.

The cowbells rang, and Jane entered the store, sidestepping Princess. The cat's yellow eyes followed Jane, confused as to why she didn't give her any affection. Customers always acknowledge her with at least a little pat.

I squatted down. Princess perked up and trotted toward me. I petted her as Princess head-butted my knee.

Underwood replicated the message to Jane about reopening. Based on her lack of excitement, I assumed Jane already knew.

"Be careful." Underwood said before fixing his gaze on Jane. "Call me if you need anything or find anything else." With that he left.

"What were you thinking?" I said, once Underwood climbed inside of his police cruiser. Jane looked puzzled. I softened my tone. "You were supposed to stay in the car, and then you go talking to the neighbors? Have you forgotten that you're a suspect in Doris's murder investigation?"

Princess walked away to roam the store. Jane watched her until the black and white cat walked past her. She then tucked an invisible hair behind her ear. "Clara wasn't going to call the police."

"What makes you think that?" I asked, recalling countless times Dad went to Clara's neighborhood. She thought her neighbors were smuggling drugs because they were acting "suspicious."

"When the police released me, I heard the cops talking about Clara. She's a suspect and she knows it. Clara was bluffing."

I felt good knowing Clara was on the police's radar. My list of suspects was on the right track.

Jane walked down an aisle, deeper into the store. "The store needs tidying. Do you know where I can donate the books and..." She glanced at the miniature football helmets along the tops of bookshelves. Princess gazed down as if she was enjoying herself. "Stuff."

For the first time, it was just the two of us. I took this opportunity to lay it on thick about the store's greatness. I had to keep trying. "Have you thought about reconsidering? Everyone loves a cute bookshop. The remodel will really open up the place. Just think—" I pointed around the store— "adding more globe lights will make it really cozy. We can move the glass to the new bargain room, and have a variety of books floating." Jane kept looking at the stack of books, waiting to be put away. "Teresa bought an iron conservatory framework she thought about adding." I had no idea how. The frame was over ten feet tall, but it looked cool. Teresa had bought it with special events in mind. Right now, it hung out in the storage unit.

Jane went behind the register. Her face scrunched with disgust.

I changed my angle. "I made a folder on the computer that shows our sales from the last five years. You'll see that we make a profit every year." Not by much, but at least it never dipped into the negative bracket. "We have the business to stay open."

"I'm curious about some things," Jane said, studying the clutter.

"Such as?" Princess leaped onto the counter, sat, and watched. I hid my excitement by rubbing my nose. Princess looked too cute.

"First, I need to know, does everyone in Sevier Oak think I killed Doris?" Jane sounded sad, hurt even.

Megan did. Jane was the only other person in the store. She voiced this once we got back to the house. Recalling my best friend's nickname from school, Meg-Yapper, I assumed her mom and boyfriend also sided with her. Grandma had made a sly comment about the same theory last night. I knew Stone enough well to at least consider Jane a suspect. And less than thirty minutes ago, Clara accused Jane of committing the crime. I pictured the town's spy sharing her opinion to anyone willing to listen, thus adding more people to the bandwagon.

"Nope," I lied, "just the police."

Jane looked a little relieved. Then I told her about the customer's paid orders waiting in the receiving room. I was about to elaborate more about the store's profits when she said, "I'll call them myself. Then I'll call a realtor about selling this place. Do you recommend anyone? The buyer from last night backed out."

My temper took over. "You can't sell. This place meant everything to Teresa. And to me and everyone in Sevier Oak. Surely that means something to you."

Jane's shoulders lowered. "I'm sorry, Garnet. Teresa's Bookstore is no more. That's what I came to tell you. I really appreciate all the work you've done, I do. Teresa was very fond of you. But I'm closing the store." She walked around the counter and headed toward the main staircase.

I hollered, "Why did Teresa give you the store? Do you even read books?"

CHAPTER 14

Jane looked as if I slapped her with a hardcover. I stood there, waiting for an answer. Then her eyes softened. Was she still mourning her aunt's death? Or did she realize how heartless she's been?

When she answered, Jane sounded like a coach explaining to a child why they didn't make the team. "You wouldn't understand."

I placed my hands on my hips, nails digging into my skin. Mom said the same thing when I asked her why she spent more time on the ocean than on land. She gave a sad smile, putting her hands on my shoulders, and gently said, *You wouldn't understand.* To me that meant, *I'd rather not talk about it.*

Now, standing in a beloved bookstore, I didn't know if I should've burst into tears or yelled at the top of my lungs.

"I'll pay you to help move and clean up," Jane said as if that would make everything better.

"I can't help you clean out the store. I can't do it." Thinking about removing one book from the store broke my heart.

"Leave Princess and Butterscotch alone. I'll find them a *new* home." I headed toward the door, possibly for the last time.

"Garnet, wait," Jane called.

I didn't stop. I shoved the door open, harder than necessary, as angry tears streaked my face.

The sun's heat added to the raging fire within me. Never had I been this upset, including the time I caught Dad following me during dates, or when I discovered my ex-boyfriend was cheating on me, or when Mom was a no-show during a Florida trip.

I leaned against the brick building and closed my eyes. I didn't want to be angry. Anger created bad choices; often leading to regret. I held onto my charm and took slow deep breaths. The pounding in my heart slowly eased.

Jane had been through a lot too, I reminded myself. A person died on her first visit to her aunt's bookstore. Then she had been accused of being the killer, thrown in jail overnight, and victimized by people she didn't know. Perhaps I judged her too harshly.

And yet, I had no desire to go back inside.

I didn't know what to do so I searched up and down Copper Street for an answer. Customers walked on the sidewalks with bags and coffee cups in their hands. Kountry Wings opened before noon for the early lunch. In the next half hour, the scent of food would fill the air. I loved living here. A part of me wanted to walk the paths of Crockett Park and get lost in nature.

But the bookstore needed rescuing.

A man's laughter startled me. He exited Old Treasure while talking into his cellphone. I entered the antique store with a new agenda.

A heavy odor greeted me like an old friend, musty with a distinct hint of wood polish. Teresa often shopped here and chit-chatted with her good friend, Karl. When not socializing, she came to find treasures, for either her home or the bookstore. Sometimes I accompanied her, mainly to talk her out of buying another table for a book display, decorations, or using this and that after the remodel.

Customers roamed around the store. A man, perhaps in his late fifties, tested a rocking chair by sitting in it and leaning back while his two grandkids, I assumed, were having a grand time, rocking fast in their chairs. Meanwhile, a couple stood in front of a dining set, talking in low voices. The place was full of treasures, but not as cluttered as the bookstore.

A part-time worker waved at me while talking to a customer about a wardrobe. I didn't have to venture far to find Karl, or rather he found me. The big guy greeted me with his famous smile. As usual, he wore jean overalls with a white shirt underneath.

"What brings you in today?" Karl asked after we said our hellos.

"I was wanting to talk to you for a few minutes, if you have the time." I glanced at his shoppers.

"Come on, upstairs." Karl waved me to follow as he turned around.

We wandered deeper into the store until we encountered a narrow staircase. With each step the wood moaned under our feet. I had traveled up and down these steps many times since I started working for Teresa. The creaking wood seemed to grow louder every year. I worried that one day I would fall through. Karl, on the other hand, trotted up without a second thought.

The top floor reminded me of a mad scientist's lab centered around furniture. Doorknobs were tossed in totes that sat on a table with different colored and shaped legs. Here and there I spotted nails or screws on the floor. There were many workbenches with a variety of tools. Screen doors and windows stacked across one wall and all were broken in some way. One area had pieces and parts of what used to be a whole appliance. I assumed Karl, or his staff, used them to either create new pieces or repair one with the broken parts.

Every time I came up here, the laboratory reminded me of Teresa. She and Karl shared a common trait— they couldn't throw anything away. The good thing going for Karl was his wife; she came here and tossed out things that were rusty, too moldy, or beyond saving. Now I thought about it, maybe that's why Teresa's clutter had gotten out of hand. She didn't have her other half.

The realization made me sad as I followed Karl. I breathed in the thick musty smell. In a strange way, the wood polish comforted me.

Karl stopped to open a door, ending my depressing thoughts. He flipped a switch, and stood off to the side, allowing me to peek inside.

"It's finished," I said, marveling at the bathroom's update. Out went the wood panel walls and in went white drywall. A modern sink with cabinet space replaced the old birdbath looking one. A part of me missed the pink toilet from the sixties, but it had to go.

"About darn time. Preston did a heck of a job. When he came," Karl grumbled.

"How long did it take him?"

"A little over two months."

I looked at Karl. "Over two months? For a small bathroom?"

"Yep. One day, he ran out of supplies. Another time, he left some of his tools at another job. Then he had a cold. Then he was waiting for a part." He pointed at the updated sink. "The list went on. But he got his butt in gear when I threatened to drop him and hire Mateo."

"I bet. But the bathroom looks nice."

"When you remodel the bookstore, go with Mateo. He's much faster and way more reliable than Preston."

"Why didn't you go with Mateo from the get-go?"

"He was busy, and I didn't wanna wait. But if I would've known Preston would take two months, then I would've waited a month for Mateo."

He turned off the bathroom light and closed the door. "But you didn't come here to admire a bathroom." Karl gave me a knowing look. "It's about that new boss of yours, ain't it?"

When I nodded, Karl led me to his office. Compared to the laboratory, his office was simple: desk, two chairs, laptop, and a filing cabinet.

While he plopped behind his desk in a roller chair, I sat in a seat that once belonged in a kitchen set. A blue leg told me the story of how it ended up here.

Karl grabbed a Diet Coke from mini fridge. "Want one?" I shook my head no. He pulled the tab and took a drink. "I miss the good stuff."

I eyed the can. Karl always drank Coca-Cola. When he came to the bookstore to have lunch with Teresa, he always drank out of the notorious red can. It was odd seeing him drink Diet Coke.

"Why the change?"

"When Preston started working, he recommended diet drinks. It didn't help that the missus was here and took his side. Now my wife only buys Diet Coke." He stared at the can as if he wished it was a regular Coke. "Sugar is sugar. Why try to tamper with it when the plain stuff is better?"

"You want me to buy you the good stuff?" I smirked.

Karl let out a bellowing laugh, one that I had to join. After a few moments, he shook his head. "Nah. I'll stick with this a little longer. Or at least until the case is gone. The problem is that it sometimes tastes funny, and makes me so darn tired. I swear some days I come up here just to take a nap." He leaned closer with a worried face. "Don't tell to my workers or the missus. I don't want them thinking that I'm slacking."

He pulled out chewing gum. As he unwrapped it, I smelled cinnamon. "This stuff wakes me up." He popped the gum into his mouth. He offered me one. I declined.

I winked my promise of secrecy and moved onto my objective. "So, Preston was working on the bathroom when Doris died?"

Karl took a quick drink; he grimaced at the aftertaste. It probably tasted funny with gum. "He was. I was napping when my phone rang. The missus told me that the police were closing Copper Street. When I check out the window, I saw all them cops. I'd told Preston, and he went out while I was stuck on the phone. When he came back, he got his butt in gear and finished installing the sink." He chuckled. "I think he was afraid that his ex-wife was going to come back and haunt him if he didn't finish the bathroom."

"Was he upset? Doris was his wife."

"Nah. Preston and Doris divorced years ago. Any love they had for each other is long gone. Preston came back yesterday to finished the last touches. He must've been a little upset to work two full days, back-to-back." Karl smirked. "Let me give you some advice about men. We stay busy to keep our minds off things. If Preston was shaken about Doris being killed, he wouldn't show."

I nodded unsure how to take his advice. The important part was that Preston couldn't be at two places at once. He didn't kill Doris.

"So, what's that new boss's big plans?" Karl sounded anxious to know the scoop.

"Jane wants to sell."

His curiosity morphed into sadness. His lips drooped, reminding me of the day when Teresa passed away. “That’s a shame,” he said softly. He slugged back his Diet Coke as if it was a shot of whiskey. Again, he grimaced.

We sat in silence, lost in our thoughts. While Karl seemed heartbroken about the bookshop closing, I was agitated. I was no closer to finding the killer than this morning. I needed information that pointed toward the murderer. Something more cohesive than a teddy bear with a blood spot, a knife with Doris’s fingerprints, a pillow as the murder weapon, and a broken tea kettle.

When Karl’s mouth opened to say something, loud creaks interrupted. We waited until the part time worker appeared. She stood in the doorway, pointing into the office. “She’s in here.”

A moment later Jane rushed in. I jumped on my feet as the chair screeched. “What’s wrong?” I asked.

“Garnet,” she said, reaching for my hand. “I need your help.”

CHAPTER 15

"That owl scratched me." Jane held up her wrist to show the red marks.

We were back at the bookstore, staring into the office. I shouldn't find this funny, but I did.

Butterscotch hissed at Boss-Lady, clearly mad at Jane for disturbing her nap. The scene felt like déjà vu. Only this time there was a paper plate on the desk with crumbles. Jane must have indulged in a piece of Megan's famous apple pie.

I walked into the office. The tortie's yellow eyes eased at the sight of me. "Butterscotch only likes certain people."

"Can you remove it?"

"Butterscotch," I corrected. The tortie cat meowed as I picked her up. I set her in the hallway. She trotted towards the back staircase. "Close the door or she'll reappear a few minutes later. Butterscotch spends most of her day in the office."

Jane cradled her hand, not looking any happier. "What's the password?" she asked, referring to the boxy computer.

I smiled.

"What?"

I stepped around her. She hovered over my shoulder while I typed the password.

"Butterscotch?" Jane scoffed then mumbled about changing it.

"All Teresa's passwords are Butterscotch. And don't change it. It's easier to remember."

"It's unwise to use the same password for everything."

Normally I would've agreed, but in this case I shrugged. Before Jane needed something else, I left. I had a mystery to solve.

Dessert Bar was busy during lunch tell they were short staffed. Megan worked the register, while Molly bounced back and forth from the kitchen and handed out treats to customers. I found a seat at an empty table and waited for the rush to pass. Four people carried red boxes out, special orders. Most customers were high school aged, eating dessert as their lunch. Thankfully, Clara Hackett and Drake Voss were elsewhere. I wasn't in the mood to see them.

Now seemed like a suitable time to write notes about Preston Powell. Before I could open the app on my phone, someone asked, "Is this seat taken?"

Leo Voss, Drake's grandson, stood next to me with a dashing smile. His facial features reminded me of a blond version of Alexander Dreymon. Leo had short honey colored hair, a strong rectangular face, green eyes, and a deep voice. But not bass like Underwood's; Leo's tone sounded smoothing. I liked it. He took a seat before I could tell him not to.

I sat up straighter, unsure what to expect. Leo and I had run into each other a few times in the two-year history of Voss-of-Books. Most of the time it involved Drake and Teresa, except that one time when Brad and I were dating.

"It's been a while." His eyes skimmed over my shirt before gazing into mine. "You look different today."

I did a quick peek at myself, forgetting that I still wore skinny jeans and a gray t-shirt. "I'm off today," I said.

"It's a nice look on you. It matches your platinum hair."

Is he hitting on me?

I checked the counter hoping my best friend could get me away from Leo. Unfortunately, Megan was bogged down by a steady flow of costumers.

"Have you tried the lava cake?" Leo asked, drawing my focus back to him. "It's to die for."

"My best friend's mom owns the place. I've tried everything." Including their failed attempts on new recipes and the ones that didn't taste good enough to keep on the menu.

Leo's lips pressed into a thin smile and an awkwardness fell upon us. I wished he sat elsewhere. He seemed nice enough but I didn't know how to act around him. At any moment, I expected Leo to turn into his grandfather.

"Have you eaten?" he asked. "I could order us something."

"No, I'm fine. Thanks. I'm just waiting on Megan."

The sound of the restaurant engulfed us with classical music, and the clanking of forks and spoons. Before I could slide off the bar stool, Leo continued. "I see you're no longer with that guy."

My eyes widened. "What?"

Leo nodded at my right hand where a fake ruby ring used to be. "I don't see a ring or any heart jewelry. And I haven't seen a man at your side."

There was a playfulness in his voice.

Definitely flirting.

I toyed with my garnet necklace. "I have high standards."

In truth, my standards weren't unreasonable: be kind, crack some jokes, have a job, and don't mind me reading books for hours on end. Other than Brad, my boyfriends didn't stay around long enough to know me, because of Dad. Every parent asked questions about their child's date but my father questioned my boyfriends like they were persons of interest in a crime. I still hadn't forgiven Dad for monitoring me a few times in high school. After my first date with Brad, I told Dad to give me some space. He did, and never tailed me after that. Then again, I hadn't dated anyone since Brad. Thankfully Stone kept his distance when it came to my dating life.

"Tell you what." Leo leaned forward. His green eyes sparkled. I hated how I found them attractive as well as the sound of his voice. "I know about your little investigation."

"Who told you I was investigating?" I asked at the same time I spotted Megan moving. She waved and darted behind the swinging door to the kitchen. *So much for keeping this a secret.*

"I'll tell you what I know, but it will cost you." Leo's grin grew to the point of being sexy.

I eyed him as his sexy grin turned mischievous. He had me where he wanted me. For the sake of the bookstore's future, I asked about his cost. *How bad could it be?*

"You have two choices," he said. "One, you buy something at Voss-of-Books." My mouth dropped and snapped it shut. His cheeks reddened, making me nervous. "Two, you go on a date with me."

"The first one," I said, quickly.

Leo looked hurt, and I instantly regretted answering too fast. I had to remind myself that Leo was a nice guy despite the family he came from. Not to mention that I was attracted to him. Was it so bad a hot guy was asking me out? Leo was the catalyst for my breakup with Brad.

"Alright," Leo said, giving what appeared to be a forced smile. He slid off his chair. "I'll be at the store the rest of the day and most afternoons." With that he said goodbye.

I watched him leave and felt terrible. Despite his grandfather's rivalry with Teresa, Leo didn't seem to be money hungry. Not once did he brag about Voss-of-Books or bring up Teresa's Bookstore. Maybe I listened to too many cop stories and thought of the worst in people.

"He's cute," Megan said, suddenly appearing at my side. I jumped in my seat. Megan side-hugged me, and said, "If I wasn't dating Austin, and if I was you… I would have taken the second option."

"You heard that?"

Her grin answered my question.

"You wouldn't go on a date with him if Voss was Dessert Bar's sworn enemy," I pointed out.

She frowned. "Yeah, you're probably right. But seriously, if Leo knows something about Doris's murder, then you better find out sooner than later." She gave me a stern look that reminded me of her mom.

"Did you tell anyone that we were investigating?" I changed the subject.

"No." Megan checked the front counter again and saw a customer needed a refill on their drink. "Gotta run. Go find out what Leo knows. I'll see you tonight."

CHAPTER 16

I SAT ON MY LIVING ROOM COUCH, SEARCHING ON INDEED. THERE were plenty of job listings, though none centered around books or libraries. Most of my choices consisted of working part time as a summer employee or going to Bristol, Tennessee. I needed a full-time job lasting me beyond August and one that didn't require an hour-long commute.

Slowly, I was starting to feel bad for myself, letting a pity party start to form. A part of me envied people who were born to do something and embraced it at an early age.

My dad knew he wanted to be a detective. He had watched Stone, start out as a beat cop and move up the ranks until he became Chief. A sense of justice took root and sprouted over time. But being a small-town cop wasn't enough. After I graduated high school, Dad transferred to Nashville to be a detective. I was proud that he achieved his dream job, and yet a little voice reminded me that I still lacked a passion.

When I was either seven or eight years old, Grandma bought me a Halloween police costume at a yard sale. I put it on and stared at myself in the mirror. I looked the part: brave and strong. However, the inner passion to seek justice wasn't there. Battling crime sounded scary. I respected Dad's job, especially after the necklace story. Law enforcement did more than tackle bad guys. They saved lives. I didn't need job shadowing to know being a cop was not for me.

Working at Teresa's Bookstore was the most fulfilled I had ever felt. I always enjoyed reading stories. Books were also an escape from my troubles, a lacking mother, the dangers of my family's job, and normal struggles everyone faces in life. I found joy within the walls of a messy bookshop. I talked to fellow readers about stories and discovered new authors. My time with Teresa was just as great as reading a storybook.

Books were my passion. According to the local job openings, being a bookworm wasn't a career option. Then again, while lounging on the couch, I realized how much I'd enjoy selling books. It had never hit me until now. I worked at Teresa's Bookstore for years and loved every moment. I didn't need to be an owner to live my purpose. The answer seemed so simple that I overlooked it, and now felt silly that it took me this long to see it.

I tossed my phone aside, feeling my happiness drain. My career choice was closing its doors. My eyes watered. If Megan's mom was here, she would've told me, when one door closes, another one opens. It happened to her when Megan's dad left, and Molly created Dessert Bar. But I didn't see a door opening, only one slamming shut and locking.

I got up from the couch to pace around the house. I toyed with my necklace charm as I walked, thinking what to do next. Voss-of-Books, kept interrupting my thoughts.

I scoffed at the name, and then chuckled. "That's not the door I want to open," I said to no one.

As I paced around the dining table, I recalled my vow to never step foot in Voss-of-Books stores. Anger stirred thinking about breaking it. After releasing an inner groan, I felt no better.

To avoid what needed to be done, I grabbed my phone and checked my email. While the page loaded, I considered if I should tell Dad about the store closing. Knowing Dad, he would suggest I move to Nashville. I had no desire to leave Sevier Oak or move to a big city. I highly doubted my life calling awaited me in the state capital.

Regan's first message remained at the top of my email, indicating that Dad hadn't written back. I ignored my "sibling's" email and pushed aside the thought of Mom serving guests on a private yacht.

A knock on the front door startled me. When I opened the door, I expected to see either Grandma or Stone. Instead, I found Jane standing on the welcome mat. Her brown eyes were slightly red as if she had been crying.

"Can I come in?" she asked.

I stepped aside. Jane stood in the living room, unsure where to sit. I extended a hand toward the couch. She sat on the far side, while I sat on the opposite side. If Princess lived here, she would have placed herself on the middle cushion, watching us.

"Sheriff Estep came to the store," Jane started. "He had some more questions about the investigation."

"That's because you're still a suspect."

Jane played with her nails. "I'm aware of how this all looks. I assure you that I had nothing to do with Doris Hackett's death. I never met the woman until that day." She paused for a moment and stopped fidgeting. "What was Teresa going to do with all the stuff during the remodel?"

"She's renting some storage units. There's some stuff already there. We planned to have a sidewalk sale for duplicate books or any unwanted stuff. Anything left over was supposed to be donated. Have you been to the storage units yet?"

She shook her head. "What about the cats?"

"Princess and Butterscotch were Teresa's cats. They were going to stay at her place."

Jane frowned.

"What's this about?" I asked.

She rolled her shoulders back as if thinking before she answered. "I'd been doing a lot of thinking since you left the bookstore. You made a lot of valid points. I'm reconsidering keeping my aunt's store."

"Really? What changed your mind?" I squirmed in my seat, struggling to contain my enthusiasm.

"Not so fast," Jane said calmly. My knee stopped bouncing; this didn't sound good. "Murder draws a crowd, good for business as the saying goes. But I don't want that kind of business. I want the traffic my aunt had: friendly, book lovers, not busybodies who think I dunnit. Before we do any work, I want to clear my name. I can't live here with a scandal hovering over me."

"Are you saying that if I solve the case, then we can move forward with the remodel?" I tried to contain my excitement, but I heard my high pitch tone. How could I not be ecstatic?

"I'm not saying *you* solve the murder." Jane took a nervous breath. "Though, I admit I'm a little worried about Sheriff Estep's abilities. He might need some extra assistance."

I snorted. He needed all the help he could get.

"Back to your question, yes, I'm considering opening the store after the murder has been solved. I'm enjoying the slower pace in Sevier Oak. I like the weather here. My aunt said her bookshop was a hidden treasure. I see potential and she had some good ideas."

They were my ideas too, but I kept my mouth shut.

"My new neighbors sitting and staring at me from their front porch is a little unnerving. People don't do that in New York."

"Welcome to the South." I beamed. "Southerners like sitting on their front porch. You'll get used to it."

Jane sighed. "I doubt it, but I'm willing to overlook it because everyone seems harmless, expect for Dori's murder," she quickly added. "Back to the store, I'd heard about your roommate's cat allergy. I'll keep the cats during the remodel but after that they are your responsibility."

"Deal," I practically shouted

Jane's posture relaxed. "Good. Now that we're a team, I have some information to share with you from this morning."

CHAPTER 17

I CLOSED MY EYES, FEELING STUPID. HOW HAD I FORGOTTEN ABOUT Jane talking to Clara's neighbors? I should have asked her on the drive back.

"Let's hear it," I said, opening my eyes.

Jane placed her hands over her lap. "According to Mr. and Mrs. Watson, Clara is the town's spy."

"Tell me something I don't know. Even children know that."

"The couple said that Clara is worse than a snoop. She's a gossiper."

Again, I knew this, but decided to keep my mouth closed. I waited patiently as Jane told me about Clara's life story from a neighbor's perspective. It seemed like forever when she finally got the juicy details.

"Clara was spying on their house the morning Doris died. Mr. and Mrs. Watson were putting on a skit for her. The whole community is in on the act."

I could see myself doing that if I had a nosy neighbor like Clara.

"Go on, I'm listening."

"Like I was saying, everyone on the block was in cahoots. They created a community app."

"Really?" I interrupted. I stopped myself from asking if the Watson's gave Jane an invite.

"According to Mr. and Mrs. Watson, yes. Now let me finish," Jane kindly scolded before continuing. "Everyone takes a turn creating a scene. Spread out drama so one household isn't dealing with Clara for a long period of time."

"Let me guess, the morning of Doris's death was the Watson's turn."

"Correct. Mr. and Mrs. Watson claimed they were walking in their front lawn, yelling at each other over buried gold, and recording each other."

"That is weird."

"What Clara saw was them actually playing a game on their phones. While they were performing, they saw Clara burst out the front door and drive off. Neither of them knows why she left in a hurry. Before you ask, they don't know what time she returned, only that her car was backed up in her driveway before they went to bed at eight."

Dad once told me that Clara owned a police scanner, and it wasn't surprising to find her at crime scenes. My 911 call from the bookstore might have lured Clara from the Watson's game of fun. She never shopped at the bookstore, but Doris did. Even the worst spy in history had to know where their sibling's shopped.

Then again, someone could have called Clara about her sister's arrival. Did she leave in a hurry to kill Doris at the bookstore? If that was the case, who tipped Clara off, and why? I had a feeling this theory was wrong.

"Do they know what time Clara left the house?" I asked.

Again, Jane shook her head. The Watson's didn't pay attention to the time.

This information was a dead end. It meant nothing because it supported nothing. If Clara heard the call from the police scanner and then left, she was innocent. But If Clara left before Doris died, then she could be the murderer.

If Clara murdered her sister, how did she enter the store without being seen? Unless the town spy knew how to pick a lock, I didn't see how she committed the crime.

I remembered Clara making her grand appearance the day of the murder. She had stormed up on Copper Street, demanding the officer bring her Doris's belongings. Was Clara's shouting an act? Did she really do it, and return to fool the police? All the what ifs were making my head spin.

"Until we know when Clara left her house, we can't eliminate her as a suspect."

Jane sat quietly either unsure how to respond or deep in thought. Her fidgeting with her nails was driving me crazy.

After a few moments, I couldn't handle it anymore. "What did the Watson's do after Clara sped away?"

"They stayed home. I'm not sure about the specifics because I was interrupted."

I didn't see how knowing the way they spent their day was relevant to the investigation. We should go door to door to find out if anyone saw what time Clara left. After seeing the time, I made a mental note to do that tomorrow.

A new thought occurred to me. "Did they see what Clara was doing before she left? What if Clara was arguing with Doris over the phone and snapped." Jane gave me a disbelieving look. "People can text, too." I struggled to remember if Doris was on her phone.

"No. And Doris wasn't on her phone when she entered the store. Besides, I don't believe Clara killed Doris."

"Why?" I asked. If I wanted to hold my end of our bargain, I needed to step up my game, including eliminating suspects.

"Based on the fact that Clara attacked you single-handedly. She wouldn't need help killing her sister. There was no forced entry in the back door. Besides, given the account she's never been in the store, how would she know the layout?"

"We need facts. Not theories. Until we can prove Clara's timeframe, she remains a suspect," I said, quoting my dad.

Gosh, I was turning into my dad. A Progressive commercial when people turned into their parents came to mind.

"I believe money is the key," Jane continued.

I hummed my agreement. "This morning Clara asked if I got Doris's inheritance. Why would she think I'd get it? Doris and I weren't friends."

Jane replied, "Sounds like Clara didn't inherit anything. Maybe she's wondering who did."

Too bad Dad wasn't here. It would've been easier to solve the case if he was sitting at Grandma's dining table, venting about the suspects. I picked up my phone and emailed him. I knew asking how to obtain phone records would result in a phone call as to why. Until we knew about Clara's records, she remained a suspect.

"Other than Clara Hackett, who else is under suspicion?" Jane asked once I set my phone aside.

"I have a list," I said then wondered where I put my notebook.

Jane must have taken my silence the wrong way. "We need to trust each other, just as I do about you not having anything to do with Doris's death."

"Me?" I gasped.

"It would be foolish of me to not consider you. You were on the same level as Doris during her time of death and you knew her. Who would suspect a Stone? Sheriff Estep doesn't.

And given your family's history, you could possess the knowledge to pull the perfect crime." Jane paused for a moment. "My aunt said you are a 'sweet gal.' I don't believe my aunt had misjudged you. So, I'm trusting you that you didn't kill Doris."

"I think we misunderstood each other. Honestly, I was thinking about where I put the list."

"Does this mean that you no longer see me as a murderer?"

I studied Jane. After spending time with her today, I struggled to picture Teresa's niece as an assassin. Plus, Princess liked her.

"No."

Jane's glare melted into relief. "Thank you," she said. "Do you remember who you put on the list?" her voice went back to normal.

"Hold that thought." I jogged to the kitchen and found my notebook on the counter. "I started with four, but it's not looking so good," I said, skimming over the page as I sat back on the couch.

Her eyebrows furrowed. "That doesn't sound promising. Tell me about them."

"Preston Powell, Doris's ex-husband, was on the list. He was working next door at Old Treasures. Karl cleared him. Sasha Whitlock was another. She's the girl who came into the bookstore wanting her job back. I talked to her last night. She was at Voss-of-Books for an interview during that time talking to Mateo. So that confirms Mateo's alibi."

"Mateo is the other contractor?"

"Yes. And he's also Doris's ex-boyfriend. The guy Doris cheated on Preston with."

"Anyone else?"

When I shook my head, Roland came to mind. The deliveries were odd, but that didn't make him a murderer.

"Can you confirm that Sasha and Mateo were at the other bookstore, or are you just taking her word for it?"

Dang it, I thought. I made another rookie mistake. Again, I shook my head.

Jane stood up, failing to hide her excitement. "Pull yourself together. We're going to Voss-of-Books and speak to the manager."

"Whoa," I said, jumping up. "Let's just wait a little bit."

Jane looked puzzled. "Why?"

"Because I'm going there at ten till eight."

Jane's expression remained fixed. I summarized Leo having a lead. The best time to go to that awful store was minutes before closing. That way no one would see me, and it would force Leo to cut to the chase, instead of flirting with me or worse...trying to hire me.

"We can go now."

"No. Closing time. If anyone sees me, rumors will circulate that I shop there." I imagined Sasha snapping a picture of me and texting it to all her friends. Everyone in Sevier Oak would know before I left the store.

"There is no better time than the present."

"No, it's not."

"Let's compromise. We go now; I'll drive so no one will see your car in the parking lot," she said, as if her suggestion resolved my problem.

"I was going to park two blocks away, but sure, your way will work too."

Stone's ringtone interrupted what Jane was about to say next. I answered, hoping to end this nonsense about going to Voss-of-Books in the middle of the day.

His voice boomed through the speaker, "I need you over to the house ASAP."

CHAPTER 18

I DROVE US TO MY GRANDPARENT'S HOUSE. LIKE THE PREVIOUS CAR ride with Jane, she talked non-stop about cleaning Teresa's home, which had more clutter than the bookstore. I tuned her out. When Stone heard that Jane was with me, he wanted her to come too and for us to hurry. His urgency made me think Sheriff Estep was on his way to question me again, just like he had done with Jane. Was I officially a suspect now? Or was there new evidence pointing to another person? Did Stone have some questions for Jane?

Before I knew it, I pulled into the driveway, and parked. Grandma and Stone were sitting in their rockers, waiting. Their lack of joy made me more worried. This was serious.

I introduced Jane to my grandparents. She greeted them with a handshake. I sensed my family already knew everything about Jane Jackson. Once the formalities were over, we all ventured inside the farmhouse.

My head kept spinning as we ventured inside. Had Dad already read my email, figured out what I was doing, and called Stone? Did Underwood call Stone? The suspense was killing me.

Grandma went straight toward the kitchen while Jane and I found a seat at the table. Stone stood behind his chair, gripping the back so hard that his fingers turned white. Clenching stuff was Stone's sign that things were really bad. I also detected a faint smell of cigarettes.

Before I could ask what was wrong, Stone asked, "Where were you two on the evening of April twenty-third?"

Jane and I glanced at each other. Teresa died that night. Stone already knew my answer, but he asked to hear Jane's reply. I held my breath as I waited for her response.

"Why?" Jane sounded anxious.

Stone pressed his lips. Despite no longer being on the police force, he was in cop mode. I answered before he snapped.

"Teresa let me go an hour before the store closed. She was in a cleaning mood and told me she was going to stay late. I was hanging out with some friends."

That was the last time I saw Teresa alive. She stared down at me from a ladder. Princess stood on top of the bookshelf, swatting at the Swiffer in Teresa's hand. When Teresa got in these moods, she accomplished a lot. Getting a head start on the remodel, she told me while playing with Princess with the duster. I left without a second thought and waved goodbye as I walked out.

When Karl called me the following morning, I had a bad feeling. Teresa was never late. Customers were either waiting on the sidewalk or going into Old Treasures asking Karl why the bookstore was closed. I called Teresa while driving over, but like Karl said, Teresa wouldn't answer. Karl accompanied me as I unlocked the door. We wandered inside, thinking she fell asleep; instead, we found her at the bottom of the bargain stairs. I called Stone. He stayed on the line with me until he arrived. He stood by my side as he phoned the authorities, doing most of the talking. The medical examiner ruled Teresa's death as an accident. She lost her balance from carrying too many books and had a bad tumble.

Movement brought me back to the present. Grandma returned from the kitchen carrying two glasses with sweet tea and a slice of lemon placed on the rim. Whatever news Stone had, he waited until Grandma sat down.

I wanted to burst. What did Teresa's death have to do with what's happening now?

"Thank you," Jane told Grandma, making no attempt to drink it. "If you must know, I was in New York. I have a friend who can confirm I was in the city."

Stone took in this information. The realization hit me all of a sudden, like an unexpected boom of thunder. The final pieces fell together, yet it still hurt when Stone confirmed my suspicion. "Teresa's death was no accident."

"What?" Jane cried out.

Before Stone could answer, we voiced a million questions.

"My aunt was murdered!? Who—" Jane began.

"Why would someone—" I said at the same time.

Stone raised his hand to silence us. "After Doris's murder, I've been looking into Teresa's death. Two deaths in a bookstore within two months, and in the same room, that's not a coincidence."

Tears welled in my eyes.

"The coroner ruled it as an accident," Jane said. Either she didn't understand what Stone was trying to say, or she was refusing to believe it. "My aunt fell down the stairs. She was carrying too many books." Jane stared off into the kitchen as her hands cupped the iced tea. Her lips trembled.

"I don't understand," I said. "Who would do such a thing?

And of all people, why Teresa? Everyone loved her." Tears slid down my cheeks.

"I already informed the police chief," Stone said. "He's away on vacation, but he's aware of the situation. I'm sure Sheriff Estep will be here shortly." He looked at me, and I understood why he wanted me here so fast. "I want to ask some questions before he gets here."

"Who wanted to kill my aunt?" Jane asked more to herself than us.

"It's now being investigated."

While Stone reassured Jane about Sevier Oak's abilities to solve her aunt's murder, I thought of one person who didn't like Teresa. The same person who wanted to buy her bookstore and became a nuisance when she refused.

Drake Voss.

"What makes you think my aunt was murdered?" Jane demanded. "If what you say is true—"

"It's true." Stone turned his attention back to me. "Teresa's phone was found."

Jane too looked at me. "Did you find it?"

"Not me," I said and then turned to Stone. "Where was it?"

Stone finally took his seat. His big hands clasped together. "Answer mine first." For the first time, I wondered if this was how criminals felt when being interrogated by Stone. He had a stern voice that didn't allow nonsense. I heard something under the table followed by Stone glancing at Grandma. His face eased a little, and I relaxed. "Please."

"I tried looking for it after the accident, thinking it was somewhere in the store, but I never found it."

"Was this the first time she lost her cell phone?"

I remembered all the times Teresa asked me to call her. She often misplaced it somewhere in the store, never in the same place twice. Butterscotch lying on it only happened on a handful of occasions. After answering the question with a simple no, Stone asked me to elaborate. "She lost it at least twice a week. Teresa got fed up one day and programmed the store's phone to call her cell. All we had to do was push and hold the number nine button, and it would call."

"When did you last call it?"

I thought for a moment. "Two or three days after Karl and I found her. When it went to voicemail, I stopped calling. I figured it was at her house and the battery died."

"I haven't found her cell phone. I haven't even thought about it. Did you find it?" she asked Stone.

"A librarian found Teresa's cell phone inside of a box while sorting through the donations. He called me, wanting me to pass it along to you." He nodded at Jane.

Teresa liked giving extra copies of books to schools or libraries. Donating had always put her in a cleaning mood. That April day was no different.

Jane rubbed her thumbs along her glass of tea. Her eyes were watery, but no tears fell. I reached out and touched her shoulder.

Stone continued, "I listened to the voicemail before I turned it into the station."

My heart pounded faster, making me lightheaded. I removed my hand form Jane and sipped some sweet tea. I had a feeling this was going to be bad.

"Teresa called herself that night. She left a disturbing message."

I closed my eyes, knowing what had happened. Teresa was calling for help; she held the number nine button too long.

"Why didn't she call the police?" Jane's voice went up an octave, clearly upset.

Stone steel blues landed on me. "You answered why."

She gasped a few seconds later, I knew it hit her, and tears flowed.

I took a long drink, pretending whiskey was mixed with the tea. The sugary beverage made my stomach sour.

"I'll summarize the voice message," Stone said. "Teresa was trying to call for help. She realized her mistake nineteen seconds in, and her tone changed. She said there was a knife hiding in the store. I couldn't hear much after this point. A cat was hissing and—" Stone studied us. "Let's just say background noise."

"What was it?" I asked.

"I believe the office door was closed, and the intruder was trying to break inside, but it also sounded like Teresa was moving stuff as well. I'm not sure. We—" he waved a finger between himself and Grandma— "couldn't understand a word during the commotion. Before the message ends, Teresa wants whoever is listening to warn Doris."

"That's it?" cried Jane. "Just warn Doris? She didn't say who was coming after her?"

My grandparent's silence gave us the answers. The room felt heavy. Ice crackled in the untouched glasses. I pieced together what happened next. The office door couldn't keep the killer out. Teresa was trapped.

Jane and I cried. Our noses dripped. Grandma brought over a tissue box. Questions raced through my mind. Was this how the knife got into the store? Someone brought it to the store, and then what, hid it? But why and where? Did Teresa catch him or her in the act? How did Teresa know Doris was in trouble? The endless questions became too much. Soon, I found myself no longer crying.

"I think I know the answer, but I need to hear it." Jane's gaze fixed on Stone. "How did my aunt end up at the bottom of the stairs?"

"Whoever killed Teresa, made it look like an accident. There were too many books to be inside that size of the box."

"Teresa wasn't that careless," I added. Teresa was the type of person who made several trips rather than carry everything in one haul. It drove me crazy when she carried one bag at a time, returned to her car, and repeated until everything had been brought inside. During my first winter working at the bookstore, I was so annoyed by her constant in and out. She explained she would rather be careful than risk breaking something.

"I'm sorry," Stone lowered his tone. "I should have looked more into it instead of dismissing it."

I looked up at Jane. Like mine, her eyes too were now dry. Our gazes locked on to each other. I knew we were both thinking the same thing. We were going to solve Teresa's murder.

CHAPTER 19

Jane and I left after Stone reassured us he would be doing his own investigating. I felt more determined to find the killer, assuming both murders were committed by the same person. Solving the cases became paramount over keeping the bookstore open. It was personal. Based on Jane's lack of talking, I sensed she felt the same as I did.

While driving back to my place, I thought about my hometown. The occasional crime consisted of trespassing, stealing lawn property, drama between spouses or neighbors, and drunks. Despite all of this, Sevier Oak was still considered a good place to live. It was even safe enough for people to leave their homes or vehicles unlocked overnight. People baked casseroles when someone came down with the flu too sick to cook, or when a farm animal escaped their pin, people put them back in without any trouble from the owner.

So how did murder slip into this friendly town? Twice? Sure, Sevier Oak residents loved to gossip and were nosey, but at the end of the day we were a community who looked out for one another. Which town folk had taken matters into their own hands?

I shook my head at these awful thoughts. Maybe I was looking at this wrong. After Doris Hackett won the lottery, she turned her back on everyone, including her only sister. Preston had built a beautiful cabin deep in the woods just to have Doris tear it down to reconstruct a mansion. Then, she added a high fence around the vast property to keep people away. Perhaps the killer wanted to be Doris. Jealousy was a powerful motive. As of now, no one *had* inherited Doris's millionaire status.

But where did Teresa come into play? Was it the killer's plan to kill her or a matter of wrong place, wrong time? Before I could formulate more questions, I was pulling into my driveway having navigated there on autopilot. I climbed out of the car and walked in the house with Jane on my heels. We sat in the same spots as before.

I watched Jane fiddle with her nails. The redness from her eyes was slowly fading back to normal. Any doubts I had of her being the killer were gone. Boss-Lady might've loved money more than a bookstore, but not more than her aunt. I couldn't see Jane harming Teresa for an inheritance or plotting murder.

In my book, Jane was innocent.

I wanted to talk about the murders, but which one? *Should I start with Teresa's death, or the day Doris died and work backwards? Or go over the suspects again to find a connection between the two women? Should I call Dad and ask for him to come back to Sevier Oak?* Jane's soft words stopped these racing thoughts.

"Teresa gave me the bookstore because I hated my job," she said. "Her original will stated for the store and everything else to go to you. She changed it after the New Year."

I stopped myself from questions. This was a keep-your-mouth-shut moment, and let her speak.

"I used to be a defense attorney. I was excited about going solo. I could prove to my father that I was as smart as him, and I could carry on the family legacy. My first case was a guy accused of attempted murder. Of course, he claimed to be innocent, but the evidence was overwhelming." Jane's spoke faster. "The more time I spent with him, the more I didn't want to defend him. I knew in my heart that he was guilty. His story kept changing, trying to hide the ugly truth. I tried talking to my dad, but he wouldn't hear it. The guy came from a rich family, willing to pay whatever to keep their son innocent. They even created a witness to testify for his whereabouts. *Do your job*, my dad told me. I knew everything about the case was a lie. It made me sick. Then the guy's brother stalked me, making sure I was, 'doing my job.' I was terrified."

She paused and looked at me. The cream jacket over her coral top still said she was a successful entrepreneur, but her facial expression told me that Jane did not put her career first.

"Dad was furious when I asked if I could drop the case. The guy was clearly guilty, and I couldn't handle someone following me. The victim was scared." Jane's hands tightened into a ball. "I did what I had to do."

I wanted to say something comforting, but I didn't know what. I couldn't image being in her shoes. I couldn't even fathom not being able to go to my dad and Stone for help.

"Teresa saw my depression during Christmas. She knew that deep down I never wanted to be like my family of lawyers, attorneys, or anything that dealt with the courtroom. It's a stressful job. One they enjoy with the perks and status. My parents said I was a good judge of character and intelligent. It took a while to see that my heart wasn't in it."

Jane talked in depth about how much she hated the career choice. For years she walked in her family's footsteps that felt impossibly too big and too steep. She ignored her desires of wanting to be a history professor, persuading herself to do what the Jackson family did.

"You're supposed to know what you want to do in life at an early age," Jane said. "I thought working in law was the correct answer. It surrounded me. But deep down, I always knew it wasn't."

Her words pained me. I knew all too well how it felt to not have a career passion, to feel lost when others joyfully found it. Going by Jane's logic, I should have been a police officer. I couldn't imagine my family forcing me into that life.

"Come to think of it, Teresa always bought you historical novels," I said, giving a little smile.

Jane smirked and nodded. Her gaze fixed on a spot on the carpet.

"Teresa offered for you to come to Tennessee," I said.

A tear escaped and ran down her cheek faster than Jane's hand moved. "I didn't even try to help the guy's case because I knew he tired to kill her. I didn't want to change his story or bring in a false witness. No money from his father or creepy stalker could sway me. The man was found guilty and charged with attempted murder. He and my shadow are now behind bars. After everything was settled, I quit. I thought I would feel better, but instead I felt like a failure. I moped around New York trying to figure out what to do with my life while my parents told me to come back. My brothers said that I was stupid for throwing away a good career. My only regret is that I didn't come here sooner."

A silence fell, and I sensed that was the end of her story. "Well, I'm glad you didn't let the guy get away and that your stalker is his cellmate." I added a wink to ease the sadness surrounding us.

Jane didn't react. During our silence, I pieced together

what happened next. Her aunt died four months later leaving her everything, including a messy bookshop.

"I thought if I sold the store and my aunt's house, then I could go back to school and do something else or..." Jane paused for a moment, sucking in her lips. "Coming to Tennessee meant a fresh start for me. I never expected any of this." She waved her hands in the air.

I sat up and scooched onto the middle cushion. I wrapped one arm over her shoulder. Jane let out a small sob as she leaned into me. A sisterly bond blossomed between us. A friendship that I found myself wanting. I misjudged Jane. She wasn't like my mother or Drake Voss. She was a kind woman who hid her pain underneath those fancy suits.

Once Jane's tears eased into sniffles, I stood up and held out my hand. She took it. We stood face-to-face as an unspoken agreement was being said.

We had work to do.

CHAPTER 20

"The killer is sneaky," I said, "but that doesn't mean we can't catch them." I smirked, trying to add some humor. "We each got skills. You're an outsider and can read people well. Maybe you see something I'm overlooking. I have my detective skills. Together, we can be a team."

Jane gave the brightest smile I'd seen yet. "Team Jane and Garnet or Jackson and Stone." Her nose crunched and her smile vanished. "That one sounds bad. I don't want people think we named ourselves after Stonewall Jackson. Let's forget that last one."

I grinned knowing Jane meant well. "We'll think of a team name later, first I need a drink."

Jane followed me into the kitchen. I poured myself a tall glass of sweet tea. Whiskey sounded better, but a virgin drink would have to satisfy me.

"Do you have unsweetened tea?" she asked.

"I have coke and water."

Jane chose water. *Crazy Yankee*, I thought as we drank our beverages of choice.

"Teresa's death was related to Doris's," she said after a sip.

I agreed, mulling over what I wanted to say next. I didn't want to upset Jane, but at the same time, I saw Teresa as family too. "Based on the voicemail, I think the killer was planning to murder Doris in the bookstore. According to Clara, it's the only place Doris went. The killer must have known that too, but the killer didn't realize Teresa was there. She must have walked in on him or her while the killer was planning their attack. Then... you know." Jane nodded that she understood. "Teresa didn't always stay late, but she did get in random cleaning moods." Unfortunately, on April 23rd she felt motivated in doing so.

"It makes sense that Teresa was trying to call for help. She must have held the button a tad longer than she intended."

I'd heard enough crime stories to know people didn't always think clearly during a moment of crisis.

"I believe you're right," agreed Jane.

"I know fingerprints on the knife belonged to Doris, except for one."

Jane perked up. "I didn't know that. What else are you keeping from me?"

I pondered for a few moments. "Deputy Underwood told me that Doris was suffocated. I can't remember if the killer hit her with the tea kettle. I wouldn't be surprised since there was some blood on her forehead."

"I heard about the cause of death. It's so strange and doesn't fit. If the killer planned on killing Doris at the bookstore, why use a pillow?"

"Maybe the killer was interrupted? Perhaps Doris saw him or her this time."

Jane brought her thumb to her lips as if she was going to start chewing on her nail. Before she did, Jane said, "What about the blood on the stuffed bear and tea kettle? Did it belong to Doris?"

"That I don't know. I'll ask Stone. Underwood would tell him before me." I sent Stone a text, hoping my theory was correct.

"There must be something that we are overlooking." Jane took a sip, staring off into the distance before back at me. "Are you sure that you know...that mess, well?"

"Positive."

"We should focus on Teresa's voicemail. The only clue she gave was that a knife was hidden in the store. It was also at Doris's murder. Let's assume Teresa saw the killer hide it somewhere to kill Doris at a later time. All that being said, that doesn't explain how Doris's prints got on the knife?"

"Let's assume that's what happened, the killer hid one in the bookstore. Maybe Doris had one for protection. Her prints were on it and the knife is small enough to hide in her purse. Maybe there were two knives. When the killer fled, he or she took the one they hid."

Jane sighed. I knew what she was thinking because I felt it too. Too many theories and not enough facts. This moment reminded me why the police needed intel.

"I've been taught to look at all angles. What if my aunt's death was not a result of the wrong-place-at-the-wrong-time scenario? Who wanted her dead and who would benefit from her death? Did Teresa have any enemies?"

One person came to mind. "Drake Voss. He's been after her store since he opened Voss-of-Books. They're a big-name company."

"I never heard of them until I arrived."

"It's a Southern thing," I added. "I think they originated in Georgia and are slowly spreading."

I got up and poured myself a refill. My stomach growled, and I checked the time. Lunch hour came and went. I needed to eat something soon before a headache came. I considered ordering a pizza, but that would've taken too long. I opened the refrigerator door, scanning the shelf for something that could be eaten without cooking or heating up in the microwave.

"Garnet?"

I peeked over the refrigerator door, finding Jane staring at me. "Sorry. What did you say?"

"I said that I believe if we find the killer's motive for wanting Doris dead, then the answer will reveal the killer, and why my aunt was murdered. Now we have a new suspect, we should go have a chat with him."

Quickly, I popped some grapes in my mouth and closed the door. Jane stood next to me with her car keys in hand. Then she asked me about Drake Voss.

"He and Teresa had disagreements, but Drake is an old geezer and a regular at Dessert Bar. I don't see him physically able to take on Teresa though. The main thing we should focus on are the facts." I really was turning into my dad. "The stuffed bear had a blood spot. We need to know who owned that knife. Oh, and Benadryl. All of those are clues."

"Benadryl?" Jane asked.

I gave a summary about finding a pink pill.

Before leaving for the bookstore, I took a big gulp of tea, embracing the sugar running through my veins. Since I was breaking a sworn vow to never step foot in Voss-of-Books, I was half tempted to add a splash of whiskey. Something told me I was going to need it.

CHAPTER 21

"ARE YOU HUNGRY? MAYBE WE SHOULD GRAB A BITE TO EAT," I suggested. "Kountry Wings?" I really wanted a hot meal, but I would've suggested every place in town to stall.

Jane gave a half smirk as if she was saying, nice try. She kept driving. My stomach no longer turned or growled. I could only go another hour before my inner Mr. Hyde involuntarily took over. My eyes lingered on restaurants while Jane drove. Everything sounded amazing. Hamburgers. French fries. Chicken nuggets. Hot dogs. Even a gas station Slim Jim sounded delicious.

"We need a plan," Jane said, slowly breaking at a stoplight.

I forced myself to stop thinking about waffle fries. "What's there to plan? I buy something and Leo tells me what he knows. And if you see Drake Voss, you talk to him. The end."

Even with sunglasses on, I knew Jane didn't like my idea. She had a look. "Your plan is to fly by the seat of your pants?"

I didn't see the problem. Voss-of-Books was a bookstore with a cafe inside, not a chemical plant where I had to steal an employee's ID to slip past security guards.

When the light turned green, Jane laid out her plan of action. “While you talk to Leo, I’ll browse nearby and eavesdrop on co-workers if Drake isn’t there. Employees always spill dirt without thinking. Better yet, just keep Leo talking and I’ll try to get them to talk to me about Drake.” She finished with a proudful head nod.

It wasn’t a bad idea. Jane had proved that she could get people to open up to her. It worked with the Watsons.

While riding in Jane’s black sports car, I felt like we were on a spy mission. If Jane went over the speed limit, I could’ve totally pictured us as undercover agents. *No.* Charlie's Angels. I smiled, wishing I changed back into something tight and sexy. Then again, I didn’t want Leo eyeing me up and down. Black jeans and a gray shirt with Ray-Bans propped over my forehead was perfect.

Something hit my foot and I jerked them up.

“What?” Jane asked. “Is it a bee?”

I looked down and saw a clear plastic container. “It’s a water bottle,” I said. The longer I stared at it, the more items came into view. Pens with no caps were tucked into the floormate’s groves. A mint container sat centimeters away from my feet. Napkins and fast-food bags were tucked into the side door. I dared myself to peek into the backseat. The first thing I spotted were two laundry baskets filled with clothes with a cluster of tangled hangers piled next to the baskets. I liked to assume the clothes were clean and Jane hadn’t gotten around to putting them away. The floorboard was invisible from all the stuff, mostly empty water bottles and hangers that slid off from the seat.

Was Jane an unorganized person or had she not gotten settled yet? I feared that Jane and Teresa shared something in common.

My cellphone dinged a notification causing me to jump.

Dad emailed me. It took no time to read his message. Good news, Dad confirmed about Clara Hackett being the neighborhood's biggest nuisance while she claimed to be on the neighborhood watch— which didn't exist. Dad and his co-workers at the station looked into Clara's complaints about her neighbor's bizarre behavior. In reality, they were teasing Clara. It seemed their skits had been ongoing for years. Dad also mentioned Clara owning a police scanner; it wasn't uncommon for her to be present at crime scenes, spying. Towards the end of the message, he gave me a chilling warning.

> *Now that her sister was murdered, I expect Clara's obsessive behavior to kick into overdrive. Best to stay away from her. But if you see her around spying on folks, tell Idris Underwood. I know you don't like it but put that pepper spray back on your keychain. Your old man will rest better. Love you very much. Dad.*

I couldn't tell if he knew about Clara attacking me or if he was just being Detective Dad.

"We need a code word," I said, going along with Jane's latest plan. If Leo was anything like his grandfather, I might need her help to escape.

"Books."

"Really? It's like going into a candy store and not expect to hear the word *candy*. Books won't work."

"Then what do you suggest?" Jane side eyed me.

I smirked. "Witcher."

Jane's eyebrows disappeared behind her sunglasses. I knew she was glaring at me while driving. "Are you trying to be funny or serious?"

"It's a book series. Remember?"

Jane waved her hand. "Yeah, yeah. But we're not using Witcher. How about Henry?"

"What if there is a guy there named Henry. Talk about an awkward situation."

"Fine." She paused for a moment. "Nancy Drew. It's bookish and her name doesn't scream violence."

"Okay, Nancy Drew."

"So, what's your history with Leo Voss," Jane asked.

"There's not much to tell," I said. "I've run into him a few times." The first being when he and his grandfather crashed a private party. The memory still made me mad.

When I added nothing more, Jane said, "I think he has a crush on you."

"No, no," I cried.

My mind flashed back to our last encounter. It was a summer night. I was fresh out of high school hanging with Brad at the county fair. I stared at a stuffed leopard, wishing to have it. Brad hated playing games and paying money for a one-minute ride. Our entire date was spent walking around while everyone else had fun. I bought us a lemonade trying to make the best of the night while Brad griped about everything. As I admired the stuffed cat, I spotted Leo amongst a group of guys. He paid the worker to throw darts at balloons. For a moment, our eyes locked. Again, I pestered Brad about winning me a prize. He refused. After my boyfriend ditched me to hang out with other friends, I walked to my car feeling low. That was when I heard Leo calling my name. I turned around and saw him holding the stuffed leopard. "That guy," Leo said, "doesn't know how to treat a lady." Then he handed me the prize along with a napkin with his number. I never called, but realized Brad wasn't for me. I remember thinking that a Voss treated me better than my boyfriend. The following day, I ended things with Brad. I hid the stuffed cat and the napkin in a tote.

I never had the heart to discard the leopard, but I also couldn't admire it either.

"Leo is just another guy," I said, hoping to satisfy Jane's curiosity.

Jane said nothing while pulling into a front parking spot. Voss-of-Books blocked the view of the distant trees. It's wide awning overwhelmed the neighboring stores. It was like sitting in the front row of a movie theater. My stomach twisted with dread.

I was about to break a sworn vow.

"Did you really have to park up front?" I asked.

Jane flashed a not-so-sorry smile. Boss-Lady had a mischievous side. I liked it and hated it at the same time.

I took two steps when someone hollered my name.

CHAPTER 22

Sasha Whitlock strolled up to me wearing tight jeans and a graphic t-shirt that read, *Go get Voss-of-Books.* Catchy. Sasha looked better than when she had worked at Teresa's Bookstore. Her hair had been brushed and her pants didn't have holes or tears, fashion that drove Teresa bonkers. Sasha's lips were as red as the fake apples in Grandma's kitchen. I wondered if these subtle changes were from dating Mateo or if she was happy about Doris's death.

Meanwhile, Jane lingered inside her car. *Now she waits in the vehicle?* I considered saying the code but decided to suck it up. No sense in becoming the boy who cried wolf too many times because someone spotted me.

"I've been wanting to talk to you," Sasha said with a chipper tone.

"Okay," I said, hoping to hear the latest town's gossip related to the investigation.

To my surprise, Sasha linked her arm with mine and escorted me straight towards the enemy lines. I wanted to dig my heels into the ground like a dog who realized he had been tricked into going to the vet's office. Maybe I was overreacting and this meeting would be easy. Who was I kidding? All I could think of was how Drake mistreated Teresa. My vow broke as Sasha opened the door.

Five minutes, I told myself, *just five minutes.*

While Sasha complimented Voss's store, I cringed. The walls were painted solid white. I expected at least one book poster, but there were none on display. Not a single bric-a-brac decorated the top of the bookshelves. The rows and rows of bare shelves made the place feel lifeless. The rest of the store was no different. A lonely spinner of bookmarks stood near two registers. I scanned the area for the usual knick-knacks of coffee mugs, mini flashlights for reading at night, and blank journals, but none were in sight. On the far right was the cafe. A tiny whiteboard hung over the counter. A cozy picture of the monthly special would bring some appeal. Adding to my disappointment, the air lacked the familiar scent of crushed coffee beans. In fact, the place smelled like...nothing.

Voss-of-Books might've sold more novels, however, it was deficient in personality. Teresa's Bookstore wasn't tidy, but blossomed with life and love. Books snuggled on shelves, vertically and horizontally. There was something magical about browsing in an old building surrounded by countless novels. One did not need to hold a book up to their nose to smell the pages. The scent floated in the air. A sweet feline accompanied shoppers while searching for their next adventure. Each figurine on the top of bookshelves held a story, which Teresa gladly told them. Booklovers came in and often wandered for hours, searching for something and nothing at the same time.

"Isn't Voss-of-Books great?" Sasha beamed, looking around. "Mateo helped build it. You should hire him for the remodel. Oh—" her smile lessened— "that is, if Teresa's Bookstore stays open. Maybe it's for the best if it closes. Just like the saying goes, it's not personal, it's business."

I didn't trust my words and said nothing.

Sasha pointed around the store as if she was a game show host, showing the audience the prize they could win. "These books are way better. No broken spines or dog-eared pages. You also can't compete with the coffee. The lattes sold here are the best in town. Not that Teresa's were bad, but it wasn't her specialty. And best of all there are no rotten cats or fur." Sasha snarled a disgusted face.

You're rotten, I thought while biting back those words.

Before I could ask what Sasha wanted to talk to me about, Leo Voss appeared behind a row of books. His narrowed eyes made his sharp traits more pronounced. For a moment, I thought I misheard him about our deal.

"Sasha." His voice sharpened loud enough for only us to have heard. "You're late again. Hurry up and clock in. It's past Miranda's lunch break."

Sasha scurried away without a goodbye.

When Leo noticed me, his stern glare melted into a pleasant smile. "Hey, Garnet. I'm surprised to see you so soon."

My cheeks warmed. His good looks had to charm women. I pushed aside my feelings, remembering why I was here, and walked toward the spinner of bookmarks. After snatching the first one, I stood by the register. "Ring me up."

Leo gave me the stink eye, adding to his charm. "A bookmark?"

"You never said what I should buy or how much. I'm willing to spend two dollars."

He walked behind the counter with his head high and informed his co-worker that she could go on break. Miranda, I assumed, gladly left.

While Leo tapped on the screen, I couldn't get a read on

him. Was he mad? Did my mouth get me in trouble again? Or was he still hurt that I rejected going on a date?

I glanced around the store. There were a few customers shopping, and none them of them seemed to notice me. Jane entered. She took a few steps in, studying the layout. Then she zeroed in on the New Releases table, and picked up a hard-cover. *So far so good*, I thought.

By the time Leo rang up my two dollars and seventeen-cent bookmarker, Sasha arrived. She wore a black apron over her clothes as if she should be working at the cafe rather than the register. She flashed Leo a smile like she had with Teresa when she got into trouble. It never worked on Teresa. Based on the look on her boss's face, Sasha's charm didn't work on him either.

Leo nodded toward the cafe. I took the hint. As I walked to the barren coffee bar, behind me I heard his harsh tone toward Sasha. I had a feeling the Voss men were not as patient as Teresa. Still, everyone had a breaking point.

When entering the cafe, Jane sat at a two-person table. Her nose was stuck in a book she had picked up. I sat facing Jane in case she said the code word. Her eyes shifted over the pages. Before I could get her attention, fearing she would get lost in the story, Leo took the seat next to me.

"Sorry about that," he said. "I had to clear something up. Do you want a coffee or a latte?" He jabbed his thumb toward the cafe.

He was halfway standing up when I said, "No, I'm good. Thanks." Even though my stomach begged for a muffin or a slice of marble bread. The sooner I got the information, the sooner I could leave. "What do you know?"

Leo straightened his back. "No, small talk, huh?" When he realized that I wasn't going to answer, he leaned forward. "First, I wanted to warn you about your new head-honcho."

His green eyes shifted towards Jane's direction and back on mine. "She tried to sell Teresa's store to Gramps."

I pretended to be surprised, mentally recalling seeing the three of them at the Kountry Wings.

"The deal didn't go through," Leo continued. "Miss Jackson's asking price was too high, and the thing with Doris Hackett."

I changed the subject. "Did you hear the news about Teresa? Her death wasn't an accident. She was murdered." I wasn't sure if I was allowed to reveal this. Stone never said not to. Besides, Sevier Oak would know sooner than later, I figured since I was investigating, the story might as well come from me.

Leo's pale skin went a shade lighter. "No, I didn't. That's terrible." He moved one hand over mine. His warmth ignited something deep inside of me; I enjoyed his touch. "I'm so sorry."

I forced myself to remove my hand. Teresa's and Doris's murders needed to be solved. Now was not the time to be wooed by Leo. Thankfully, Leo didn't look hurt by my motion. "Thank you. I want to know why Drake wanted to buy the bookstore. What were his plans?"

"Nothing."

My head tilted like when Princess first saw a slice of lemon floating in my tea. "Nothing?"

Leo gave a sheepish smile. "I know that's not what you want to hear. Gramps and Teresa never got along. But you already knew that."

I almost mentioned the time when Drake called Teresa a horrible name because she sold used books, instead I gave a little nod.

"Gramps was using his personal funds to buy the place— if

Teresa sold it, that is. He planned on reselling it once the books and shelves were removed."

Leo's tone surprised me. I expected to hear a hint of arrogance, something that would indicate that their bookstore was better than Teresa's. In contrast, he sounded disappointed at his grandfather's plans. Like with Jane Jackson because she wore suits, perhaps I misjudged Leo too.

The stuffed leopard flashed in my mind.

"Why not do something with the space?" I asked, unable to contain my curiosity. "I mean it's silly to buy a place, just to resell it. I thought he wanted to use it to sell clearance books or host big name authors. It's makes no sense."

Leo frowned. I wished I didn't say that last comment. His tone turned serious and folded his hands over the table like businessmen often did. "Mr. Voss doesn't like competition, including a little used bookstore. It bothers him that the pharmacy has a tiny section of paperbacks. He's a businessman and aims to be the best."

"Drake is a bully," I said without thinking, letting my anger control me. "Maybe Drake murdered Teresa and made it look like an accident, hoping Jane would sell him the store. Teresa's an easy target."

As the story spilled from my mouth, I knew it sounded ridiculous. I had no evidence to support this story. Meanwhile, Leo's face morphed into the same look he gave Sasha. This time my mouth had gotten me into trouble. Deep trouble. I braced myself for him to kick me out and call me horrible names. Instead, he took some long breaths. Slowly his shoulders relaxed. When he talked, it sounded calmly as if I never insulted his grandfather.

"Gramps was in Germany when Teresa died. Dealing with family business over there. Between you and me, he was upset that he couldn't attend her funeral."

Drake Voss was bummed that he couldn't come to Teresa's funeral? The same Drake who mistreated Teresa? It took me a few moments to gather my thoughts.

"He was?"

"It was no secret that Gramps didn't like Teresa very much, but he did respect her though. He holds high regards to any owner who fights for their business. Did her willpower annoy Gramps? Absolutely, but he still thought highly of Teresa."

I let the information sink in. It sounded strange, and yet made sense. Teresa, on the other hand, had no respect for him. She once told me she hoped Voss-of-Books would burn to the ground, after the fire department rescued all the books.

I hated to ask the next question, but for the sake of the investigation I had to. "Where was Drake when Doris died?" After I said the words, I instantly regretted them. I just now remembered seeing Drake at Dessert Bar after Underwood questioned me. Megan often vented about how much time he spent there, eating pie while making phone calls and typing away on his laptop as if Dessert Bar was his office rather than a restaurant.

"Nevermind," I said. "I re—"

"Gramps and I were here. We had a conference call that morning. My father is having some problems in some of the stores in North Carolina. It took three hours to deal with the situation. Afterwards, he went to Dessert Bar."

Eliminating Drake off the suspect list felt good. I was also slightly annoyed that another suspect provided an alibi. Why did all my suspects have an excuse?

"You said you knew something about Doris's murder," I said.

Leo gave a sheepish smile. "I'm afraid I lied."

"Lied?" My voice sounded funny. A mixture of feelings swooshed inside: upset, smitten, touched. If only he wasn't a

Voss, then this would be the perfect scene from a romance. Or was it a perfect scene happening in my own story?

"Please don't be mad." He went to move his hand over mine again but stopped. "I wanted to spend time with you now that I'm permanently living here, and that guy is out of the picture. Tricking you here was the only way I knew how."

Butterflies fluttered in my stomach as I felt myself blushing. I wanted to be angry at him for making me break a sworn vow. Leo was a Voss, not a hero that Bonnie Tyler sang about. People who wore suits were money hungry bodies who put their career before family, like my mom. Then again, Jane proved me wrong. But as long as both outlets remained open, Leo and I would be rivals. He was the villain, however, there was something about his blushing face that made me think he was a knight in shining armor. He had shown several acts of kindness. Maybe, just maybe, Leo was more like Mr. Darcy in Pride and Prejudice than Tamlin in A Court of Thorns and Roses.

In the corner of my eye, I spotted movement. I glanced in Jane's direction. She shifted in her seat before turning a page. She was either really wrapped up in the story, or had taken acting lessons.

"I should get going," I said, not knowing what else to say. I stood up, and he followed suit. When I gazed into his green eyes, I felt like I was seeing Leo for the first time. He was a great guy who smelled of musty cologne and had a handsome smile. A part of me wanted to sit back down and get to know him better. The next time he gave me options, I would choose the second one.

"Thank you for your time," I said a little louder than normal. "I think I'll go read some Nancy Drew books."

"We have a great selection." Leo smirked. "We also have a

great book club that meets on the last Thursday of every month. I can arrange for one of her books to be read in July."

I rubbed my nose to hide my warming face, telling him that I needed to go. Before leaving, Leo invited me to come again, and handed me a business card with his personal phone number written on the back. With my purchase in hand, I headed toward the door, hoping Jane was following. After stepping into the summer heat, my head swimming with lust, I bumped into someone.

"Sor—" I started to say, only to see the person was Grandma Stone.

CHAPTER 23

"What are you doing here?" I hissed.

Grandma's outfit reminded me of how Megan dressed this morning. Instead of a white shirt with yellow shorts, Grandma's shirt was yellow and she wore white capris. As usual, her hair was tucked under a straw hat with a pink bandana and she wore massive sunglasses she'd owned for years. Her tiny nose stud sparkled in the sunlight.

"Are you shopping at Voss-of-Books?" I asked.

Without notice, a red sedan zoomed into a parking spot a short distance behind Grandma.

Clara Hackett.

She barely had the car in park before she was half hanging out the driver's window with binoculars pressed against her face. Dad was right about Clara's nosiness being kicked into overdrive. Why was she even here? She and Doris never shopped here.

"Excuse me," Mateo said, approaching us.

Grandma and I stepped aside as Mateo entered the bookstore. I stopped myself from following. Jane could handle him while I dealt with Grandma and keep an eye on the town's spy.

"Garnet?" Grandma's voice brought me back to the present.

"Sorry," I said, ignoring Clara. "Are you buying from the enemy?" I pointed behind me at Voss-of-Books.

Grandma's chin lowered. "You did."

I wadded the bag under my arm. "It's just a bookmark."

"It starts somewhere."

"It's not what you think."

Grandma raised her eyebrows. "I heard you're warming up to the young Voss at Dessert Bar. And now I find you here."

Thinking of Leo stirred butterflies in my stomach again. If Grandma knew that I had a small crush on him, she would pester me to call him. Before I could argue that we were just friends, I spotted movement. I glanced over Grandma's shoulder. Clara was walking towards us, and she didn't look happy. I shifted my gaze in Clara's direction, hoping Grandma understood. She didn't get the hint and started talking about Leo moving into a condo at the edge of town until Clara interrupted.

"Is Sterling Stone looking into my request?" Clara asked Grandma. Her eyes were puffy as if she hadn't slept in days. She also stank of sweat. "I need to know."

What was Clara mad about? I wondered, and what was Stone doing for her? I looked at Grandma for her response.

Grandma plastered on a smile she reserved for difficult people, and her tone turned deeply Southern. "Oh, darling. Lawyers make everything difficult. Don't you worry honey, Stone is digging hard into your request."

Maybe Sasha should take lessons from Grandma's charm because Clara mellowed.

"I appreciate it. But I am in a hurry. You understand, right?"

"Patience, darling."

"When will he arrest that new woman?"

"You mean Jane Jackson?" I said while pretending that Grandma wasn't glaring at me behind those sunglasses.

"Yeah, that's her name," Clara said, turning her attention to me while pointing a finger at me. "Why did you and your friend bring Jane to my house? Don't you know that she murdered my sister in cold blood?"

Grandma's thick eyebrows raised in question. There went my cover for stopping at Clara's house without Stone knowing. Since I was going to get lectured anyway, I figured might as well keep going. "Why would Jane want to kill your sister? She never met Doris until that day."

Clara's jaw tightened and moved her pointed finger near Grandma's chest. "You tell Sterling to hurry up. I want that woman behind bars, and tell him to get my ring back."

"Don't you worry, darling." Grandma smiled sweetly. "Let him do all the work and worry. You just rest up now. Get some sleep. Take a load off from packing."

Clara scowled at the same time cool air brushed behind me. I closed my eyes for a moment. Jane's timing was the worst. Why couldn't she stay inside and read one more chapter? Grandma took the opportunity to dart inside. I shook my head at her sudden departure. *Traitor and a coward*, I thought.

Clara grabbed my upper arm, and whispered, "You make sure your grandaddy brings me justice before someone else gets killed," Then she added, "And that he finds my ring."

I yanked my hand away, giving her my most hateful glare. "Touch me again and I will press charges." For a moment I considered giving her a light hip toss to prove my point, but chose not to because I didn't want to give her a reason to press charges against me. Fortunately, Clara understood and power-walked to her car.

"Ready to go?" Jane asked, watching Clara get in her vehicle. Within moments, she then brought her binoculars up. At least she wasn't hanging out of the window.

"Not yet, I'm waiting for Mateo to come out."

"I did."

"Can we talk about this elsewhere." I shifted my eyes towards Clara.

"Let's talk at our bookstore," suggested Jane.

Hearing Jane say *our bookstore* was music to my ears.

CHAPTER 24

PRINCESS GREETED US WHEN WE ENTERED THE BOOKSTORE. SHE snaked between our legs, purring. Butterscotch, on the other hand, glared daggers while sitting next to her half-full food dish. As I refilled the cat's bowls, Jane sat in the reading nook with her new book open across her lap.

Once the cats were fed, I brushed off Princess's fur, and sat in the second chair. My body eased into the comfy chair. I didn't realize how much my legs ached until that moment. Other than having an hour to myself at home and after running into Leo at Dessert Bar, this was the first time I had stopped. It felt great, yet more sleuthing needed to be done.

"I'm almost done with this chapter," Jane said, flipping through the pages before returning to her spot.

I was eager to know what Jane learned at Voss-of-Books. For now, I welcomed the rest.

While Jane read, I glanced around the store. I had vacuumed the morning of Jane's arrival. If all went well the green carpet would be removed during the renovation, and I wouldn't have to crawl on my hands and knees with the vacuum hose. I also wanted to move one genre out of the romance/horror room. To where was the million-dollar question. Teresa never decided where. In a messy bookshop, one thing had to be relocated before something moved in its place. That was a lot of moving that required more time than I had been given.

I took a deep breath, changing my perspective. Work always needed to be done in retail, and it didn't have to be negative. I focused on my view. From my spot, I saw a section of the front counter through an aisle. It felt like staring down a long tunnel, but instead of thick ivy along the walls there were hundreds of books. I would' rather be here among the cluster of books with worn out carpet and cat fur than in a dull store.

Excitement rose inside of me. I imagined this store being featured online after the remodel. People and travelers to Bristol would stop here to shop. Teresa's Bookstore wouldn't be viewed as an unorganized store that overflowed with more books than it could carry, but a messy one with organization while maintaining a cozy beauty. The floating books idea could hover over from the loft area, or have it above it, so people standing on the second level could be spellbound by the sight. It now occurred to me that the cast iron conservatory would be perfect for a sitting area. That way the coffee bar would be safe from Princess's nosiness.

The whole layout would change. Teresa and I agreed that removing a part of the second floor would open up the place. Chairs and other small furniture would be moved to the upstairs loft to host book clubs. Each genre had its own section with signs adorned in stunning handwriting. During the Christmas season, I imagined a sixteen-foot tree in the middle. A smile grew across my face thinking about draping garland with lights over the shelves. On warmer days, carts of clearance books could be wheeled onto the sidewalks.

I wanted to get started right now, but Boss-Lady turned the page.

A sweet meow came from above. I looked up and spotted Princess. She perched herself on top of a shelf, gazing down at me. She reminded me that if we added the conservatory, then we had to restore the missing glass, otherwise, Princes would turn into Godzilla and wreak havoc. Like the first and only time we served coffee.

When I heard Jane's book close I asked, "What did Mateo say?" If Megan hadn't called on the ride here, asking for updates, then I would've known the details.

"Mateo went straight to the counter and talked with Sasha. I see why my aunt let Sasha go. She was totally flirting with him. I don't approve of that kind of behavior, and there was a line of customers. Leo looked furious. At least Mateo had some sense to walk away so she could do her job. When he came into the cafe, I waved him over." Jane glanced at her phone. "He should be here soon."

I sat up straighter. "Here?"

"Yes, here. I want his professional opinion about the store's layout. Plus, we can question him about his alibi." She looked proud of herself. "I thought he would open up without his girlfriend staring at us."

It was a good plan, except that Jane invited a possible murderer. I held my phone, telling myself to hang onto it at all times.

"Before Mateo gets here, I meant to tell you that Drake Voss called me about my aunt's store." She held up a hand to stop me asking questions. "Mr. Voss called me over a week ago. And yes, I was about to sell him the store. We discussed the terms over the phone, but at dinner Drake backed out because murder is bad business. But that is behind us now. What did you learn from the cute Voss?"

Leo's stunning eyes flashed to mind. *Gorgeous.*

"Garnet?"

Girl, stop daydreaming, I scolded myself. "Leo sa—"

Loud banging cut me off. We jumped up. Princess landed with a thud and rushed to the front door. I peeked from the bay window but could only make out the figure of a man. He stood too close to the door to determine the identity. I assumed it was Mateo. Jane was already walking, and I followed. In the next window, I saw it was Preston Powell. I grabbed Jane's arm. She stopped, giving me a confused look. I pointed at Preston. Unless he looked to his right, Preston couldn't see us. His gaze focused on the view through the glass door. He wore what I called Sunday's best, a dress shirt tucked into a clean pair of dark blue jeans. He had shaved his beard since we last met. In his hands he carried a storage clipboard. The aluminum board looked like it had seen better days with a hole at the bottom and some dents in a few spots as if it had been thrown a few times.

As much as I wanted to start working on the update, I didn't want to hear how Preston thought the new layout should be. His idea was to remove more of the second floor, making Cat's Lounge nonexistent. He also wanted to replace the hardwood floors and stain them a dark color rather than a lighter color to brighten up the place. When Karl and Teresa had peeked under the green carpet after Preston left, they agreed the subfloor was in good condition. At the end of the consultation, Mr. Powell's asking price seemed high, and he couldn't promise a finish date.

Preston never came across as a bad person or contractor, but his insistence at doing things his way made Teresa sway more towards Mateo. Unlike Mr. Powell, Mateo listened and tried to stay close to Teresa's original plan and within budget. He said the layout might need some tweaking based on the location of support beams, which sounded more understandable than Preston wanting the loft to be bigger, because bigger was always better.

He knocked again. I shook my head, thinking now might be a good time to tell Jane about Karl's experience with Preston.

"Let's just hear him out," she said.

"It can wait another day."

"He might know something that could solve the case."

After talking to Karl, I highly doubted he did. Preston was working next door, on the second floor's bathroom. He and Doris had divorced years ago. And he never quarreled with Teresa. End of story.

"Besides," Jane continued, "I also want to hear his professional opinion."

"I can tell you that. Teresa's plans are upstairs. I know exactly where they are. We should go over them before talking to Preston. Or Mateo."

"I'm respecting the Stone." Jane held head higher as she walked away.

I chased after her. "That's not what the saying means," I muttered.

Jane unlocked the front door. "Mr. Powell, come in." She stepped aside, flashing him a welcoming smile as Doris's ex-husband entered.

"Call me Preston," he said. He glanced at Princess, and she darted away.

I detected a hint of his citrus cologne. Orange seemed like an odd choice for a guy, but I'd rather he smell fruity than sweaty.

"I came by to see if you're considering moving forward with Teresa's renovations. I wrote a quote a few months back, but the price of lumber changed." Preston gave a sympathetic frown. I assumed the price had gone up. "But you're the new owner. It all depends on what *you* want, Miss Jackson."

While Jane and Preston chatted, I went upstairs to find the store's blueprints. Listening to Preston's plans for a third time sounded as interesting as a bear's snore. Butterscotch laid across the desk. She sat up when I entered while Princess batted at a pen until it fell onto the floor. If I needed a pen, a highlighter, or a pencil, I only needed to look down. The floor had a great selection, all thanks to Princess.

I kicked a Zebrite highlighter from under the desk. The quick movement across the floor sparked Butterscotch's senses. While the boxy computer hummed to life, the cats played with the pink highlighter. Their little paws rippled across the carpet. I watched until Butterscotch stopped and began cleaning herself. Princess continued playing into the hallway, not realizing her sister used all her energy for the day.

The office looked different than it had this morning. Had it really been hours ago since helping Jane with Butterscotch? *What a day it has been*, I thought while studying the desk. The stack of old fliers was tossed in the recycle bin, supplies in the top drawer had been emptied, and the intertwined bundles of yarns that Teresa vowed to untangle were too disposed of. Some things remained untouched. Jane probably would have cleaned more if Sheriff Estep hadn't come here to question her again, prompting her to come to my house before Stone called.

I rubbed my face, glancing at the time. It was coming up on four o'clock. It felt like it should've been later, like eight or nine. A part of me wanted to go home and crawl in bed, while the other part wanted to get more done. Teresa, my friend, had been murdered in her own bookshop.

"It's just four," I told myself, thinking of the times Dad ran on fumes. If he could solve cases on a few hours of sleep, then so could I.

Now the computer was ready to work, I noticed the sticky note about calling the online orders was gone. *Looks like Jane has been busy as me.*

"Wait," I said, standing up. I jogged downstairs to the receiving room. The large box Roland had brought was gone as well. I still needed to ask him why only one came and not three smaller ones, but that seemed petty compared to solving two murders. Still, something nagged me to ask Roland.

I heard Preston talking. I pictured him waving a pen in the air, mentally showing Jane his ideas. I darted back upstairs to print the store's blueprints and Teresa's drawn plan she doodled on Microsoft paint. *One thing at a time*, I mentally told myself.

Ten minutes later, I had the printed copies in hand, and headed downstairs. I followed the voices towards the bargain room. Jane disappeared into the room followed by her footsteps creaking up the stairs, while Preston leaned against the doorframe. He wrote something on a piece of paper, unaware of my presence. I noticed his hand was wrapped in a nude bandage. Alarms went off in my head.

The morning Doris died, he had a dirty rag wrapped around his hand.

"Are you okay?" I asked while keeping a clear distance between us.

He startled for a moment before studying himself. "Oh. I hurt my hand last week. It happens a lot in my field of work."

"How?"

He tensed. Preston clearly didn't like to be questioned. I pressed the papers against my chest, giving him the same tough expression I had done with Clara.

After a few beats of silence, Preston grinned. "I scraped it on a rusty nail when I was finishing a job at Old Treasures."

"A rusty nail? Shouldn't you get a tetanus shot?"

Preston shifted his weight to one side. "I've been in this line of work since I was a teenager. I know when I need to see a doctor. You wanna see?" He put the clipboard under his armpit and reached for the bandage.

"No," I said quickly, not wanting to see dry blood or a nasty cut. If Preston injured his hand while attacking Doris, then I doubted he could have finished Karl's bathroom. *Besides, why was I questioning him like a suspect*, I wondered. Karl said he was working during the time of Doris's murder. Preston wasn't a suspect.

An awkward silence fell. I wanted to ask him questions about the murders, if he knew something that would crack open the case, but I couldn't think of how to say it without sounding like I was suspecting him.

Thankfully, Jane reappeared. "Here." She handed Preston a little white card. "My new number is written underneath the old one."

Preston's eyebrows rose while reading the business card. "You are a defense attorney?"

Jane placed a hand over her chest as if she was flattered. "I was, but I left New York to find a new career. You wouldn't believe how much paperwork is involved. And interviewing eyewitnesses." She gave a weary sigh. "I can only imagine the interviews the police are having with eyewitnesses. Lots of people must have seen Doris walking on the sidewalk before coming here. Did you know her?"

I saw why the Watson's opened up to her. Jane was cunning.

"I'm her ex-husband," he said in a kind tone.

Jane's eyes went huge and her mouth formed into a round O shape. "Oh, really? I'm so sorry. That's awful." Jane paused to let Preston talk, but he said nothing. "Did you see anything? Garnet was telling me that you finished a bathroom next door that day, by the way it looks wonderful. Did you see Doris when you went into Old Treasures? She seemed flustered when she came into the bookstore."

I was proud of Jane. She was taking advantage of being the new person in town.

"Afraid not." Preston cleared his throat. "How about we walk through the bargain room. I was thinking that we might be able to knock down a wall."

"It's a mess. I haven't had time to clean it."

He insisted. Jane led him into the room. When Preston walked ahead, Jane gave me a look over her shoulder. I didn't understand it, but had a funny feeling that she was going to try again.

With nothing to do until Preston left, I headed to the front to keep a lookout for Mateo. I could get his alibi while Jane occupied Preston. Plus, I didn't want them in the same building. Maybe nothing would happen. Or one of them strangled the other. Those guys hated each other, and I'd rather avoid male drama.

Something pink on the floor caught my attention. I kneeled down for a closer look. *Another Benadryl pill? Or was this the first one that got kicked over here?* I thought I threw it away before Underwood escorted me out, but now I couldn't remember. I struggled to recall that morning, but my mind felt sluggish. So much stuff happened that day and today. I needed a break and food.

Princess appeared, blocking my view. A paw lifted.

"Don't play with it." I scowled.

Princess made no attempt to obey as she tapped it. I snatched her up, along with the pill. Princess sniffed my hand but I refused to let her play with medicine. Maybe Jane took Benadryl. East Tennessee probably had more pollen than New York City.

I set Princess back on the floor and tucked the allergy medicine in my pocket. She disappeared into the store as voices came in my direction.

When I got to the register, Jane trotted away. "Be right back," she told Preston.

Now what is she doing, I wondered, wishing she stayed. She was better with Preston than I was. When Preston saw me, I knew I couldn't sneak away to see what Jane was up to. The awkward silence returned. Preston leaned against the counter reading over his papers. I walked behind the counter, pretending to be tidying when in reality I was shifting stuff around within the space. I had to break this unbearable tension. A question came to mind. I couldn't use the same method as Jane did. I grew up here and knew better than pull the I-forgot-card. Being blunt was the only way to get answers. Surely Preston knew who else hated his ex-wife.

"I heard you hated Doris."

CHAPTER 25

PRESTON SHRUGGED AS IF HATING HIS FORMER WIFE WAS OLD NEWS—which it probably was. "I hated everything about that woman. Marrying her was my biggest mistake," he said, his voice growing louder and louder. "She took everything from me. Even my tools. Doris couldn't tell the difference between a screwdriver and a pencil. She took them just to be spiteful. When she won the lottery, she didn't give me a penny. Not a damn one. She should've given me something after tearing down the cabin I built and for stealing my tools. I wasted fifteen years of my life. But don't ask just me. Doris took a ring from Clara. I wouldn't be surprised if ol' Clara-Bell killed Doris."

When Preston paused to take a breath, I squeezed in a question. "Why did Doris steal a ring from her sister? Was it valuable?"

"It's more sentimental than valuable. Their granny gave the ring to Clara. Doris was always jealous because she wasn't the favorite. Their parents also left Clara the house. That really ticked Doris off when the will was read." He grinned. "I think their parents thought Clara would be a loner. Finding a crazy man ain't easy." Preston chuckled at his own joke. "Living in the same house your whole life can give you a loose screw, or two in her case."

I didn't care about Clara living in her childhood home. She mentioned the ring to Grandma. I was starting to ask more about it when Preston talked over me.

"Shortly after Doris won the money, she threw bricks at Clara's windows. Doris denied it of course, but Clara and I knew it was her. Doris was a spiteful soul."

"That's horrible," I said. "Did Doris break into the house to steal the ring?"

"I heard that Clara gave Doris the ring for safe keeping. Don't ask me why because I never understood crazy. Now she's dead, I doubt Clara will get her ring back. Police closed off the driveway, and nobody is saying a word about Doris's will." He shrugged again. "But I don't care about her stuff like everyone else in town does. I got nothing from Doris when she was alive, her death won't be any different."

Before I could ask more about the ring, cowbells jingled. Jane forgot to lock the door when she let Preston in. I power walked to the front, secretly hoping Grandma popped in with food. Unfortunately, Mateo stood at the store's entrance.

"Hello." He smiled before it morphed into a deep frown. The lines on the sides of his mouth revealed his age.

Oh no.

"Is Jane Jackson here?" Mateo asked as his dark eyes fixed over my shoulder.

Preston's heavy footsteps crossed in front of me. He stood taller, gripping the clipboard tightly. Mateo seemed to have forgotten me as he matched Preston's stance. The men's postures reminded me of a western standoff. I placed myself between them, fearing they might resolve their personal issues in a final showdown. Then I realized my mistake. Playing monkey-in-the-middle never worked well for a short girl. *Too late to back out now.*

At any moment I expected them to bull rush each other or start a yelling match. Instead, they puffed their chests out, giving each other a hard stare. In a way, the display of dominance was funny, but it wouldn't have been if one of the men made a move. I broke the tension before one of them exploded.

"I have the blueprints—"

Preston's chuckle silenced me. It sounded far from being humorous. "Why would Miss Jackson want to hire you? You're lazy and cut corners."

Mateo's face hardened. His Spanish accent came out thick. "You're dead wrong, *amigo*. Your work is sloppy. *Mi abuela* could do a better job. I've been hired so many times just to fix your mistakes."

"Like my ex-wife?"

My heart pounded as my head bounced between them.

"I did. Because that was another mistake that needed fixing man."

Preston smirked and gave a thumbs up. "You did a great job at fixin' that piece of work."

Mateo's face turned red.

"You know what, I should be thanking you, because you took care of that mistake, by killing her."

I gasped then slapped my hand over my mouth.

"No way man, I didn't kill her," Mateo shouted. "I wasn't even here when she died. I was at Voss-of-Books painting their breakroom. You know, working...unlike you."

Preston stepped closer. I used the opportunity to get myself out of the middle.

"She ditched ya after you built that house. All those gifts and flowers you bought her meant nothing. She dumped your ass and you couldn't take it anymore. You weren't far from where she was killed."

So were you, I thought but didn't dare let the words fly.

"Man, you were next door *amigo*." Mateo countered. His eyes narrowed so much I wondered if Mateo could still see. "I know you're still bitter."

"I'm not the one who knows how to sneak into places," Preston said.

Mateo stepped closer. Preston matched his move.

"Say that again?" Mateo's tone dangerously low.

"You sneaked into my house and into my bed." Preston spat in his face. "Killer."

Their arms were cocking back the same time Jane's voice screamed out, "Get out! Get out!"

Both men straightened up as if the school principal entered the room. Apologies quickly followed.

"So sorry, Miss Jackson." Preston pleaded.

Mateo folded his hands into a praying motion. "I'm sorry. I was out of line. My sincere apologies."

"Get out!" Jane repeated herself, pointing at the door. "Leave!"

"Will you think about my offer?" Preston squeaked, giving her a weak smile while Mateo asked about giving him another chance.

Jane shooed them toward the exit without an answer for either of them. After slamming the door shut, she locked it behind them crossing her arms over her chest.

"Some partner you are," I said, jokingly, "you let them in."

CHAPTER 26

JANE AND I WATCHED AS THE MEN CONTINUED THEIR HEATED argument on the sidewalk. They stood inches from each other's faces. Words were being said, but not loud enough to hear behind glass doors. I expected if one of them threw a punch, the police would have to come to end it. Their voices attracted a crowd, Clara being one of them. Preston and Mateo left in opposite directions, but their body language suggested that this wasn't over. I doubted it ever would be as long as they both lived in Sevier Oak.

Once Copper Street returned to normal, I told Jane about my chat with Leo. Drake Voss had an alibi for both murders. Jane looked pleased at the news. Then I told her about Mateo's alibi, the one he shouted at Preston. Again, she seemed relieved. We stood in place emotionally drained, lost in our thoughts.

"I don't know about you, but I'm beat," she said, staring at the new book resting on the chair. "My aunt's house needs a lot of cleaning. She only had enough money in the bank to cover funeral expenses. I have to figure out how to have a yard sale or something." Her body sagged a little, still gazing at the novel.

Deep down I think she just wanted to sit down, relax, and escape into a story. Now that the action stopped, I felt worn out, too. My stomach longed for food, and to crawl out of these clothes in exchange for loose lounging ones. We had been on the go all day. Despite wanting to find more information, taking a short break won me over.

After Jane dropped me off at my house, I scarfed down a peanut butter sandwich to hold me over. I felt more like myself after a quick shower. I enjoyed being home, despite my thoughts refusing to let me rest.

Why was Stone helping Clara retrieve her family heirloom? Was a ring worth plotting and killing Doris in a bookstore for? I supposed that question depended on it's worth. Was that why she attacked me, thinking Doris gave me the ring?

I changed out of my robe and drove to my grandparent's house. I knew may not get all the answers, but I'd get some, and hopefully dinner.

While driving there, I pondered about Grandma Stone. I never knew her to go into Voss-of-Books. If Teresa didn't have the book she wanted, Grandma bought it off of Amazon. She was up to something.

I turned on music to stop my mind from racing. Worrying never gave me answers, it only led to stress eating and sleepless nights. As Justin Moore sang, my body eased. The weight of today's adventure started to take its toll. Country music had a way to both calm and lift my spirits.

Now I understood why Dad often fell asleep on the couch or why Stone refused to go anywhere on his days off. Investigating was exhausting, and yet the nagging questions pushed me forward.

I decided after this trip that I would stop for the day. Stone and Dad had short tempers, if they went too long without sleep or ate a warm meal. They often yelled their frustrations at the dinner tables while Grandma and I ate in silence, half tuning them out.

At least there is hope for the bookstore, I thought.

My phone chirped. I silenced Justin Moore to steal a peek at the text message. Megan. Call me, it said. I pulled over and tapped on Megan's picture.

She answered during the second ring. "Hey, you won't believe this."

I was about to say the news about Teresa being murdered, but Megan didn't give me a chance to answer.

"Ivy was just in here. Mad as a hornet. I heard her phone conversation the whole time she was waiting on her order."

"Whoa, back up, who's Ivy again?" After today's events, I needed a friendly reminder.

"Seriously?" Megan gasped over the phone. "Ivy Fremont. Roland's mom. Dr. Poison Ivy."

I wanted to smack myself. Dr. Poison Ivy was notorious for being a perfectionist. She was head of PTO for years, driving parents and school members crazy, demanding greatness from everyone. Rumors say that she was the reason the science club ended. One by one students dropped out until there were none. After several visits to the Fremont house with Brad, I believed the rumors.

"It's been a while," I told Megan. I hadn't been to the Fremont residence since breaking up with Brad. "I remember her. What about her?"

Mentally, I hoped Megan wasn't about to suggest her as a suspect. I didn't want to interview her.

"She was on the phone, talking about Roland. Ivy said, 'Roland is old enough, let it be a hard lesson.' I swear that was word for word. I think she was talking to Roland's dad. You remember him too?"

"Yep, and that was a good impression Dr. Poison Ivy," I joked.

Megan giggled before turning serious. "Do you think Roland had something to do with Doris's murder? Clara said she was watching him. I don't think I've ever seen Roland scurry so fast."

It took me a second to catch my breath. Roland was also at the bookstore to drop off a package. One box instead of three. The orders were for separate customers and ordered on different days. Like many business owners on Copper Street, Teresa gave him a key. Megan spoke as if she heard my thoughts.

"Roland has the perfect alibi, driving a mail truck. Maybe Roland brought the knife? Wanna go question him now? I'm not meeting Austin for another hour."

"Tomorrow," I said, and gave a short explanation as to why. After ending the call, I got back on the road, and pondered more about Roland. He was a troublemaker in school. Dad once told me he believed Roland's actions were due to his overbearing mother. I agreed. Roland was rough around the edges. The years only made him distant and short tempered, especially when his best friend Brad, my ex-Brad, left Sevier Oak.

If Roland killed Doris, then it had to be an accident. His fights were typically spur of the moment, not plotting for revenge or out of jealousy. He had no motive for wanting Doris dead. Him hurting Teresa seemed farfetched. She always treated him with kindness. Other than Drake, Teresa went out of her way to help others. One time she drove Roland to the post office because the mail truck got a flat tire. On another occasion, she cleaned a dress shirt because he spilled coffee on it. Roland being a murderer didn't fit the Roland that I knew.

The single package weighed on me. I had a feeling that Roland harbored a secret, and his parents knew. So naturally, I had to find out.

CHAPTER 27

STONE'S TRUCK WAS MISSING WHEN I PULLED INTO THE HORSESHOE driveway. My grandparents often stayed home on Wednesday nights; unless Stone wanted to go to the lake to find rocks for his latest hobby. The thought of him walking on the muddy shoreline with a bucket in hand made me chuckle.

I let myself inside thinking Grandma might be home. "Grandma?" I called out, heading towards the kitchen. She wasn't there. I grabbed a muffin from under the glass dome and continued searching. In a matter of seconds, I discovered that I had the farmhouse to myself. Both of their absences made me more suspicious. Grandma didn't like riding in Stone's truck. She said it was too jerky. Which was true. The Nissan truck was from the 1940's, and often jerked while accelerating. Stone said he would fix it once he retired. I wondered how that would turn out. Stone and machines never mixed well.

My stomach growled, demanding for more food. I went back to the kitchen for another muffin. As I ate, I noticed the time. Six o'clock. No wonder I was starving. I leaned against the island, staring into the pantry. I debated if I should leave and get fast food or stay and hope Grandma would whip something up. Home cooking sounded better. For now, I grabbed another muffin.

I wandered around the house with a third chocolate chip muffin in hand. Old and new pictures dotted the living room walls. Some were black and white from Stone and Grandma's younger days, to one of Dad and me four months ago when he visited. Our family's notorious picture hung over the couch. It was Stone's idea to go on a three-mile hike on the hottest day of the year. The journey back to the vehicle wore me out. Dad had heaved my seven-year-old body onto his shoulders and carried me the rest of the way. Grandma stopped us to get a family photo. She gracefully slipped into her spot before the timer ran out. Her urgent screech made the three of us laugh. Grandma chuckled at herself just in time for the camera to snap the image. That day was marked as one of our best family moments.

Seeing the family all together like that I couldn't help but think of Regan.

Did I have a brother or a sister?

Not knowing the answer bothered me, almost as much as Mom failing to mention that she had another child. Why didn't she say anything after all these years? Why am I not saying anything to her now?

Right now, solving two murders were more important than seeking answers. Those decisions could wait a little longer. I shoved the last bit of muffin into my mouth then walked out of the living room, leaving behind memories and what could have been.

The stairs leading to the basement were behind a white door in the dining room. As a kid it used to be creepy. The single light bulb casted shadows rather than giving off light. It didn't help that the air grew colder as the stairs descended. Once Grandma told me to think of the basement as Stone's man cave, it wasn't as creepy.

The air smelled stale and musty like all basements. It was spacious and not well-lit compared to the top of the stairs. To the left was the laundry while the other side was Stone's man cave. His space wasn't glamorous— just a small couch, a coffee table made by Karl, and a TV on an old dresser. He often came here to clear his mind by sitting on the couch and watching a movie.

Since Stone's retirement he had placed a workbench and table lamp. Paint brushes and unfinished projects were scattered around a sand bucket filled with smooth rocks. A few completed pieces rested under the lamp as if they were still drying. I smirked. They looked like they came from a Kindergartener's classroom.

Stone's second addition was the white board resting on an easel. Two pictures were typed in the center. One was a news clipping of Doris Hackett winning the lottery, and the second was a photograph of Teresa. Red lines connected either between notes written in blue or toward a picture.

My grandparents were investigating.

I quickly scanned the board, eager to know what they discovered. According to the information, the only connection between the women was the bookstore. The names Preston Powell, Mateo Navarro, and Clara Hackett were written next to Doris's picture. Stone also believed the three were suspects. Sasha Whitlock's name wasn't there.

Under Doris's picture, Stone wrote the word "clues" and then a square. Inside the shape were the suspicious items found at the scene: knife, tea kettle, pillow, and bear. Each item had a small description. I was bummed to see that the mysterious fingerprint remained unanswered, and nothing about the blood found on the bear. I still found it strange; a weapon that was normally found in a crime scene was the oddest clue. Doris was suffocated by a pillow, and Teresa was pushed down the steps. The knife still didn't fit in either murder.

Who the heck brought the knife? I wondered.

In the top corner I spotted a sticky note. It read, "Bear. Not Doris's Blood." I re-read the note, feeling more confused. The blood spot had to be Doris's. There was some blood on the scene from when she had been hit with the tea kettle. Unless the killer got cut during the struggle and touched the bear. If so, that didn't answer how the stuffed animal got inside the bookstore.

Next, I saw a word written over Doris's picture. I stared at the single word, wondering what it meant.

Gone.

CHAPTER 28

FOOTSTEPS CREAKED ABOVE ME, FOLLOWED BY MY NAME BEING called. Grandma and Stone finally came home. I hollered from my spot and studied the board as they came down. Stone stood next to me.

"Investigating, are we?" I asked. "Isn't this called, interfering with police business?"

Grandma hummed a laugh.

"We raised you well," Stone said.

I crossed my arms over my chest. "Spill the beans."

He reached for the green marker and handed it to me. "Ladies first."

I hid my disappointment. At least he didn't lecture me like he had after my unpleasant encounter with Clara. I held the dry erase marker, debating what to say. When Megan and I went to Clara's house, I purposely left my cell phone behind so he couldn't track my whereabouts. I knew my grandfather well enough to know that he'd been watching.

"Spit it out," Grandma said, impatiently. "I know you went

to Clara's house this morning and you've been hanging with Jane Jackson most of the day."

Stone frowned. Yep, I thought, I blew my cover when Grandma was going into Voss-of-Books. I asked Grandma why she was there before I got sidetracked.

They gave each other a knowing look. They were definitely hiding something. Stone let out a sigh, clearly overruled by his wife. He went to the workbench and returned with another green marker.

"I'm doing what I would be if I was still on the force."

His answer didn't surprise me. I nodded at their crime board. "Jane Jackson isn't up there. Is she officially off the suspect list?"

"I'll ask the questions and then I'll answer yours."

I rolled my eyes as Stone removed the cap.

Gosh, he sounded like he was still the police chief.

He held the green marker up, waiting. The marker squeaked while I talked. I gave a summary of my day, also adding Sasha Whitlock as a possible suspect and the two Benadryl I found. I considered telling him about Roland Fremont, but I'd rather talk to him first before Stone or Underwood did. Roland had a rocky history with the police and might open up to me instead. Once Stone wrote the last of the information, he stood back. The three of us reading over the board.

Four suspects. Each hated Doris Hackett. Then take Teresa's disturbing voice message. It proved that she had walked in on the killer's prep work on the intended victim. Wrong place at the wrong time.

The only suspect who had a beef against Teresa was Sasha. Teresa fired her. I didn't believe she lost the store key. Murderer or not, I could see Sasha keeping the key, just to be spiteful.

Did I talk to a killer a few hours ago? Walk beside her into a store? Those thoughts gave me a cold chill.

"Let's start with what we know," Stone said, eyeing the board. He started gnawing at the bottom of the marker. Then I noticed the one I was holding had bite marks. I tossed the marker on the couch. *Gross.* When Stone spoke again, it sounded as if Grandma and I were his squad. "Jane's off the hook. She was initially a suspect until I spoke to her parents. They claim she was with them the night of Teresa's death. Her bank released a recording of Jane in the bank. She couldn't have flown to Tennessee and return to the city before dinner. Her phone records don't show any suspicious activity, or any correlation to Doris. I believe Jane and Teresa were close. Every Wednesday, Jane called her roughly around seven pm. In my book, Jane Jackson is clear."

I felt relieved that Stone didn't suspect Jane. If the former police chief had this information, then I assumed Sheriff Estep did too. The police wouldn't bother her anymore.

"I wonder—"

"Facts," said Stone, interrupting me. "Tonight, we are discussing the facts. Theories are distractions."

Grandma shook her head and *tsked.* Despite Stone being serious, I concealed a smirk. It was one thing to listen to cases, but another to be involved. I felt a little giddy.

Stone tapped the marker at the clue section: tea kettle, pillow, knife, and teddy bear. When I explained the allergy medicine, he had written it outside the square with two question marks. I guessed he didn't consider it much of a clue. *Stay with the facts*, I reminded myself. The problem with the facts was that the clues made no sense.

"Who was physically strong enough to hit Doris with a tea kettle and hold her down while suffocating her," added Grandma.

Stone hummed his agreement.

"Wait a minute." I turned to look at Grandma. "Have you helped the police in the past?" Not that Dad and Stone had a problem listening to people's opinion, however, this felt different. Leo was a bookstore owner, but it didn't mean that I would take his advice on how to run my store.

Great, now I'm thinking about Leo.

"I'll get us some tea," Grandma said.

"Avoiding my question?" I teased, watching Grandma climb the stairs.

"People tell her stuff," Stone replied. "I've solved cases based on the gossip people told her."

"Does Dad know?"

"If Onyx is as good a detective as Nashville claims, then he should already know."

I shook my head. The Stone family was a gang of spies. It made me wonder if I had what it took to be one. I liked to think so.

While Grandma's footsteps roamed within the kitchen area above us, Stone asked me about Sasha Whitlock. I told him the short version about her terrible work ethic, supposedly losing the store key, and her cruel comments to Doris the morning of the incident. I studied his face, but he gave nothing away. By the time I finished, Stone said he would talk to Underwood, and Grandma returned with a tray and three glasses of sweet tea.

Other than the ice crunching between my teeth, the basement went quiet. We studied the white board, lost in our thoughts. I had a feeling the murderer was on the board, but everything I had learned didn't lead to them as the killer.

Karl had confirmed Preston was working in the upstairs bathroom next door. Mateo had claimed he was painting the employee's break room at Voss-of-Books while Sasha was at a job interview. Clara might have been at her house, spying on her neighbors.

Each suspect had a motive *and* an alibi.

My stomach growled loud enough for my grandparents to turn their gazes on me. Before I suggested dinner, I wanted one answer. I pointed to the word above Doris's pictures. "What does *gone* mean?"

Stone set down his drink. "Clara will find out soon enough, but for now, this stays inside this room." He looked at me.

"I have to tell Jane and Megan," I said. "They're helping me."

"Just them. No one else." When I promised he continued, "Doris's money is gone."

"Gone?" I said, "As in stolen *gone* or spent *gone*?"

"Spent. Doris spent all her winnings."

I stopped chewing ice, unable to say a word. Doris spent eight million dollars in two years? Why? How? This information made me sad and upset at the same time. Sad as in Doris being penniless, yet upset at the fact that Doris had been irresponsible with that amount of money.

"Doris developed a gambling problem," Stone continued. "Her accounts have been in the negative since February."

"And maxed out five credit cards," added Grandma.

"The bank foreclosed the house to pay off her debt."

"Her house isn't paid off?" I asked, shocked.

They both shook their heads.

"What about her beach house?" I recalled Clara's words.

Grandma answered. "Sold it before Christmas. She blew the money by February. She's been selling stuff on eBay to stay afloat."

It sounded crazy. And yet made sense. When Doris got her winnings, it was common to see her in different clothes and fancy cars. Now that my grandparents mentioned it, I can only recall Doris wearing the same outfits and driving the same BMW. Some people might get a kick out of Doris's loss, but I found it depressing. Living in a big house on her own had to be lonely. Her only outlet was the bookstore and online gambling.

Back to the facts, I thought with Stone's voice filling my head. "Did Doris sell Clara's ring?" My hands reached for my necklace.

Stone took a deep breath. "Doris was wearing it at the time of the murder."

"What?" I cried.

"Clara thought I could get her grandmother's ring back. She described it to me. I accompanied an officer—"

"Underwood."

Grandma said to Stone, "We don't need to be so secretive. Garnet can know that Underwood is reaching out to you for help." Then she turned to me. "Since I was never on the force, I can be blunt. Underwood isn't liking how Estep is running the case. He hinted that Stone and me to come to the jewelers to get our wedding bands cleaned, conveniently bumping into him and discussing the case. Based on Clara's description, we confirmed that the ring found on Doris is the family heirloom she's been asking about, and it's not worth much."

Stone jumped in, clearly getting irritable. After this, I thought, we all needed dinner. "The ring was half way on Doris's finger. If she was standing upright, it would have fallen off."

"You're saying the ring was too big?" I asked, running my garnet charm up and down the chain.

"Two sizes too big."

This didn't make sense. Grandma noticed my confusion and said, "Underwood thinks someone planted the ring on Doris."

"Maybe Doris was wearing it to be spiteful, and the killer

was in the process of stealing it," I said. "Clara said she gave it to Doris for safe keeping. It couldn't have been planted."

Grandma grinned while Stone did not. I sensed they had a disagreement.

"If the killer was stealing it," said Stone, "why let go and leave it? It takes a split second to slide it off, why stop midway?"

"The killer must have heard Jane and me. We were pretty loud."

Stone's voice deepened. "But, why stop? It weighs nothing. Why let go of the ring?" He shook his head. "No, I believe the killer put the ring on Doris's finger. It was two sizes too big. Doris would have had her hand clenched just to keep the ring on. No. It was planted."

I pondered for a moment. "If she was scared enough, she would've naturally let go. But, knowing Doris, I think she wore it just to be mean to her sister."

"Yes," Grandma agreed in a tone that suggested that they had an argument over the ring theory. "Clara gave it to her sister."

Stone said nothing more on the matter. He saw no point in debating. It was a theory, not a fact.

I sighed. Another piece added to the puzzle. If I had to point to the killer based on the board and new information, Clara Hackett was the killer.

"Oh," I gasped at a new discovery. "What if the teddy bear was planted?" I pointed at the clue written on the board. "It wasn't there before. I would have noticed. The killer must have left it."

Stone sighed. "I'm going to be frank with ya, the store is a mess. A big one. Teresa might have bought the bear from Doris or Doris tossed it there herself to get rid of it. We can speculate all night how it got there. I will say, the blood spot is our focus." He glaring at the board. "I just haven't figured out how it got there."

Before I suggested food, Stone kept talking. "Mateo got a lawyer. He's not talking, but cooperating by giving a sample of his DNA. The sheriff is really harping on him. The results should be in no later than tomorrow afternoon." He narrowed his eyes. "Then we can finally cross one person off the list."

"And then what?"

"If the blood matches Mateo, then the police will question him further. Needless to say, it won't look good for him. And if not, well..." Stone left the rest unspoken.

Back to square one.

"When we find Doris's murderer, we also found who killed Teresa," Grandma said.

"We as in *us*." Stone waved a finger between himself and his wife. "You've done enough sleuthing."

I rolled my shoulders back. No way was I going to sit back and do nothing. "I can help."

"I know what can happen," Stone said. "I've seen things and I don't want you becoming..." he trailed off.

I understood. He didn't want to see his only grandchild end up as a victim.

"The killer knew Doris was going to be at the bookstore. He or she was preparing," I said, pointing at Teresa's picture. "It makes it personal."

I watched my grandparents give each other a look. Unlike Stone, Grandma seemed fine with me snooping. She gave me a wink as she drank the last of her tea. Seconds later, his eyebrows lowered in defeat. "Fine. But you tell me everything and stop purposely leaving your phone at home."

"I promise," I agreed. "I don't know about ya'll," Grandma said, "but I'm starving, and I need a break." She headed toward the stairs without seeing if we were coming. Stone and I followed.

While walking up the stairs I asked, "You still haven't answered why you visited Voss-of-Books."

She walked into the kitchen. "I was there for a lead."

I perked up and cringed at the same time. Had Leo lied to me about his grandfather's whereabouts? Was Drake Voss a suspect? Then again, his name wasn't on the board.

My grandparents got to work in the kitchen. Grandma pulled out two packages of steak from the refrigerator. Stone answered as he found the cutting board. "Someone has been sending Doris messages through a PlayStation account. I believed Doris used it to play movies." He started cutting the fat around the meat's edges.

"The task force is working with the company to get the person's ID," Grandma said, working the can opener on a can of green beans. My stomach kept sinking by the moment. I went to the cabinet to get the box of instant potatoes.

"Do you remember the ID?" I asked.

"Yennefer something," Stone said.

I nearly dropped the box. I knew that name, and from what series it originated.

The Witcher, a video game Sasha played.

CHAPTER 29

THE FOLLOWING MORNING TURNED OUT TO BE ANOTHER HOT AND humid day, causing the AC to kick on sooner than usual. Shorts and pulling my hair back into a ponytail were a must. I dragged myself out of bed after eight-thirty, Megan had already gone to work. She left a note by the coffee pot, reminding me about her date with Austin, and to keep sleuthing.

After I took a shower and ate breakfast, I left the house. The inside of my car already felt like an oven. I rolled down the windows until the vents blew out cold air. I glanced at the sky as I drove toward the bookstore. Not a cloud in sight, making the view stunning. I loved it when the blue sky touched the green hills. Some people admired the leaves changing, or snow falling, but for me, I loved the bright colors of blue and green that could only be seen in summer.

Traffic flowed at a steady pace. Nothing unusual for a Thursday morning. Copper Street was almost bare at this hour. Other than the coffee house further down the street, most businesses opened at nine. Hopefully soon, Teresa's Bookstore could reopen.

Jane's sports car was parked in front of her aunt's store when I pulled up. She hollered my name when the cowbells announced my arrival. I followed the sound of her voice toward the front counter. I stopped in my tracks when I spotted her. Jane wore black yoga capris, a solid purple shirt, and tennis shoes. Her brown hair flowed loosely midway down her back. I liked this attire much better than suits. The style made her look relaxed and easygoing.

Princess's meow startled me. She purred loudly as if she got a good night's sleep. I petted her before turning my attention back on Jane.

"I was about to call you," Jane said. "I've been thinking." She picked up a small box of cleaning supplies and headed toward the stairs. Princess and I followed. "I think we are overlooking a crucial clue."

Before she discussed her latest theory, I told Jane my grandparent's findings as we walked. We entered the office, and Jane placed the box on a clear spot on the desk. I leaned against the entrance, taking in the new changes. The holiday decorations were gone, and Butterscotch wasn't sleeping on the desk, but lounging on the filing cabinet. She glared at Princess as she jumped in Jane's lap when she sat down.

"I think I figured out how the killer did it," Jane said as Princess kneaded her thighs.

"How?"

Jane picked up the black and white cat. Princess purred. "I'll show you. Follow me."

She led me toward the second stairs, heading toward the bargain room. The room remained untouched. A mess of fallen books dotted the floor, mostly caused by the police in their attempt to get Princess out of the crime scene.

Jane set Princess down and spread her arms out wide.

"There's one last clue. One that ties all the weird ones together."

Princess and I stared at her.

"The killer planned to kill Doris here."

I resisted the urge to say duh. "You're still not making sense."

Jane's arms flapped to her side. Her face sharpened, reminding me how she would look if she stood before a judge, defending a client. "Something happened, something that ruined the killer's plan, because up until killing Doris, the killer got away with one murder. Their plan was flawless. He or she hid a clue in the perfect place. A messy bookstore."

If Jane was right about a hidden clue, then finding it would literally be a needle in a haystack. "I know the place is unorganized, but you're still not explaining your theory."

"It's inside the books. Think about it. The killer came that night for a reason. If we find the last clue, then the police can get fingerprints off the book."

I stared at the fallen books. "Like a hollowed-out book?" Only a killer would do such a horrific thing to a book.

"It all makes sense." Jane's voice rose to excitement. "First, the killer made a hollowed book with the knife. I believe that's why Teresa died; she caught the killer in the planning phase. After making Teresa's death look like an accident, the killer finished what they were doing. It also makes sense why you didn't see the knife while you worked or during the search with Deputy Underwood." Jane's voice went up another octave. "The last clue is hidden in plain sight."

Her theory sounded convincing. It also explained why Doris's murder happened a month after Teresa's death. The bookstore was closed for a week as a gesture of respect for Teresa. It was no secret Doris shopped here either. The killer's problem was that she didn't come here every day. Sometimes it was weeks between visits. He or she must have been stalking her or casing the bookstore.

The downfall with Jane's theory was that I didn't recall any of our suspects coming into the bookstore or hanging around during the time I ran the store solo.

"If the knife was here," I said, "and I mean a big if, then why did Doris die from a pillow? The pillow was one of Teresa's projects. It was stashed in the receiving room where...the bear was found."

Jane raised an eyebrow, clearly having more fun explaining this than I was. "That's how the killer got inside without being seen. Through the back door. All he or she had to do was pick up the book with the supplies to kill Doris fast." Jane picked up a random book, flipped through it before disappointingly tossing it down. "You said Doris always shopped in the bargain room. I bet the killer knew that too."

I wanted to stop the theory, but resisted, not wanting to quote my dad again. Instead, I suggested a system on how to tackle the mess while searching for a supposed hollowed book. After we grabbed the cart with three wheels from upstairs, we picked up a book, and began our long daunting mission.

It didn't take long for Princess to be a nosy-rosy. As I flipped through the book, she put her face in. Her nose scrunched and pulled back, but still sniffed the book I held. I kindly pushed her aside and reached for another book. Princess did the same thing except this time, she kept her face away from the moving pages. Then she playfully pawed the book.

Meanwhile, Jane set another book on the cart. The pile of books on the cart was growing fast. I added my second book and picked up another with Princess on my heels.

"If there is a hollowed book, I doubt there'll be any fingerprints," I said, flipping through the book. Princess sat in front of me, wondering why I wasn't kneeling like before.

A hardcover thudded on the cart, and Jane picked up the next one. "It's worth a try."

I heard the desperation in her voice. Like her, I too wanted to solve the murders, and for life to get back to normal. I decided that after searching for this needle in the haystack, I planned to question Sasha again. Despite having an alibi, I wanted to know why Sasha threatened Doris online. It was one thing to bad mouth someone in person, but online? I felt like Sasha had gone out of her way to do so.

I also needed to track down Roland. Teresa gave him a key and he delivered a package before the murder. Perhaps he saw something. If so, why hadn't he said anything? Roland wasn't the type of guy who got scared easily. Then I remembered Megan telling me about eavesdropping on his mother's phone call. *Roland is old enough, let it be a hard lesson.* If Roland Fremont feared anyone, it would be his mother.

I ignored the unanswered questions and tried to keep up with Jane's pace. Once Princess noticed there was nothing of interest, she climbed up a bookshelf and watched us from above.

The silence didn't last long. "Tell me a little about yourself," Jane said as she started piling the books next to the full cart.

"Is this an interview?" I joked.

"No." Pages flipped, followed by a thud. "I have the sense that you know more about me than I do of you."

Jane was probably right. Since Teresa said little about her family, I assumed that she didn't say much to them about me. I decided to tell Jane the basics of my life. I was an only child and grew up in a law enforcement family. Overall, my childhood was good. Things changed after graduating high school; Dad moved to Nashville to become a detective, and my yearly visits with Mom happened less. It made me sad acknowledging that the last time I saw her was three summers ago, and since it was June, I doubted I would see her this year. Then before I knew it, I was talking about Regan.

"It makes me mad that Mom kept Regan from me. Like she was ashamed or didn't want to upset me. It feels like Mom also chose her other child over me. Regan must have spent more time with Mom and her family. She was probably around on Christmas, birthdays, and school events. I don't even know my grandparent's names or if Mom had any siblings. She showered me with gifts, but Regan gets the best thing."

A mom.

I grabbed another paperback and rummaged through the pages. "The only good thing Mom did was bring me to Tennessee and gave me a rock name." I tossed the book perhaps a little too hard and picked up another one. "Mom just dropped me off and lived the life she really wanted. One without me. One that allowed her to cruise on yachts and to be with Regan." I slammed the book on top of another one. "And it's really bugging me that I don't know if I have a brother or a sister."

I picked up another paperback. The thickness told me that it wasn't a hollowed book. Princess stepped on my foot, rubbing her head against my leg while Jane stared at me with a sad expression. I didn't need a machine to tell me that my blood pressure spiked high. After I took some slow breaths, I said, "What do you think I should do? Ignore Regan or write back?"

Jane came to my side and rested a hand on my shoulder. "I think you're overthinking this. Assuming that your mom picked Regan over you." Her next words came out as a whisper.

"Maybe your mom left Regan too. Maybe he or she has been just as lonely as you."

Her words soothed my inner fire like cool water as questions flooded my mind. Who's to say that Mom didn't have another fling and left Regan with her family or with Regan's father? What if Regan had been wanting Mom's affection just as much as I had? Maybe they up wondering, why did Mom choose the sea over me? I wondered if Regan checked his or her email every day, hoping I wrote back. These questions made me feel like a heartless person. I should have written back instead of jumping to conclusions that Regan was Mom's favorite.

Someone banged on the door hard enough for the cowbells to clang. Princess ran ahead of us toward the front. Jane and I paused for a moment when we saw Sheriff Estep and three figures standing next to him. Deputy Underwood was among the mix. I scanned their faces as I forced my feet to move. None of them looked thrilled to be here. The sheriff banged on the door harder before thrusting a finger at the door handle. I unlocked the door.

The atmosphere changed. Princess must have sensed it because she climbed up a bookshelf. The sheriff marched inside with a sullen disposition. His baby face didn't look cute, but rather menacing. I wished I had the power to transform into a cat and hide with Princess.

Sheriff Estep didn't waste a moment. He pointed at Jane, and an officer walked towards her. "Jane Jackson, you have the right to remain silent."

"What? Why are you arresting her?" I cried as the sounds of handcuffs blended with Sheriff Estep reciting the Miranda Rights.

Jane said nothing as her eyes fixed on me. She gently shook her head, as if she was trying to tell me that she didn't kill

Doris or her aunt. Underwood whispered something to me, but I couldn't hear. I stood in place, watching the scene unfold. This didn't make sense. Stone and I eliminated Jane. She was in New York when Teresa died. She didn't know Doris until she walked into the bookstore. How did the police get it wrong?

Once the officer escorted Jane into the backseat of a squad car, I spun on my heels, and blocked the sheriff from leaving. "I demand to know why you are arresting her."

Sheriff Estep leaned over me. In the corner of my eye, I saw Underwood. He didn't like the sheriff towing over me like a bully, yet he couldn't say anything. I held my ground, refusing to shy away.

"A witness came forward, claiming that Jane and Doris talked the day before," Sheriff Estep explained with a hint of cockiness in his tone. "The witness overheard Jane demanding money or else." I hated how he tilted his head. "Sounds like motive for murder, missy."

"That's a lie," I said. Underwood gave me a look to stop talking. I ignored him. "Who was this so-called witness?"

Sheriff Estep stood up straighter. "Just sell your little books, and let the men handle the rest." With one hand, he pushed me aside to exit the store.

It took every ounce of self-control to not react. "Whose blood was on the bear?" I raised my voice. "Was it Mateo's?"

"Garnet," Underwood's deep voice muttered.

Sheriff Estep put on sunglasses as he strutted into the sunlight. "Let's go," he addressed his crew.

Princess came beside me. Together we watched Jane being taken away for the second time.

CHAPTER 30

PRINCESS MEOWED.

"You said it," I said, shaking my head watching the last of the police cars drive away. "I can't stay here."

I stomped around the store, searching for my purse while Princess trailed behind me. I screamed and grunted my frustration. I had to get some of this energy out, and the only way I knew was to find some hard evidence. Flipping through books in hopes of finding the killer's fingerprint didn't sound promising.

After finding my purse, I texted Stone about what had happened. Maybe he knew this mysterious witness or could talk some sense into Sheriff Estep. I doubt the new sheriff would listen, but knowing my grandfather, he would at least try.

I refilled the cat's bowls and marched outside. The summer heat added to my anger. Instead of driving, I walked. I knew myself well enough to not get behind the wheel. Besides, doing something physical always helped calm me down.

Jane was arrested. Those words rang over and over in my mind.

Did Stone overlook something? I reflected on the white board and our conversation. I didn't see how or why she had been arrested. Jane had an alibi when her aunt died and was in another state. As for Doris, Jane was upstairs. She had no motive for either crime. Now I wondered who this mystery witness was. Only one person came to mind; the one who's been insisting it was Jane, and also happened to be Sevier Oaks's biggest spy. Clara Hackett. The longer I thought about it, the more it made sense.

When I arrived at Voss-of-Books, I didn't feel any calmer. If anything, I felt sweaty. I tugged on my shirt a little for some fresh air but it didn't help. In the glass door, I caught a glimpse of myself. Other than red cheeks, I didn't look as bad as I felt.

I hoped Leo wasn't working.

"Stop it." I scowled at myself and yanked the door handle.

I cringed when walking inside the store. It dawned on me that this was the second time I stepped foot inside enemy territory. And within twenty-four hours. *Gosh, I can't make this a habit.*

I scanned the store. More shoppers browsed today compared to yesterday. One was a former fourth grade teacher. A few people I didn't recognize and I assumed they were from neighboring towns. A handful of teenagers sat at the cafe, talking over iced coffees. Two little girls reminded me of myself at their age. They smiled big while holding their book. The eight or nine-year-old girl had it opened, reading as she walked down the main aisle while the younger sister had a book in each hand. She kept stopping, eyeing one book to the other, as if she could only pick one, and then walked before stopping again. Behind them trailed their mother. I recognize the family as regulars in Teresa's Bookstore. The sight should've been upsetting, but it wasn't. It motivated me to solve the case and reopen the store.

While the family passed me, I gazed at the rows of bookshelves. I missed working at Teresa's Bookstore. From talking to customers about stories, to reorganizing a shelf for the millionth time in a day. When a customer brought in a stack of books to exchange for store credit, I got excited. Sometimes my money magically disappeared into the cash register and the books ended up inside my tote bag. I loved discovering new authors and reading familiar ones. The magic writer's scribe onto the pages never got old.

The door opened behind me, forcing me to step aside for the new customer. I ventured further inside, pushing aside my daydreaming. There wouldn't be a bookstore if Jane stayed behind bars for crimes she didn't commit.

I found Sasha at the registers. She was leaning over the counter with her booty popping out, talking to Mateo. Sasha laughed while Mateo talked. Both were oblivious to the store's surveillance camera that faced the registers. I walked up to the happy couple, ready to interrogate them.

Sasha stopped laughing and lowered her voice. "What did you tell the police?"

I stopped in my tracks and scurried behind the bookmark rack. At this angle I only saw Mateo. Thankfully, they had loud voices.

"Nothing," said Mateo. "My lawyer did all the talking."

They were silent for a moment. I studied Mateo's face for any signs of being afraid or nervous. He revealed nothing.

"Everything will be alright." Mateo leaned over to touch her.

"I want this to be over. The woman is dead. Who cares how she died. It's not like she was a saint."

My heart raced. They were talking about Doris. I dug in my purse for my phone. I had to record this.

"It is over," he said.

"It's not over until that sheriff arrests someone."

Where was my phone? my mind screamed. Then my elbow hit something. Everything happened in slow motion. When I realized the bookmark rack was falling, it was too late.

I reached out to catch it, only for my purse to fall from my grasp. The rack, and everything inside my purse crashed onto the floor. My eyes shot up. Sasha and Mateo were staring at me. I felt like a kid who had been caught in the cookie jar.

I forced myself to react. "Oh, no. I'm so sorry." I reached for the rack.

Mateo rushed over. He helped me pick up the spinner—not an easy task when the thing kept moving. Up close Mateo looked strong. Stronger and taller than Preston. He definitely had the body to hurt someone. I did a quick scan to see if he had any injuries from when he possibly attacked Doris.

"You okay?" Mateo asked.

I stopped staring at his biceps and looked him in the eye. "Yeah. I'm totally fine. Just embarrassed." I picked up the few contents that spilled from my purse.

Sasha appeared next to me, arching her eyebrows. "What are you doing here? I thought you hated this place."

Mateo gave me a funny look as if he just realized who I was.

I got straight to the point. "I was looking for you."

"Why?" she asked.

"We never finished talking yesterday."

Sasha's expression lightened. "We didn't, did we."

"Is anyone working here?" a costumer called out.

The three of us checked the counter. Not only was there a man waiting, but a middle-aged couple, and the two girls with their mom. Sasha groaned.

"I'll pick you up after work," Mateo said, giving Sasha a quick hug before he left.

I stood off to the side, away from the bookmark rack, while Sasha rang up everyone. Her customer service skills hadn't improved since working at Voss-of-Books. She didn't say a word and never made eye contact with anybody.

Once the customers had been rung up, her co-worker from the cafe came over. Based on his face expression, he wasn't coming over for a casual chit-chat. When Sasha spotted him, she flashed a smile. "Hey, can you watch the front for a few minutes?" she said while zipping around the counter, not giving him the chance to say no. Sasha looped her arm into mine and steered me towards the back.

"I don't want to get you in trouble," I said, fearing she was taking me to the employee's break room. I wanted to talk to her on the sales floor. A killer wouldn't strike when people were around, *right?*

Sasha dismissed my question by rambling about the store's clearance section. I ignored the tidy area and focused on where I was being led. Moments later, Sasha directed me toward the narrow hallway with a sign above stating, EMPLOYEES ONLY. The only reason why I didn't wiggle out of her grasp was that I desperately needed answers. We walked past two empty offices, and I sat in a folding chair at a long white table.

While Sasha bought herself a Coke from the machine, I studied the room. It was small, but comfortable enough for employees to eat. Like the rest of the store, it had white walls. Not a single picture or the store's logo hung in sight. The room looked bland with just two vending machines, a line of gray lockers against one wall, and a coffee maker in need of cleaning. In the mix with the faint paint smell, something stank from the trash can. I mentally pulled myself together as Sasha took the seat across from me.

"Sorry that Leo barged in on us yesterday." Her coke fizzed after she cracked it open. "Leo is a jerk and so bossy. He makes Teresa look like a saint, but Drake—" her eyes widened— "is the worst. It's always a bad day when he's here." She took a loud sip. "Anyway, I was wanting to talk to you about giving Mateo a chance to remodel the store. He'll do a great job. You won't regret it. Or Jane, I should say. Do you know what she wants to do? She looks bossier than these Voss's. Hopefully, she has an open mind and will hire Mateo."

I struggled to keep up with her various topics. I ignored them all. "Actually, I'm here for a different reason today."

"Oh?"

I placed my hands on the table and held them like actors did in cop shows. "I know you threatened Doris. Why?"

"You mean just before someone killed her? I was just messing with her since I couldn't while I was working there. It felt good telling her that."

"I meant online, more specifically, through the PlayStation."

Sasha was about to take a drink when I said the user's ID name. Her hand froze halfway to her mouth. Fear was written all over her face.

After a few beats, Sasha put down the drink. "I don't know what you're talking about. You're mistaking me for someone else."

"The Witcher is one of your favorite games and you raved about the actress playing Yennefer on Netflix. The pieces fit."

She snorted. "Lots of people love Yennefer."

"Move or you'll end up dead like the Suicide King," I quoted one of Sasha's threats.

"I don't know—"

"Leave or I'll jack up your brakes. Your hair is the same color as clubs, but I'll turn it red as diamonds." Saying the threats aloud sounded bizarre, and slightly kiddish. I wondered if the police dismissed them for being so unusual.

Sasha shifted in her seat, narrowing her eyes. “You’re accusing me because you don’t know any other gamers. Anyone in the world could have messaged her.”

I removed my hands off the table and sat up straighter. Now was the time to reveal my trump card. “I’m a Stone. My family may not be on the force anymore, but I still know people. Powerful people, and they will believe anything I say.” Not entirely the truth, but Sasha didn’t need to know.

Sasha held up her hands in defeat. “Alright, alright.” She then leaned forward and lowered her voice. “Yes, I sent those messages to Doris. She was blackmailing Mateo.”

“Blackmailing?”

“*Shhh*,” she snapped, gesturing her hand to lower my tone. Her eyes shifted to the doorway, making sure we were alone. “Doris was broke. That stupid woman spent all her money gambling. She used Mateo just like when they dated. She knew Mateo saved his money, and she went after him. Doris said she would tell the police that his sister and momma were illegals, if he didn’t pay her. She went as far as stalking Mateo at job sites and destroyed some of his equipment to prove her point. Mateo had to pay. She didn't care about his reputation or that it hurt him financially. She just wanted the money.”

“How much did he pay her?”

Sasha’s voice grew dangerously low. “A lot. Doris made him drive to a restaurant in Bristol to hand her the money and made him pay for her dinner. She did it so Clara wouldn’t find out.”

“That’s awful.”

“Mateo wanted us to be a secret because he was afraid she would come after me too. You know I can’t sit around and do nothing.”

I almost pointed out that she sat at home for over months before she got a job at Voss-of-Books, but I kept the thought to myself.

"So yeah, I threatened Doris so she would leave Mateo and his family alone. Doris has caused enough damage."

A connection clicked. "Doris figured out it was you who was sending her the online messages. That day when you warned her in the store." It made sense why Doris didn't argue back. She was stunned. Maybe a little afraid.

"But I didn't kill her. I was trying to scare her off."

"How did you know Doris spent all her money?"

Sasha smirked and took a long pause before answering. "She let it slip when she was blackmailing Mateo."

"How long has this been going on?" I asked.

She took a drink, pondering. "Valentine's Day. Doris thought it was hilarious. She even had the nerve to say that getting money on Valentine's Day was better than getting a stuffed animal." Sasha grunted in disgust.

As Sasha babbled more about Doris's dinner meetings with Mateo, I studied her body language. I believed Sasha in regards to Doris's blackmailing Mateo. The part about not killing her, no. As police would say, Sasha became a person of interest. Mateo too. Sasha got them inside with the store key while Mateo did the deed. It also explained why Sasha was late to her job interview. She wasn't flirting with Mateo in the break room. They were tag teaming a murder.

I wanted to leave.

"You know me," Sasha said. "We're friends. We worked together. I hated Doris before, and I hated her more after dating Mateo. I swear I was just trying to scare her out of town. She could've sold her mansion and moved anywhere she wanted."

All I heard was what she said to Doris the day she died. *One day somebody is going to hack you up with a jack of spades, and on that day, I'm going to laugh at it.*

Love and revenge were powerful motives.

I had to get away. I stood up, thinking how to end this conversation without sounding mad or suspicious. "I should let you get back to work."

Sasha jumped to her feet. "Yeah, I think my five-minute break ended five minutes ago."

After saying a quick goodbye, I walked out of the break-room first. I didn't get far. A man dressed in a black suit stepped out of the office and I bumped into him. I froze when I realized who blocked my path to freedom.

Drake Voss.

CHAPTER 31

"What are you doing here?" Drake snarled. He spoke perfect English with a thick German accent behind his words. I saw where Leo inherited his furious expression.

Words stumbled out, but nothing made sense. I couldn't find a reasonable explanation on the spot. Instead of coming to my aid, Sasha slipped past us. I got the sense she used the opportunity to escape a lecture or a write up.

"I was talking to Sasha during her break," I said, once she disappeared around the corner.

"You're not welcome here. My business doesn't need junk walking in my perfectly good store."

I held back the words I yearned to say. I was on his turf.

"Don't worry. I'll never come back." I walked around Drake, making sure to not accidentally bump into him.

"Stay away from Leo too," he added once my back faced him.

I stopped and turned around. His expression darkened before me. Drake never gave this look to Teresa. This observation frightened me.

"Listen well, Garnet." I hated how Drake pronounced my name. It sounded like he growled my name out of disgust. "The Voss staple represents a higher class than yours. We have standards. Qualities you lack." He stepped closer. I held my ground, refusing to budge. "Leo doesn't need a girl like you. Go back to your junk store."

A vile smile crossed his lips. "Forgive me, I forgot that Teresa's Bookstore is closed."

I narrowed my eyes. "There is nothing happening between your grandson and me and there never will be. My future husband will have *respectable* qualities; ones that a Voss lacks."

"Watch your tone, Garnet."

"Keep Leo away from me."

Drake took another step closer. He wore strong cologne I didn't like. It was overpowering as if he applied too much. His next words came out slowly, stressing each word. "If you come into any of my stores again, I'll call the police." He smirked again. "It would be a pleasure seeing your daddy's friends escort you out."

Anger rose within me. I turned around before I said something that would get me into trouble. While storming down the main aisle, I vowed to never come here again and eliminated my feelings for Leo. He might not have been like his grandfather but down the road, Leo would probably be just like Drake. I didn't need drama, most certainly not in my love life. If I wanted any, then I'd call Brad.

A line of customers waited at the register. Leo stood next to Sasha, bagging up items while she rang up their purchase. Drake's grandson caught my eye. Leo greeted me with a warm smile as he waved.

I turned my focus ahead and strolled out the door.

CHAPTER 32

"Crazy right?" I asked.

Megan laid on the couch, watching me pace around the living room while I vented. She didn't appear as upset as me—which drove me crazier than I already was. Then again, she worked a full shift at Dessert Bar. She was probably tired.

"Are you one-hundred-percent positive that Jane didn't do it?" Megan asked. "I mean the police ain't stupid."

"The witness is lying," I said, raising my voice.

Megan threw her hand up in surrender. "I'm just saying."

I made another lap in the living room, thinking. After I stormed out of Voss-of-Books, I called Stone about an update on Jane. My boss's future didn't look bright. The sheriff seemed fixated on the eyewitness's account and was charging Jane for the murder of Doris Hackett. As for Teresa's case, the investigation was ongoing. By the sound of Stone, who heard everything through Underwood, the sheriff hoped that Jane would break and confess to committing both crimes.

Unless I wanted to leave Jane's fate to a judge and let the real killer get away, solving these murders was a must.

"Feelings aside," Megan said, "are you really sure that Jane didn't kill anyone? Like really think, could she have flown into Bristol's airport, and flown back to New York to establish her alibi? Maybe she knew about Teresa's will and wanted her inheritance."

"Teresa had less than a thousand dollars in her bank account." I know because I had seen it. If I got a dollar for each time I logged her out on the store's computer, that nine hundred and thirty-seven dollars would be in my account. "And Jane didn't know about the inheritance until after Teresa died."

Megan remained unconvinced.

I thought back to Jane's and my time together. In the last four days, Jane fired me, and almost sold the bookshop. I also saw Jane cry at my grandparent's table over her aunt's death. She tagged along with me during my investigation. I opened up to her about Mom and Regan, and Jane had shown me a new revelation. We went from being enemies to forming a friendship. I wanted it to continue.

"Jane didn't do it," I said with confidence. "She loved her aunt."

"People lie," Megan pointed out.

I sat beside her. "True, but I can't see Jane being a killer. She helped too much. And—" I perked up— "if Princess likes Jane, then that means she's innocent."

Megan raised an eyebrow.

"Animals are a good judge of character. If Jane killed her aunt or Doris, then Princess would remember and tear her up."

Megan's lips shifted. "Okay, that's true."

"Does that mean you believe me?"

"I believe Princess."

We both chuckled. I felt better, and yet the mystery of these cases was still driving me bonkers.

"Great." I stood up and paced again. "If I had to point to someone, it would be Clara. She attacked me. She had a motive—"

"The ring?" Megan sat up straight with a determined look about her.

I nodded. "I can also see Mateo and Sasha doing it. Or Preston. He hated Doris, too." I rubbed my face and sat on the carpet. I felt a headache coming on. "This is crazy. How can my dad do this for a living?"

"Speaking of crazy." Megan came up to push me over. "Leo came into the bar, asking where you were. And he wanted a phone number to reach you at."

I glared at her.

"Don't worry, I didn't give him your number."

I briefly recalled Drake's warning. "I don't want to date Leo, and besides, I'm happily single." I added a smile for good measure. Megan wasn't buying it.

"Come on," she said, "you know Leo isn't so...well Voss."

My best friend had a point, but that didn't mean I wanted to date Leo. The relationship wouldn't survive. Our bookstores were rivals— which they wouldn't be if Drake treated Teresa decently. Leo was part owner, while I was a regular employee. The only thing we had in common was that we sold books. Nothing more.

"Let's talk about something else," I said, playing with my garnet charm. "How was your date with Austin?"

Megan sat back on the couch. "It was more of a late lunch hang out than a date. Austin wants me to meet his family." Her face turned pink.

"That's a good sign."

Megan hesitated. "I guess."

I pulled myself off the floor and sat on the couch, placing my legs over her lap. Megan shifted to where her feet pressed against my side It felt as if we were teenagers again, staying up late chit-chatting about boys.

"You don't need to be nervous," I said.

"I don't think they'll like me. They're rich, Garnet. They have this huge house and they vacation in Europe every year and...and I'm a country girl who bakes. What if they hate me? Austin said his sister is a little difficult."

"Austin will stand up for you."

Megan sighed. "What if I go with him to Memphis to meet his family, and he wants to move back. I can't leave Mom."

"Small towns have a way of holding onto people, and I think it has a hold on Austin through you."

"I really love Austin. I just don't want his family to hate me, and I most certainly don't want to move to the other side of the state." Megan eyed me. "You wanna go on a road trip with me?"

I shook my head. "No, thanks. I don't want to be a third wheel. Besides, maybe his family will come here."

Megan's eyes widened. "Oh no. Don't say that. I'm not ready for them to be here." After a playful glare, she switched subjects. "Have you thought anymore about Regan?"

I wasn't in the mood to talk about Regan or tell Megan about Jane's thoughts on the matter. Megan must have sensed my vibe and suggested watching a movie.

"I can't, not while Jane's in jail."

"You need a break. Nothing does a better job than a movie." Megan hopped off the couch.

I felt bad, but Megan wasn't taking no for an answer. Her walk into the kitchen was followed by the sound of cabinets opening and closing. I glanced at the time while waiting. Almost nine o'clock. Unless I wanted to search for a hollowed book at night, nothing more could be done. Maybe a visit to the station tomorrow would reveal something and ensure Jane was holding up okay.

While I heard popcorn popping, I checked my email. I hoped Dad wrote back. Unfortunately, he didn't. My eyes landed on Regan's name. Jane's words echoed in my thoughts. I read the message again, except this time I pictured Regan being as lonely as I had been instead of being Mom's favorite. My heart went out to Regan. So many times I wished Dad married someone who had kids, or even Molly. I really wanted siblings. Now staring at Regan's name, the least I could do was give Regan a chance.

I typed a message, then deleted it, and wrote another message before deleting it again. Until now, I hadn't thought about what to say.

I couldn't write: *Hey, did Mom leave you too? Does she shower you with gifts? Have you always wanted her to pay more attention to you? I always wanted a brother or a sister. By the way, are you my brother or sister?*

Gosh, what do I say? I wondered.

I wanted to sound normal, not ask Regan a million revealing questions or make it weird. Finally, I decided on a short and simple response about wanting to get to know Regan more and hit send before I second guessed myself.

After I hit send, I felt relieved to get rid of the should-I-write-back question. Yet I found myself with a new fear. What if Regan didn't reply? What if I made Regan upset by ignoring the message for two months?

Megan entered the room with a huge bowl of popcorn, ceasing my thoughts of Regan. "Did you pick a movie?" She nearly sat on me, forcing me to scooch over.

The buttery smell of popcorn made me instantly hungry. I set my phone aside before grabbing a handful. "Are you busy tomorrow?"

Megan narrowed her eyes. She finished chewing and said, "I'm hanging out with Austin at two tomorrow. Why?"

"I need my partner in crime."

"I am the best."

Before we settled on a movie, Megan's phone rang.

"That's your phone." Megan nudged me.

"Is it?" I glanced at where I put my phone. Surely enough it lit up with a familiar picture on my screen. Grandma Stone. I answered while Megan searched on Netflix.

"What are you doing tomorrow?" Grandma asked, sweetly.

Megan must have heard because she snorted a chuckle. Nothing good happened when Grandma asked that question. She wanted me to do something, and most of the time it involved something I rather not do.

CHAPTER 33

I SAW THE LINE OF CARS ON BOTH SIDES OF THE ROAD BEFORE I spotted the yard sale sign, right next to the for-sale sign with a sold stamp over top of it. Megan had to park her hatchback four houses down. When a truck left, another one took its place.

"You see Nora's van?" Megan asked as she leaned over the steering wheel.

I scanned the parked vehicles. "I think we beat Grandma."

A loud car zoomed by for a second time, searching for a closer spot. People walked either to or from their vehicles. A few neighbors sat on their porches, staring in the direction of Clara's house.

"There are a lot of people here," Megan muttered.

"Everyone wants to know what the town's spy is selling."

We stepped out of the air-conditioned car and into the stinking heat. *Only two more months of summer*, I thought. Thankfully, I wore cool gear clothes by Under Armour. I may not look dressed up compared to Megan in a knee length skirt and thick tank top, but I wasn't sweaty.

The yard sale was bigger than I expected. It stretched as far as the lawn permitted. Wide particle boards were used as tables with chairs holding them up. Each one was filled with items, ranging from home decor to half used lotion bottles. Various shoes sat underneath. Clothes hung on a rope draping from a big maple tree to the porch's flagpole. Winter jackets and mittens decorated the top of Clara's car. Numbers on the windshield indicated the vehicle was for sale as well.

As I scanned over the lot, I wondered why Clara was selling so much stuff. This amount was usually found at a multiple family lot, not at a single woman's house. This yard sale smelled suspicious.

Megan wasted no time. She walked up to the first table, eyeing everything. I glanced over the table seeing mostly everyday tools and kitchen utensils.

"I won't take anything less than five hundred," Clara told an older gentleman. They stood in front of a sleigh bed frame that had been disassembled. "It's in great condition. There are no scratch marks."

Clara wore a bright pink Hawaiian shirt with orange flowers and white capris. It was a different look on her compared to the simple jeans and t-shirt style. She looked years younger, especially without a pair of binoculars glued to her hand. For a moment, I wondered if the binoculars sat on one of these tables, or if it was one of the few things she kept.

I hovered back, waiting for Clara to have a moment alone. When I glanced around the yard sale, I realized that moment might be awhile. Some people had an armful of stuff while others stood in front of the bigger priced items. I had a feeling they were going to be haggling with Clara soon.

"Three hundred," the older gentleman bargained with Clara.

While Clara and the man debated, I found Megan, and

head nodded toward them. Megan understood my silent que. She walked over. "Hi, Mr. Hagan. It's so good to see you."

The man broke into a smile and made a joke about bringing him a piece of coffee cake. I went to seize my chance with Clara, but a man beat me first, asking if a lawn mower still worked. Meanwhile, a woman with an armful of Christmas decor stood at the dining table where the money box and grocery bags sat. Her gaze focused on Clara as she talked to the man about the lawn mower.

I considered coming back later when I spotted Karl and his wife walking up. His wife swooped toward a coffee table as Karl moseyed behind her. He drank Diet Coke, looking at other items for sale. When seeing me, he gave a friendly wave. He looked wide awake. *Guess, he's getting used to the diet drinks.*

The woman waiting swayed side to side. I'd been in customer service long enough to know that she was getting impatient. Clara finished talking to the man about the lawn mower when Karl's wife stopped her. Clara noticed the woman waiting, but Karl's wife sounded like she had lots of concerns about a coffee table.

I groaned, debating whether to help Clara or not. In the end, Dad's lessons about being kind to everyone won. "Are you ready?" I asked the women with the Christmas decor.

She nodded. "Yes."

I pulled out my phone and calculated her total amount. Thankfully, Clara placed price stickers on everything. By the time I wrapped the fragile ornaments, another person was ready to check out. A steady flow of people came to me with their purchases. Every now and then, I spotted Clara. She was constantly on the move. I heard people call her name and she'd answer their questions.

Megan, accompanied by Grandma, waved at me while I waited for a little boy to count his pennies to pay for a fishing rod. They laughed as if they were getting a kick out of me working. I wanted to escape, but I couldn't find it in my heart to abandon Clara. I gave them a playful look before pointing my finger at them to get back to work.

Ten or so customers later, including Karl's wife with candles, three bags of clothes, and the coffee table, I had a free moment. Clara too had escaped and came up to me. I scanned the front yard and was glad to see no one coming up or hollering Clara's name. Grandma distracted one shopper while Megan tagged the new people walking up.

Clara gave a heavy sighed as she leaned against the dining table. She looked like she needed a cup of joe.

"I see your house sold." I nodded at the realtor's sign.

"I'm moving. I'm finally getting out of this place." She sounded relieved with a hint of bitterness.

"Where are you going?"

Clara considered the question for a moment. "Hawaii."

"Really?" I skimmed over the lawn. The huge yard sale made sense. It was probably cheaper to buy new stuff rather than haul everything over the Pacific Ocean. "Why there?"

Clara looked at me. When she spoke, her voice didn't sound as cheerful. "I never liked Sevier Oak. Everybody knows ya and your family's life story. People think they know me based on my actions from kindergarten." Her eyes grew heavy. "I always wanted to live by the ocean. I felt the ocean breeze once; I want to feel it again. Hawaii seems like the perfect place. I've been saving my money for years. Now that I have enough, I sold this house and am leaving. And I'm never coming back."

My heart softened. Clara sounded desperate like Bilbo Baggins when he explained to Frodo that he was leaving. She had been wanting to leave for some time.

I noticed the Watson couple walking across the road as

they eyed the lot. I got the impression they were taking the opportunity to be nosy. I got to the point before they or anyone else interrupted this moment.

"Did you get your ring back?" I asked.

"No. Apparently, it's evidence. And since the police found it on Doris—" her words turned cold at her sister's name— "it will most likely be sold to settle her debt."

"I'm sorry to hear that."

"It was *my* ring. Our granny gave it to me. Doris stole it." Clara clenched her fists. "It was supposed to be a temporary thing."

When Clara didn't continue, I asked her about what happened.

"I was getting the entire house recarpeted. I didn't want anyone taking the ring or losing it while I moved furniture around, so I asked Doris to hang onto it. She promised to give it back, but she kept it, claiming that the ring should have gone to her since she was the oldest and that I tricked our parents into giving me the house. Why would my parents give her the house? I spent more time with them, and Doris had a nice cabin with Preston."

"Did you tell the police?" I asked.

Clara nodded hard. "Of course. But they said since I 'gave' it to her, they couldn't do anything. Then Doris had the nerve to say that she lost it. Liar. She was jealous and wanted it for herself."

If Clara was the killer, I understood her reasoning.

"I know I sound like a suspect," she said as if she heard my thoughts. "I'll tell you like I told that new sheriff, my house was on the market almost a week before my sister died. I had plans to move. That morning my realtor called." She smiled. "Someone gave me an offer. Best news I got in a long time." Then her happiness vanished. "After I got off the phone, I heard the police scanner going haywire at Teresa's Bookstore. I got there as soon as I could and found out about Doris."

Another perfect alibi, I thought, more concrete than Sasha's and Mateo's.

"The police got the right person."

"Jane didn't do it," I said calmly instead of shouting like I wanted to.

"You sound like your daddy. But if you really wanna know, the police confirmed my phone call with my realtor. It was the same time when Doris was in the bookstore. I can't be in two places at once."

I froze. The police eliminated Clara? How did I not know this? Then again, if Stone didn't know, then neither did I.

"Watch your back," Clara said so softly that I almost didn't hear her. Her gaze then shifted over the yard sale. "No one believes me, but I swear someone has been following Doris for months. I saw him in the shadows. He stands in the woods, staring into her house. The night you got attacked, I saw someone running through my back yard when I returned home. I thought it was one of my nosy neighbors, but I think it was the same person who's been stalking Doris. They planted your purse in my house."

New pieces were falling into place. I eyed her, believing her account. Clara may not be the best spy, but she did see things. Doris's death in the bookstore proved that someone had been watching her. Tailing her. Replaying my attack, the shove seemed to be more believable from a guy than petite Clara.

"Okay." I relaxed my tense shoulders. "I need to get going now."

"Sure. Thanks for helping."

As I made my way to Megan's hatchback, my little spies followed. We stood next to her vehicle, talking in low voices. Grandma and Megan learned nothing from the neighbors or other people at the sale. No one confirmed when Clara left her house the day Doris died, let alone remembered what Clara did the night Teresa died. When I gave them the short version of what Clara said, their faces fell.

"Do you believe her?" I asked once I finished the story.

"It sounds legit," Megan said.

We turned toward Grandma.

"I'll ask Stone to verify with her realtor." Grandma sighed. "I gotta admit, ladies, the pieces fit. I think she's clear."

Megan turned to me. "But she attacked you?"

"I don't think she did," I replied. "I never saw my attacker, and Clara is a terrible spy. I believe her. Someone planted my purse in her house." This meant the killer did. I tried not to shudder at the thought or how bad things could've been.

"Underwood doesn't think Clara did it either," Grandma said. "He and Stone had a long talk last night over supper."

Too bad none of this absolved Jane, our sole reason for coming to the yard sale.

"Let's regroup later, I've decided that I do want those rugs." Grandma waved goodbye over her shoulder as she walked away.

Once she was out of earshot, Megan asked, "You still game for visiting Roland?"

CHAPTER 34

A TALL GATE BLOCKED THE REMAINING DRIVEWAY, LEADING DEEPER into the woods. A roaring lion stood on each side of the path. They gave off a dark omen, warning strangers that the Fremont family was not friendly. Even years after my last visit, the lions remained untouched by weather. They were well cared for.

They creeped me out.

"I never liked coming here," Megan said.

"Me either," I agreed.

"Do you think Roland's here?" Megan asked. "He could be hanging out at a bar. Maybe he's at one in Bristol."

I shook my head. A month before Stone retired, he had enough of Roland's bar fights. Stone took advantage of a Friday night by placing Roland in a prison cell. The long weekend must have knocked some sense into him because, according to Stone and Underwood, he hadn't been spotted in the local bars since. Yet the rumors remained.

"He's here because a different guy delivers stuff on Fridays," I said. "Now come on, push the button already." I gestured toward the speaker box.

Megan groaned and rolled down the window. By the time she moved her finger from the button a voice crackled through. Clearly he saw us through a surveillance camera.

"You have no business here. Go away."

I unbuckled my seatbelt and leaned into Megan's personal space. "Did you swallow something? You sound like Professor Snape."

Megan snorted a laugh "He does sound like him," she mouthed.

"What do you want?" Roland's normal voice snapped out of the speaker.

"We need to talk to you," I said.

"About?"

Megan leaned her seat back. I yelped at the sudden moment, almost falling out of the window. Roland had to be laughing at us. Hopefully, he wasn't recording this and later post it online.

After I glared at my best friend and collected myself, I said, "It's about your last delivery to the store."

"It wasn't damaged when I left it." His voice grew impatient.

"I know what happened," Megan said.

I gave her a look to stop talking. If anyone could get under Roland's skin faster than his mother, it was Megan.

"Speak up, Mega," Roland said.

"Don't call me that," Megan snapped at the former nickname he gave her.

I crawled back to the passenger seat. A Stone or not, I didn't want to be in the middle of this fight. Again.

"Your mom told me your secret."

"No, she didn't. Now beat it."

Megan faced me with fury in her eyes. Our plan was falling

apart. I should have known Roland would see through our lie. Dr. Poison Ivy hated Megan. A baker's daughter wasn't good enough to date her son. One time she called Megan the criminal's daughter instead of the baker's daughter. Roland's mother would never reveal any secrets to Megan.

"Garnet," Megan mumbled through clenched teeth, "what do we do now?"

I leaned over Megan again to talk. I said the only thing that would allow us to talk in person. "You're hiding something. Clara Hackett isn't the only one watching you. I have eyes too."

I kept my face stern, hoping he didn't see through my lie. The silence drove me crazy. After a few long moments, I looked back at Megan. She faced the other way, probably because I was blocking her air space.

"We just want to talk," I said after a minute passed.

Megan muttered, "I should have asked Austin to come with us."

I slithered back to my seat and put on my seat belt. To our surprise the gate creaked open. We gave a high five, low enough to avoid being seen on the surveillance, before Megan put the car in drive. The gates closed behind us as we ascended the mountain.

Trees towered around us. It was a beautiful sight on a sunny day. I scanned the forest for deer. Just because I didn't see them, didn't mean they weren't there. They blended easily into nature, even when the trees were bare. Still, I hoped to see one.

My mind drifted during the half mile drive. The last visit here was when Brad and I were dating. I was angry at Roland for how he had ended his relationship with Megan, and how fast he got a new girlfriend. I forgot the reason for coming here, but I remember stewing in silence while everyone drank.

Roland constantly draped one arm over the new girl, glancing every now and then in my direction as if he wanted to make sure that I saw. After a while I had enough and walked down the long driveway. Megan met me at the gates. We had fun bashing about males over a hot fudge brownie sundae.

The forest opened around the final turn, revealing a large open space. The two-story log home screamed money. The Fremont's had a sense of class; they knew how to spend their wealth. Unlike Doris's modern style home, the Fremont's log home belonged in the forest, from the stone walkway to the tall bay windows. They had installed a gate to ensure their private lifestyle.

A guest house sat off in the corner of the lot. It was a third the size of the main house, yet maintained elegance. Roland's pickup truck parked near the front door. It was the same truck he had since high school. It looked like it had been well loved due to the mud splatters and rust. The truck reminded me of days he and Brad drove around a dried lake bottom for fun. Riding in the truck was one of the better days.

I pushed aside the memories of Brad and focused on the reason for being here. Brad was long gone. My thoughts went back to Roland and the man he became. If I hadn't known Roland my whole life, I would've said he was a spoiled rich kid who lived on Mommy and Daddy's money. But that was far from the truth. Roland was the black sheep of the family. It's been a few years, and after a breakup with Brad, to see that Roland struggled to live in his family's shadow. He lived on his parent's property because he had no other choice. Before Stone put him in jail, Roland had a history of being fired from every workplace. Rumors circulated that his parents pulled some strings to be hired at the post office. I didn't doubt them.

I got out first when Megan parked. She followed, always

staying a step or two behind me. I understood why she didn't want to be here. Roland said hurtful things, words that I knew really came from Dr. Poison Ivy. For a moment I wondered if Roland thought of Megan as the girl he let get away.

Before we knocked on the door, Roland came out. He looked muscular without his post office uniform. His black hair was unkempt, either from laziness or enjoying his day off. His jeans and t-shirt had been well worn. I was glad he dressed like this instead of pajamas.

"Are you stalking me, Garnet?" His dark brown eyes stared at me as he folded his arms over his chest. "Doesn't seem very Stone like."

"I'm not stalking you," I said.

Megan voiced what she heard his mother say over the phone two days ago, unfortunately she didn't mimic Dr. Ivy's voice, but I understood why she chose not to. "Roland is old enough, let it be a hard lesson."

Roland scoffed. "You think I killed Doris Hackett. Is that it?"

If he and Teresa had bad blood between them, then yes, but I didn't think he murdered Teresa. Before I could tell him, I thought he had seen something related to her murder Roland said, "That sheriff already questioned me. But I'll tell y'all too. I dropped off the store's package before Doris died. And no, I didn't see or hear anyone. I dropped it off like a good boy and left. Lots of people and cameras can testify that I was working." He leaned closer. "Anything else, Detective Garnet Stone?"

Once again, I was interrupted. This time by Megan. "So, what do you have to say for yourself? Why did you murder Doris? Did she get under your skin?"

For the first time since we arrived, Roland looked at Megan. I did too. Did she really believe that her ex-boyfriend murdered two people, or was she releasing years of pent up anger? I guessed the latter.

Roland turned to me. “I hope the police invest in a battering ram to get through my gate. Cause that’s the only way they’re gettin' to me.”

Megan and I stepped back. Roland let out a bellowed laugh. “Is that what you two really think? That I killed Doris Hackett?”

I said no while Megan answered yes.

Roland eyed us with a hint of a smile. He was finding us amusing. “You two are not very good at playing cop, are ya?”

I spoke before Megan did. “The package has been bothering me.”

“It wasn’t damaged,” his words quickly hardened.

“Sorry, let me rephrase that. The books weren’t damaged, but it’s odd. It should have been in three separate boxes, not one. I ordered them on different days for three different customers. Why did the books come in one box?”

Roland shrugged, but I saw his hesitation. “So.”

“Why is Clara spying on you?” Megan asked.

“She spies on everyone,” he said. “I’m glad that crazy bat is moving to Hawaii.”

“How do you know she’s moving to Hawaii?” Megan asked.

The realtor’s sign was a giveaway, but to Hawaii? Unless Clara told more people than I thought, how would Roland know?

He chuckled, I couldn’t tell if he was still amused or was getting annoyed. “You two are really bad at this. I work at the post office. She’s been mailing stuff to Honolulu for the past week. It’s not hard to put two and two together, unlike you two.” He laughed at his own joke.

I needed him back on track. The reason why we were here. “Then why the one box?”

"And why was my package late?" added Megan.

I wanted her to hush and let me do the talking, but that wouldn't happen.

I expected Roland to snap, instead he laughed. We stayed quiet as he settled down.

"Alright detectives, here's the truth— I messed up." Roland opened his arms out and let them fall to his sides. "I went through a car wash to avoid getting a speeding ticket. The back door was open. Surely you two can figure what happened next. So, then I had to find and re-buy everything. I lied to people about the deliveries being delayed. My parents figured out what happened. If I lose this job, they'll kick me out." He looked at Megan. "I delivered them as soon as I could."

"So, you have some shark oven mitts in your kitchen?" Megan asked curiously.

Roland didn't answer.

"Why didn't you just re-pack the items in a new box?" I asked, assuming some things might be okay once dried.

Roland's face turned red. "Have you been through a drive through car wash before? It's a lot of water in case you forgot. Anything else detectives?" Roland's tone went back to harsh and annoyed.

"No," said Megan. "Thanks for the info." She walked back to her hatchback while humming the car wash song.

"Thanks for telling me," I said. "I know you didn't do it. I figured you was hiding something." I smiled big. "I was right about that."

"Don't tell anyone about this. I can't afford to live on my own." He grunted. "I lost most of my savings because of this. A ticket would have been a heck of a lot cheaper." He grumbled something else, probably remembering that his parents would have kicked him out.

I promised to keep his secret and walked back to the car feeling a weight off my shoulders.

“And mind your own business,” he shouted before I heard the front door shut.

I hummed the chorus of the car wash song along with Megan as we drove away.

CHAPTER 35

Megan and I ate lunch at home. We chatted about the case in between bites. Despite our mild victory with Roland's car wash disaster, he was no help. Jane remained behind bars and everyone still had an alibi. I felt like I was playing a board game, stuck on the first square. We brainstormed about our next course of action. Other than searching for a possible hollowed book, we came up with nothing.

"I don't know about you—" Megan said after eating the last bite of her sandwich— "but I'll stick with cooking over sleuthing." She got up and grabbed the coffee pot. "We really do suck at being cops."

"We need to un-alibi someone."

"That's not even a word," Megan said with a laugh.

Solving a murder was frustrating. Secretly, I hoped Roland had seen or heard something. Something that would point to someone. I stewed on our suspects as coffee scented the kitchen. Nothing new came to mind. *How does Dad do this for a living?* I wondered. It had to be the most maddening job in the world.

After drinking coffee, Megan got ready for her date with Austin while I took a hot shower. I considered things I needed to do today, other than fight crime.

One, visit Jane to make sure she hadn't gone mad in there. Perhaps she learned something.

Two, deal with the cats. Living in a closed bookstore with little human contact wasn't the life for felines. Until things settled, they had to be relocated. Where was the painful question.

When I got out of the bathroom, I heard my grandparents' voices. "Hi," I greeted them, entering the living room.

Everyone had coffee mugs, which should be a joyous occasion, yet they all shared a look. Something happened.

"What's wrong?" I asked.

Stone got to the point. "I wanted to let you know that Clara Hackett's story has checked out."

"I told you that," Grandma kindly snapped at him. "Garnet was there when Clara told me." Grandma gave me a look to ignore her little white lie. I didn't argue.

"The police had to confirm it with the realtor. Clara should have said that sooner."

Grandma shook her head. "This is why people don't tell ya'll anything. Ya'll so formal, and never take the word of people."

"If people always told the truth, then the word *suspects* wouldn't exist."

"I know when people are lying," Grandma said, defending herself.

Megan and I kept quiet as my grandparent's bickered back and forth on how to interrogate people. I rarely saw them like this. In a way it was funny, despite Stone being dead serious. A classic example of Stone being snappy and annoyed at everything. He really wasn't mad at Grandma; he was upset that the case wasn't solved.

"Sounds like you two need an afternoon nap," I teased.

Stone ignored Grandma's last comment and said to me, "I want to let you know that we're not giving up on either case. Underwood has been upfront with me about the ongoing investigation, which stays in this room. He can lose his job if word gets out. I also have a message from Jane. She wants you working the bookstore."

"Wait," I said, perking up. "You saw Jane?"

Grandma answered first. "He was at the station while we were out at the yard sale. Jane refused to hire a lawyer. She's representing herself." She shook her head, disagreeing with Jane's action.

"Not a wise idea," Stone agreed. "She needs someone on her side. And you—" he pointed at me— "don't count. I'm doing what I can to aid the police, and also asked Onyx's professional opinion."

I wouldn't be surprised if I saw Dad for dinner tonight. A part of me hoped so. It would be like old times, only this time I was part of the investigation.

Stone continued, "Sheriff Estep isn't viewing the ring as evidence, and dismissed the blood on the bear."

"Why?" I cried. "That's ridiculous."

Stone frowned. "The blood doesn't match Mateo's. According to the sheriff, the blood could have been from Teresa." He held up his hand to silence me. "Which is being tested. Until further notice, it's a dead end."

Grandma grumbled something under her breath.

This was frustrating. Another piece of evidence the sheriff was ignoring. "Do the police have any evidence against Jane?"

"The witness," Grandma and Stone said at the same time.

Then Stone added that Jane was present during the crime, and there was no forced entry on the back door.

I paced around the living room. "I was there too. Does that make me a suspect? Plus, Sasha and Mateo had a motive. Sasha still has the store's key. Did that stupid sheriff think of that?"

"Don't get all upset," Stone said calmly, making me more agitated. "Deputy Underwood is still reviewing the case. I don't want you sleuthing anymore. The killer is relaxed now Jane is taking the blame. He or she will lash out if they feel threaten—"

"Yes, we know the stories," Grandma interrupted. She winked at me. Stone saw but said nothing. "Now tell me, when are you bringing Leo for dinner?"

Megan spat out her coffee, laughing.

I stopped pacing and stared at Grandma. "Never because there is no Leo and me."

Grandma arched one eyebrow. She believed otherwise.

"The Voss's are stingy people. Drake said that I wasn't good enough for his precious grandson and to go back to my junk store. He's treating me like he did Teresa."

"Give Leo a chance," said Grandma.

Megan's smirk grew. It was tempting to chuck a pillow at her. How dare she take Grandma's side.

"Why Leo?" I asked. "He could turn into his grandfather. And who knows, maybe his dad is even worse."

"I want you to be with someone. Onyx is happily single. Stone and I accepted a long time ago that we ain't going to get anymore grandchildren, but that doesn't mean you should be alone. You're too good Garnet."

That warmed my heart.

"I agree, but the Voss men are not good enough for my granddaughter," Stone said. His words also warmed my heart. "There are other fine young men who are worthy of Garnet."

Grandma patted his knee. A sign for him to be quiet. Meanwhile, I glanced at Megan for support. Her face buried into the coffee mug.

"Don't judge a guy based on his family," said Grandma. "Kind of like, don't judge a book by its cover."

I rolled my eyes while ignoring Megan struggling to not burst out laughing. Too bad Austin didn't have a brother, then I would've asked Megan to set me up with him just to avoid this sudden awkward conversation.

Grandma kept going, "If your father was here, he would say something like, 'every man can say the same about you.' Sweetheart, I know it's not easy being a Stone. People are intimidated by you based on your family. Some folks think that cops are bullies, but they're not, and you're not. I hope you understand what I'm trying to say."

"Don't be oblivious that Onyx and I do background checks," Stone said while Grandma shot him a look. I couldn't tell if Stone was annoyed at the ongoing case or if he really disliked Leo.

Megan couldn't control herself anymore. "Sounds like Leo has a clean record," she said with a laugh.

Grandma was giving the worst advice, yet her words rang true. It seemed like I misjudged a lot of people— Jane, Regan, and now Leo. I had to get out of here.

"I'm going to the bookstore," I said, and stopped in my tracks. "To Teresa's Bookstore, not Voss-of-Books."

"Why?" Stone asked, concerned.

"I need to check on the cats." And to search for a hollowed-out book, but I kept that part to myself.

CHAPTER 36

WHILE DRIVING TO TERESA'S BOOKSTORE IN MY SCORCHING HOT CAR, I replayed what my grandparents said, ignoring the part about Leo or me settling down. Things didn't sound good for Jane. It annoyed the crap out of me how much Sheriff Estep overlooked clues. Then again, he dismissed the Benadryls so why should I be surprised? I was already motivated to solve the murders before, yet the urge grew stronger. I didn't know what I wanted most: get Jane out of prison, reopen the bookstore, or seek justice for Teresa. All three? But I knew all too well that we don't always get what we want.

Copper Street was busy. Cars lined up on both sides. People walked on the sidewalk either shopping or dining out. The sight made my heart ache. Teresa's Bookstore should've been busy. I had to park in the municipal lot behind Copper Street.

When I unlocked the front door, Princess and Butterscotch greeted me. "Hello," I told them, mainly Butterscotch. It had been months since she roamed the sales floor. She really must've been missing human contact. I petted them both until someone knocked on the door. I jumped up and saw Grandma Stone waving at me.

As I unlocked the door, I checked Grandma's surroundings. No sign of Stone.

"That man," Grandma said, entering the store in a huff. She stopped for a moment to pet the cats.

I locked the door again and ventured further into the store before anyone else showed up. Grandma followed me with Princess cuddling in her arms.

"Sheriff Estep is wrong," I said. "Jane didn't do it."

"I'm talking about your grandfather." Grandma put Princess down.

"Where is he?"

Grandma waved her hand around. "Busy. Probably smoking a pack of Marlboros." She walked up to the front counter to set down her purse. Princess was on her heels. "Stone is driving me crazy. Future reference, if a case goes unsolved for more than a few days, it gets under his skin." She drummed her fingers on the counter. "Grouchy old man," she grumbled.

I didn't want to add that I already knew Stone acted this way. Sometimes it was best to let a person vent and keep my mouth shut.

Princess perched herself on the counter while Butterscotch disappeared into the unknown. The tortie cat's social moment had come and gone. I stroked Princess from her head and down her back. She purred.

"This case is making him especially crabby," Grandma continued. "After he came home from the station, he threw all the paint supplies and rocks in the trash. Then he started cleaning my kitchen! He was about to throw away my best wooden spoon because it has a teeny tiny crack."

I wondered what Leo did when he was upset. I scowled at myself. Why was I thinking about Leo so much? Maybe I would get lucky, and he would move back to Georgia. Leo's visits to Sevier Oak were always short. By the end of the month, Leo would be gone. Then again, he mentioned staying when I talked to him at Voss-of-Books. Princess's meow brought me back.

"Before we get started, has Stone learned anything new in the last hour?" I had a feeling there was more evidence than they said.

Grandma sighed. "Sheriff Estep wants to prove himself. This was the first murder since I was a teenager. Unless you get the killer, the real one, to confess, it doesn't look good for Jane." Grandma clapped her hands. "I want to know why you're really here?"

While walking toward the bargain room, I explained Jane's hollow book theory. Grandma wasted no time by picking up the nearest book, flipped through it, and put it on the already searched through pile.

"How long have you been helping Stone with cases?" I asked, picking Princess up to move her to another spot in the room. The moment I turned to leave back to my spot, she followed.

"He never asked. He was really fussy one time, slamming dishes and yelled at Onyx over not taking out the trash." She rolled her eyes at the memory as she picked up another paperback. "So, I decided to snoop a little to help Stone. Turns out, I found the robber through the grapevine. Stone knew it was me who tipped off the police, but he never questioned it. He told me to be careful and we formed some code words in case I was ever in trouble."

Grandma's words made me happy. Stone didn't lecture

non-law enforcement to mind their own business. He saw the value in gossip and from that, developed facts.

"It's in your blood," she continued. "I understand better than Stone why you're looking into the murders. You got what it takes."

I hoped so but feared otherwise. Since Doris's death, I had interviewed suspects, visited Clara's home twice, been in Voss-of-Books more times than I wanted, talked to Roland, and all I had to show was a little bruise on my forehead from being attacked.

We worked in silence with the occasional light push for Princess to move aside. With each book I tossed in the pile, I feared Jane's theory might be wrong. But it was the only thing I had left. While working, my mind raced at a million miles an hour. What would happen to the bookstore with Jane sitting in jail? Would the bank take it and Teresa's home? I didn't have enough money or credit to get a loan. If I miraculously got a loan, I would have to pay it back on top of paying bills, gas, food, and half the month's rent. What if Megan moved in with Austin? Then I had to pay double the rent I was used to. I couldn't forget about Princess and Butterscotch. They needed a new home, but where? Grandma and Stone?

Crap, I also had to find a new job.

The weight of solving all these problems became heavier by the moment. I wanted to cry frustrated tears, but locked them inside a vault. I hated this feeling that my best wasn't enough. Crying never solved anything.

When I picked up a third copy of The Body in the Library by Agatha Christie, something felt off. The hardcover book was noticeably lighter. I opened it as something fell out. Princess rushed towards the item. I stared at the insides of the book as the hole stared back at me. The book was no longer readable since someone cut a tiny square in the center, yet it told me this was the last clue. I opened my mouth, but nothing came out. Hope removed all my doubts. Jane was right.

"Garnet?" I heard Grandma's voice.

After a few moments I finally spoke. "I found it," I said, looking at my grandmother. "A hollowed book. It's here." I held it up, showing her.

Grandma pointed at me. "Don't touch anything else and freeze."

"Shouldn't it be the other way around?"

Grandma nibbled on her lips and said, "Perhaps we should have worn gloves. Don't move, I need to call this in."

While she darted toward the front of the store for her cellphone, I stared at Princess. Her big yellow eyes gazed up at me. "Sorry," I told her. "Can't pet you right now."

Grandma returned talking on her cellphone. "Garnet found something crucial. I'll be waiting for you." With that, she ended the call.

"Is Stone on the way?" My arms were burning.

Grandma shook her head and warned me again not to move as if the Agatha Christie novel was a bomb. I felt like a model as Grandma snapped a million pictures of me, before she claimed to be sending them to Stone. Meanwhile, Princess batted at the item on the floor. I tried to see what it was, but Princess hovered over it. Every time I moved, Grandma scowled at me to stand still.

The moment grandma left the bargain room, I took the opportunity to bend over to see what captivated Princess's attention. The air ran out of me when I realized what fell out of the book.

A ring box.

"What's going on?" Underwood asked, coming into the room.

I snapped up to attention and saw him and Grandma.

Instead of a navy uniform Underwood wore gray sweatpants and a tank top. His muscles were bigger than I would have guessed.

“I thought you found everything the day we asked you to search the premises.” Underwood sounded tired. There were deep bags under his eyes.

“Jane thought of it the other day and Sheriff Estep interrupted us,” I said.

Grandma stood between us. “No need to get all riled up.”

Underwood said nothing as he came up to me. Grandma picked up Princess as he examined the book and noticed the ring box. Underwood opened an evidence bag that was hidden in his grasp, and I slipped the items inside. In the following minutes, I explained Jane’s theory and how I found the book and ring box. Underwood nodded along, asked a few questions, and left without saying goodbye.

“Boy was he cheerful,” I noted after Underwood left.

“He’s probably as stressed as Stone,” replied Grandma.

“Hopefully, the police will find a fingerprint,” I said, feeling hopeful.

“You know what this means?” Grandma said, looking at me.

I did. “Stone was right about the ring being planted on Doris. The killer was framing someone.”

“Not someone. Clara Hackett.”

“I see why the killer chose Clara. She makes a good suspect.”

Grandma nodded.

The bookstore’s phone rang, ending the surreal moment. I felt obligated to answer it. We headed toward the counter. “Hello Teresa’s Bookstore, how can I help you,” I said my usual greeting. I felt Grandma's eyes on me.

“Hello,” a distinctly male voice said. “I’m looking for Garnet Stone.”

“This is her,” I said just as Princess jumped up, making me jerk back a step.

“Hello, Garnet,” his voice perked up, “I’m Hank Bingham. I’m Teresa’s lawyer.”

CHAPTER 37

An hour later I sat at Spaghetti Tree, the best Italian restaurant in my opinion. The owners weren't from Italy, yet they perfected their skills up north before setting their roots just outside of Sevier Oak. I loved the logo, a maple tree made out of spaghetti noodles. Spaghetti Tree was notorious for hosting parties like graduations, holiday dinners, and birthdays.

And business meetings.

A headache was coming, a sign that I'd been overworked, overthinking, and overly stressed. Hank Bingham didn't say what was so important, just that he needed to talk to me. I ran my garnet charm up and down the chain. My thoughts circled around the same questions. What is this about? Why now?

I took several sips of water, waiting for Teresa's lawyer. Glancing at other people, I suddenly felt underdressed. Megan offered me one of her sundresses. It was a little big, but I didn't want to sweat in dress pants. If I had more time, my hair would've been curled or wrapped up. Since I had a moment, I found a pen and a thin hair bow at the bottom of my purse and wrapped my hair into a cute messy bun. I'd done this enough at the bookstore to know it was an improvement.

For the millionth time, I checked the time on my phone. For a man claiming this was urgent, he seemed to be taking his sweet time. After the waiter refilled my water, a short-rounded man appeared. He gave an apologetic smile.

"Sorry, Miss Stone," he said, taking the chair across from me. "I accidentally passed the place and had to do a U-turn." He held out his hand and we shook. "Hank Bingham. Teresa's good friend and lawyer."

"Please, call me Garnet."

Hank beamed. My nervous jitters eased as I sensed a friendly, bubbly vibe from him.

"Do you know what you're ordering?" he asked, scanning the laminate menu. "It's been a while since I've been here." A waiter walked by, and he waved two fingers over.

Quickly, I looked over the menu while Hank gave his order. I picked a chicken salad with extra croutons and handed the waiter my menu.

Hank hadn't stopped smiling since he sat down. He was bald at the top of his head with short combed hair on both sides. His brown eyes were full of life. His cheeks were slightly red, adding to his friendly personality. I understood why Teresa chose Hank Bingham to be her lawyer.

"I've heard so many good things about you," said Hank. "Teresa was very fond of you. I also heard you ran the bookstore all by yourself. Bravo." He gave me two thumbs up. "It shows me that you're independent and self-sufficient. Very good qualities."

"Thank you," I said, not knowing how to respond.

Hank's smile grew, revealing very white teeth. "You have a very strong case. A very good thing to have in a position like this."

"What case?"

Did Hank know something about Teresa's murder?

"When Teresa rewrote her will back in January, I tried to convince her to leave it as it was." Hank frowned, without completely losing his cheerfulness. "Teresa always had a soft spot for her niece. Originally, she wanted Jane to only inherit the house and some personal belongings, but as you know now, Jane also inherited the bookstore, Teresa's car, and everything inside her home."

I shifted in my seat, not knowing where this meeting was going. I felt compelled to nod. Hank's wide smile returned. Then he placed a briefcase over his lap and began searching inside.

I sipped on my water, trying to figure out why I had been brought here. Did Hank stumble upon a clue? Did Teresa's will point to the killer? Was Teresa the intended victim and Doris's death became a red herring? I had no way of answering these questions, since the will had been read in New York among Teresa's family. The suspense made my leg bounce.

Finally, Hank set down his briefcase and flashed another smile. "The look on your face tells me that Jane Jackson failed to inform you about the second part of the will."

"Second part?"

"Correct. Teresa wrote in her will that if Jane refused any part of the inheritance, then it would go to you, Garnet. Including the bookstore."

"Me?" I nearly choked on the air. I took a drink as Hank waited. "Let me get this straight." I set the glass down a little too hard by accident. "If Jane had turned down Teresa's offer... then I would have gotten everything?"

Hank beamed. "Yes."

I took a deep breath and then another drink. Then it dawned on me. "You want me to contest the will?"

His big hands clapped, momentarily silencing the room. "Correct. When I address this matter to the judge, I'll add that you are very wise and intelligent."

I wanted to say something, but my voice refused to come.

"I called you as soon as I heard about Jane Jackson being charged for the murder of Doris Hackett." He spoke as if this was great news. "Murder gives you a very strong case. You can take what should've been yours from the start."

This news didn't set well because Jane didn't kill anyone. Still, a little voice reminded me about Jane's deceitfulness. She planned on selling her aunt's bookstore from the get go. I ran it on my own, and her emails never hinted about closing its doors.

Why didn't Jane tell me about the second part?

"I thought Teresa was being too kind to her niece, and tried to reason with her," Hank said. "I've dealt with other family's dramas more than my own. Teresa's family never came to Tennessee. Why is that? I wondered." He paused to let it sink in, but I already knew why Jane never visited. She was too busy following her family's career path to notice that she could leave. "Teresa loved Jane more than Jane loved her. Jane's arrest gives you a very strong case. You're already proven you can run a business."

While Hank repeated the same information, just in a different way, I daydreamed about myself as the new owner. The remodel could start by next week. I would choose the contractor— probably someone near Bristol to avoid Mateo and Preston. Princess and Butterscotch didn't have to find a new home. I could reorganize the layout the way I'd always wanted: cozy and well organized.

My way. My rules.

Then I recalled my recent memories of Jane. She went from wearing suits to yoga pants and tennis shoes. Her flipping through a book, even though it had been purchased at Voss-of-Books. The words she said about Regan was what made me write back. Even Jane's messy backseat made me miss her.

"You are a Stone," Hank's words brought me back to the present. He briefly extended his arms out wide, blocking a waitress's path. "Everyone in Sevier Oak knows the good name. Heck, people in Bristol know Stone and Onyx. I strongly believe the judge will rule in your favor."

"Can I ask you something?"

"Yes, of course."

"I want to cover all my bases. What if the police made a mistake and Jane is innocent? Then what?" Deep down I didn't want to go behind Jane's back to get ownership, but curiosity compelled me to ask.

If Hank was nervous by my question, he didn't show it. His smile kept going like the energizer bunny. "Based on the information I received, that would be unlikely. If Miss Jackson is found innocent, then her reputation is forever ruined. Court cases take months if not years to resolve, by that time you could have a year's worth of profit."

I listened for the part if Jane's case was dropped, instead Hank talked about Jane being jobless and how she quit after losing her first case. Before I could defend why Jane didn't want to be a defense attorney, our waiter arrived with our dinner. This gave me the chance to consider this opportunity.

I knew in my heart that the police arrested the wrong person. But if I contested Teresa's will, then I knew for a fact that Teresa's Bookstore would reopen. I felt like the little girl in Voss-of-Books from the other day. I held two books in my hands, but could only pick one.

CHAPTER 38

THE FRESH AIR FELT GOOD. I SAT ON A WOODEN BENCH, ADMIRING Crockett Park. The summer evening lost some of its heat making it tolerable as night approached. Light posts dotted along the walking path; one by one they automatically came to life. In the near distance, traffic flowed at a steady pace while the woods surrounding the park, slowly darkened by the minute. Behind me, a baseball game was being played. Every now and then, the crack from a metal bat dinged, followed by erupting cheers. Then everything went quiet once more. This was the perfect location for both worlds— a city life and peaceful nature. I was alone, yet not completely so.

A handful of dog walkers and people walked along the paved path. One jogger came by and we gave each other a friendly wave as he ran by. As his footsteps faded away, I welcomed the sound of the nightly crickets.

I often came here during difficult times to unwind my thoughts, by sitting on this very bench. My visits started after I obtained my driver's license. I needed to be alone without anyone hovering over me. Crockett Park gave me the space I desired. During my teens, my worries mostly consisted of Mom and Brad. Then it slowly faded to other things; normal stress of work, worrying about my future, and other everyday drama. I also sat here shortly after Dad moved to Nashville. I didn't realize how much I missed him until our main communication went from talking at my grandparent's dinner table to emails. Regan's email also brought me here. I cried on this spot after I learned about Teresa's passing.

Now my thoughts raced on other things.

A stick snapped close by. I spun to my right, scanning the forest. It sounded close. Too close. Yet as I stared from tree to tree, I saw nothing. The tiny hairs on my neck prickled. A strange sense told me that I was being watched, and it wasn't a cute forest animal.

Is Clara spying on me? Or the mysterious stalker?

I screamed when something wet touched my hand and jerked my hands up. I gasped seeing a big blotch of black. It took me a few seconds to realize it was a dog. Its big brown eyes gazed at me as if wondering why I wasn't giving it love. The dog's nose twitched, looking sad. I recognized the dog's stocky build and the black coat with the famous brown patches over its eyes. A rottweiler. The only unusual feature was its long tail. *At least it's wagging*, I thought.

"Jade," a man called. The dog tilted its head back, causing its tongue to roll out.

I looked over and saw a man jogging up to us. "Leo?"

Leo slowed his pace to a walk. When he reached us, he picked up Jade's leash. He stood in front of me, catching his breath. Instead of business casual apparel, Leo wore athletic wear with the Under Armour logo showing. He looked like a jogger who was out of practice.

I turned away and found Jade staring at me. When our eyes met, the dog saw this as an invitation to lick me.

"Stop licking," Leo said. "Sit." The dog obeyed. Those big brown eyes gazed up at him. "Sorry," he said to me, "she's still learning."

"She's big." I petted her large head. Jade closed her eyes, enjoying this moment.

"Jade is a German rottweiler. They're bigger and their fur is darker compared to American rotties."

I smiled. Jade's head was huge. She leaned into me as I stroked her side.

Leo took a seat next to me. "You look nice."

I crossed my legs, secretly glancing at myself. I forgot I had borrowed one of Megan's summer dresses. It did look nice on me.

"You came to the store yesterday. I wanted to say hi, but you left."

I almost forgot about being at Voss-of-Books for a second time, but not Drake's words. An awkward silence fell upon us when I didn't acknowledge it. After Jane's arrest, finding a hollowed book with a ring box, and Hank's offer, I didn't know how to respond. Instead, I kept petting Jade. She didn't mind.

"Rough day?" Leo shifted, and our knees barely touched. I tried to ignore the sensation by focusing on Jade.

I realized my silence was making things weird. It wasn't Leo's fault that Drake said harsh things to me. Deep down, I knew Leo wasn't like his gramps. We didn't have to be enemies or boyfriend and girlfriend, but friends. I debated a few moments about how much I should tell Leo. "It's been a long week."

"Sounds like we're in the same boat."

I moved so I could see him and Jade. The light from the streetlamp gave Leo a sexy glow.

Stop it, I mentally chided myself. If I wanted us to be friends, I couldn't find him attractive. "What happened?"

"Work drama. I see why Teresa let Sasha go."

"Let me guess, she's not doing her job. Playing on her phone. Not talking to customers."

He gave an annoyed look. "Every employee is complaining about her. Gramps also doesn't handle drama well. His first reaction is to get rid of the problem, but I would rather give someone the chance to correct their mistakes." He paused, staring into the distance as if contemplating of he should reveal more. I waited for him to work through his thoughts. After a long moment, Leo continued. "Gramps can be difficult to work with. Job applicants are non-existent. We can't afford to lose one, including one who barely works."

"Please don't offer me a position," I said.

Leo smirked. "I would never insult you."

My face warmed. This time, I didn't care if he saw. For a moment I wished he acted like Drake so it would be easy to hate him.

Leo leaned back. For a moment I thought he was going to drape one arm along the bench, covertly putting it around me. Thankfully, he didn't. I didn't want us to get much closer, physically, or emotionally. Grandma's words popped to mind about the Stone family being difficult. I shoved that thought away.

Jade laid down with a heavy huff. Part of her body laid over my feet. I couldn't find it in my heart to move them.

"I think your dog is tired."

Leo nodded as he glanced down before turning his full attention on me. "I'm sorry to hear about Jane." He sounded sincere.

"She didn't kill anyone."

"I hope you're right. She doesn't come across as that malicious. It seems like Jane was...bait? That's not the right word but you know what I mean." He thought for a moment. "Collateral damage, so to speak."

"It's frustrating," I admitted. All the clues pointed to different suspects, yet Jane was getting blamed for it.

"I'm frustrated, too. My dad has some issues at one of his stores in North Carolina." He eased his tense face and his shoulders relaxed. "Sorry. My drama is nothing compared to yours."

"It's okay. We all have troubles." I huffed. "I turned down the chance to take over Teresa's Bookstore."

Leo's eyebrows shot up.

I gave him the short version of the case, the unusual clues, the suspects, and Teresa's voice message. While telling him this, it felt good. Peaceful even.

A smile grew over his lips. "Spying on my employees? I thought you were better than Clara."

I laughed the same time Jade shot to her feet. Her ears perked up, staring into the woods. Leo and I perked up too, listening. The only sounds were from vehicles driving. I realized the baseball game had ended.

"It's probably just a squirrel." Leo petted Jade's back while her focus remained locked on the forest.

My heart raced, hoping Leo was right about it being a furry, forest animal. I had my doubts as the nagging feeling of being watched intensified. Someone was out there. I studied the trees, trying to see a figure. But it was too dark to see anything.

Leo was about to say something when Jade growled. Shivers shot up my spine. Leo wrapped one arm around me, holding me close. I leaned in, looking where Jade was staring. Again, I didn't see anything.

"I say let the police solve it," Leo said. Unlike me, he sounded calm, yet kept watch. "If there are any fingerprints on the book or ring box, they have to investigate."

"But what if there's not. I can't sit back and let Jane go to prison. None of the clues point to her. I have a theory on how the killer dun-it."

"Let's hear it. I like a good—"

Jade barked, lunging forward. Leo jumped to his feet, nearly knocking me over, to stop her from bolting. Leo commanded something in German, stopping Jade, yet her attention never wavered. Even in the growing darkness, I noticed her stiff body and raised fur. I stood up at the same time something ran within the forest. The crunched leaves and breaking sticks froze me in place. It sounded much larger than a squirrel. Thankfully, whatever was running travelled further away. It wasn't long before the air went quiet again. Jade relaxed and gazed up at her owner. She had a prideful look about her.

It was over, yet my heart kept pounding.

Leo touched my elbow. "You wanna grab some coffee or dinner?"

"Thank you, but I'm not hungry."

We stood in place as katydids and crickets sang their nightly tune. It calmed me. I sensed Leo didn't want to leave. Neither did I.

"Well," he finally said, "Jade and I should get going. Maybe we should do this again. Vent to one another." He reached into his pocket and pulled out his wallet. A moment later, he handed me his card. "Ignore the front. My personal number is on the back."

I smiled as I took the business card. His number was hand written in blue on the back side. A warm feeling blossomed inside of me. It was like he handed me the stuffed leopard all over again.

"If you ever wanna talk or buy another bookmark, just give me a text."

The bookmark comment made my smile grow. "Maybe I will."

He and Jade started to leave when he stopped. "Let me at least walk you to your car."

Jade walked between us as we headed toward the parking lot. Stars slowly made their appearance as the sun lowered behind the Smoky Mountains. I enjoyed this moment. Yet, I couldn't completely relish it. Jade focused on the tree line. I tried to dismiss the creepy sensation of being followed. Jade could've been seeing deer, they'd been known to be loud when running. I petted Jade's back, hoping to ease my fears. Her body felt tense, and I removed my hand.

"Next time we meet up," Leo said, "I'll give you a copy of that book."

I turned my head away from the forest. Leo still looked handsome. I liked this look better than business casual. "What book?"

"The hollowed out one. It was an Agatha Christie book, right?" I nodded. "It's a crime for someone to rip out pages and throw them away." He flashed a grin, showing me that he was teasing.

I froze. A thought just hit me.

Leo's lips frowned. "What? Did I say something wrong?"

My mind repeated what Leo said. If there weren't any fingerprints on the book or the ring box, what about the ripped paper? The ones the killer removed to hide a velvet box. If I remembered correctly, the hole was a few pages shy from the back cover. Over a hundred little pieces from Agatha's story went somewhere. Could those pages still be at the store? There was one way to find out.

"Garnet?"

Without thinking, I hugged Leo. He stiffened before easing

into me. Leo smelled like a mixture of men's deodorant and dog. I liked it.

"Sorry," I said, feeling my face warming. When I stepped back, Leo's green eyes gazed into mine. "You gave me an idea. I need to check something at the store."

A dorky grin crossed his face. "No need for apologies."

After saying our goodbyes and a final head rub for Jade, I power walked to my car. Once driving down the road, I called Megan.

Dishes clanked in the background when she answered. "Hey. Austin just left. I have leftover—"

"Leo gave me a crazy idea."

"Let's hear it."

CHAPTER 39

The receiving room looked like a tornado passed through. Armed with kitchen gloves, I dumped all Teresa's projects onto the floor and ripped open the trash bags from the past week. Thankfully, it wasn't much. After everything was scattered on the floor, I got on my hands and knees, making sure I didn't overlook anything.

Meanwhile, Princess stared at me from the entryway. Her yellow eyes were wide as if she was unsure if she should come in or not. For once I was glad Princess kept her distance. If the pages were here, I would find them faster without a nosy kittycat.

"Anything?" Megan's voice came from my phone, sounding tired.

I took in the mess I created. Nothing stood out or resembled ripped pages from a book. I let out a heavy sigh. "No."

"I don't think the killer was dumb enough to hide papers inside the receiving room. If I was them, I would've taken the pages home or thrown them in a random dumpster. Face it Garnet, those pages are long gone."

She had a point. The killer had a key, it made sense to throw the pages in a different location. Searching for another clue among the clutter was wishful thinking.

"I'll lock up and come home," I said, feeling defeated.

Megan gladly hung up. I wondered if the case was too much for her too, or if Austin had pushed her to visit his family, or maybe my grandparents had said something after I abandoned her. Perhaps all three. It seemed like all my problems now weighed a ton.

I turned off the light and walked toward the back staircase, leaving my mess for another day. Since I was here a few hours ago, I doubted the cats needed anything, yet it didn't feel right to ignore them. Butterscotch laid across the hallway floor. Her head perked up when she saw me. Princess headbutted her sister. Butterscotch playfully batted at her when Princess walked by.

The Cat's Lounge had a single window, overlooking Copper Street. Since daylight was gone, my reflection stared back at me in the window. It always unsettled me, knowing someone from outside could see me, but not the other way around at night. Yet the thought of turning off the light terrified me more. I suddenly felt alone, which was silly. I'd been alone in the store countless times. Somehow, this time felt differently. I had an urge to leave.

"Stop it," I muttered under my breath, blaming the uneasiness on the killer.

Something touched my leg. I jumped back, giving out a cry.

"Princess," I hissed.

The tuxedo cat gazed up at me, purring. My pounding heart slowly eased.

"I'm going to have a heart attack before the end of the night," I said.

Princess meowed.

I squatted and petted her for a few moments. Her purrs brought some peace, but I did want to leave. When I stood up to go, I noticed the trash can in Cat's Lounge hadn't been changed. Crumbled papers were visible. I didn't recall throwing anything away recently. If I threw something out, I normally used the office's trash can.

Wait? Could this be the ripped paper? My heart raced once more.

I snatched them up. The edges were jagged that fit in the palm of my hand. When I uncrumpled them, a flash of pink fell out. I knew what it was before it landed on the floor. Benadryl. Princess pounced on it.

"Oh my gosh," I said, putting the pieces together. The killer carried the allergy medicine. But why? I knew deep down it wasn't used to cure itchy watery eyes, coughing, or sneezing.

Then I focused on the pages still in my hands. Names jumped out at me as I read a few sections, Miss Marple, Mrs. Bantry, and Ruby Keene. Characters from a book I read. The Body in the Library, by no other than Agatha Christie.

I placed the torn pages on the floor. I had to take a picture before I called Stone or Underwood. Then I glanced around. *Darn it*, I left my phone in the receiving room.

When I went into the hallway, I stopped in place. Butterscotch was gone. Princess's claws raced in front of me, running toward the main staircase. An eerie sense overwhelmed me. I hugged myself, feeling something in my dress. I forgot there were pockets in Megan's dress and found my phone.

Settle down, I thought to myself while stepping back into Cat's Lounge. The cats were probably playing.

First, I texted Stone a picture the ripped pages. I sent him another text message when the hardwood floor groaned.

I spun around. It came again. Closer. Without taking my eyes off the entryway, I tried calling Stone. My muscles tightened, feeling my blood pressure sky rocketing. I glanced down for a moment, hoping my fingers were calling Stone. Instead, I sent him a weird text message with a bunch of jumbled letters.

"Put the phone down," a voice spoke out loud and clear.

The phone slipped out of my hand when I saw the gun.

CHAPTER 40

"It was you," I said. My legs trembled.

Preston Powell stepped into the room, closing the gap between us. Anger fueled his eyes while keeping the gun pointed at me.

I was trapped.

Quickly, I scanned the room. Cat toys wouldn't help and breaking the window to scream for help took too much time. My breathing rapidly increased. I had to calm my nerves to escape. *Distract him*, my thoughts screamed. Tough mode style.

"You killed them," I said. "Why?"

Preston's face twitched. "I want those back. Pick them up and hand them over. Nice and slow."

My heart rate lessened. "I want to know why you killed Teresa," I said, hoping to sound brave. "You killed Doris because you hated her, but why Teresa?"

Preston studied me as if he was weighing how much to tell me. Before he could, my cell phone rang. Stone.

"Kick it toward me." He nodded toward my feet. I did. While keeping his eyes on me, he picked up my phone. He held it up, reading the name while keeping an eye on me. As the ringtone played, I managed to slow my breathing and was able to concentrate. Moves replayed through my mind. If he lowered the gun, or stepped closer, I could escape.

"Other than Leo and Megan, did you tell anyone you were here?" he asked.

"You followed me from the park."

Jade sensed him.

"Answer my question," Preston's tone deepened.

"No," I lied, hoping Stone was on the way. "Just them." I almost added that Megan would be suspicious if I wasn't home in another ten minutes. I needed more time. "Now answer my question. Why?"

Preston slipped my cell phone into the back pocket of his jeans. At that moment, I saw a finger bandaged. Unanswered clues started to add up. I bet it was Preston's bloods on the stuffed bear.

"Doris was always selfish. She always wanted more money. In order to make my sweetheart happy, that meant I had to work longer hours and stay out later." His tone didn't match the fury in his eyes. He sounded happy to get this off his chest. "But Doris didn't like me working more either. I bent over backwards for her. She didn't understand hard work. I had a business to run."

He paused for a moment, feeling he was getting carried away. The gun moved while Preston rolled his shoulders. *Keep him talking.*

"You stole Sasha's keys," I said. "When you were walking around the store, taking notes for the remodel. You used the opportunity to steal them."

Preston frowned as if he was impressed.

"You've been following Doris." Preston was the mysterious stalker Clara saw snooping around Doris's house. He was spying on his ex-wife to learn her routine. "But something went wrong when you were hiding the knife and box," I added. "Teresa was here."

"I thought the store was empty." He shrugged. "I'm sorry for your loss, but Teresa saw too much. I had to silence her."

Tears stung my eyes, but I refused to let one fall. "After you made Teresa's death look like an accident, you finished your plan. By that time, you already broke into Doris's house to steal Clara's ring. Then you put the ring in a hollowed book along with the knife you planned to kill Doris with." I pointed my finger, hearing my voice go up an octave. "That's why you took your sweet time repairing Karl's upstairs bathroom. You convinced him to switch to Diet Coke and put in Benadryl when he wasn't looking. All that was left was to wait for Doris to show up and make your move. It was supposed to be a quick attack without having to carry the items to do it."

"It was about time Doris showed up." He sneered. "Karl was getting on my case." He came a step closer.

"Doris threatened you with the knife," I practically spat out. Just a little more time. "She found the book before you got to it."

He chuckled. I didn't like it. "Doris didn't know how to use a drill, let alone a pocketknife. I always have one, but it's stupid to carry the one I plan to kill my ex-wife with." Then he shook his head, annoyed. "Of all the damn books, she picked up that one. She looked so confused staring at the ring in that box. I bet she didn't even realize it was gone." Preston shook his head at his comment before turning serious. "I did what I had to do. I grabbed the tea kettle and that pillow. After I whacked her a good one, I suffocated her. Turns out that I didn't need the knife after all, just used the junk around me."

Don't stop

"You planted the ring on Doris, trying to target Clara. The bear must have had your blood when Doris attacked you."

Preston laughed. Unfortunately, his eyes didn't waver. "I told you the truth. I did cut myself while working on Karl's bathroom. When I heard you and Jane running, I had to get out of there real quick. I didn't realize I had cut myself until later. That sheriff never suspected me. He never asked *me* for a DNA sample." He sounded proud of himself.

That answered the blood, but not the bear. Then, the final piece clicked. "You stole more than just Clara's ring. Doris kept the stuffed bear from Mateo. The night you killed Teresa, you hid the bear somewhere in the store, and put it in plain sight after the crime." It bugged me that I didn't notice the bear while cleaning the store, yet I didn't feel the need to look through Teresa's projects tucked away in the receiving room.

"You made a mistake," I continued. "You tried to put the blame on two people. All the clues didn't point to one person, it confused authorities. But if you had focused on just one person, you might have pulled off the perfect crime."

"It doesn't matter now. That new owner is taking the blame."

While Preston nonchalantly confessed to being the mysterious witness, I listened for the cowbells. Stone should be here any moment. Then I realized my mistake. The doors were locked. Unless they broke the glass, Stone had to find another way inside. If Preston heard Stone, this would turn into a hostage situation.

I had to disarm him.

Preston took another step. I sensed my time drawing to an end. When I shifted my feet, Preston's glare hardened. "Don't be doing any funny business, little Stone. I can make this fast."

Something moved behind Preston. I forced myself to not

look, fearing Preston would fire the gun. I asked another question to buy myself more time.

"You attacked me and planted my purse at Clara's house. Why?"

I ignored the moving figures behind him. Staring Preston in the eye was frightening. My chest tightened, forcing me to breathe slowly.

"You're right. I did make a mistake. When I saw Jane being arrested, I thought that went better than I planned. But then they let her go. I figured there was no better way to add suspicion on the town's spy than to attack a Stone." He gave a cocky smile. "In a way it worked, because the police never suspected me."

The hardwood creaked loudly as if the gun had gone off. Everything happened so quickly. Preston turned around at the same time there was shouting. I made my move by leaping toward Preston. I hip-checked him to the floor at the same time Stone grabbed Preston's arm that held the gun. The weapon went off, shooting a hole into the ceiling, before Preston thudded to the floor. He cried out in pain.

"Let go of the weapon," Underwood shouted over him with his own gun drawn out.

Preston did as he was ordered. Stone and I held Preston in place until Underwood cuffed him.

"Ha," I laughed at myself, "I solved the murders after all."

CHAPTER 41

Grandma handed me a glass of sweet tea with two lemon slices. I took a large gulp, welcoming the taste. Later, when everyone was gone, I would fix myself a bourbon iced tea.

Megan sat across from me, staring at her untouched tea.

"I'm fine," I told her for the millionth time. "Preston didn't even touch me."

"You shouldn't have been there at night by yourself." Grandma used the tone she reserved for Dad. She plopped in a chair next to me, giving me a concerned glare. "It's a good thing Stone broke the back door's lock. Otherwise, things could have ended very badly."

"How was I supposed to know I was being followed," I explained. "At least I remembered how to defend myself." I gave her my best smile.

While Grandma remained upset, Stone walked to his chair with a proud face. Grandma noticed and glared at him. I knew their car ride home wouldn't be a quiet one.

"It's over," I said, trying to ease the tension. Once I said those words, reality sunk in. Everything would go back to normal. Jane was innocent. Teresa got justice. Best of all, the bookstore was saved.

Grandma patted my hand, easing further tension. "I'll give you a piece of advice that I learned while sleuthing— if you're going to do something stupid, be smart about it."

Being alone at the bookstore wasn't stupid, but now wasn't the time to argue. Yes, Preston could have shot me, making me his third victim, but how was I supposed to know that I was being followed? Instead of arguing, I nodded at Grandma's words of wisdom and sipped my tea.

"I should have been there," Megan said.

"Yes, because your sneezing fit would have scared Preston away," I teased.

That earned me a chuckle from Megan and Stone, but Grandma still didn't have a spot of humor.

"What's done is done," Grandma said to Megan. "Hopefully this will be the last time you'll be in danger." Her eyes landed on me.

We sat in silence drinking our tea. Megan brought out a cheesecake from the refrigerator, leftovers from her date with Austin. With forks in hand, we dove in. While we ate, the remaining discomfort faded. Nothing could go wrong with dessert and sweet tea.

I eyed Megan. "I told you Jane didn't do it."

"Yeah, yeah." She waved a hand at me, her way of showing that she was also joking.

"Your father is going to be upset," said Grandma. "I'm letting you tell him what happened."

I looked at Megan shaking my head as she resisted a giggle. Grandma finally gave a little grin. All was forgiven— not that I did anything wrong, but again I wouldn't argue.

"There is one thing that I don't understand," I said.

Megan sighed. "Just one thing?"

"Why did Preston do it? I mean, he and Doris divorced years ago. Why kill her now?"

We turned to Stone. He took his time chewing and taking a drink of his beverage. My foot started tapping while Megan widened her eyes, growing impatient. Only Grandma seemed relaxed.

Finally, Stone said, "He snapped."

Megan lowered her head, confused. "Snapped?

"Plotting to kill his ex-wife at a bookstore doesn't sound like he just 'snapped,'" I added.

"Before I retired," Stone replied, "Preston called the station often. He complained that Doris showed up at job sites or raced by his home. I don't think he was completely lying, but I think he blew the story out of proportion. Preston was furious about the cabin and how Doris won that money. I think he just had enough and thought the only way to deal with Doris was to kill her. He snapped and then he planned."

"Why couldn't he just move?" Megan said.

I agreed. Moving away seemed easier than trying to get away with murder.

"We suggested that too. But Preston's business was here. He couldn't afford to leave and start over again."

"And he was stubborn," Grandma grumbled. "I think he thought Doris would move first."

"Some people think death is the solution," said Stone.

It was nice listening to crime stories once more, but as enjoyable as it was to participate, I never wanted to be in the action again. Books were my kind of thrill.

"Why did Doris keep that bear?" Megan asked. "It's weird to keep something an ex-boyfriend gave you. I threw away everything Roland gave me the day we broke up."

I understood why. I never dated Leo, but I didn't have the heart to get rid of the stuffed leopard. "Perhaps Doris had feelings for Mateo but didn't like him working long hours, just like with Preston."

The doorbell rang. I raced to the front door before Stone. I expected to see Deputy Underwood, but when I opened the door, I saw a happier face. "Jane," I said as we embraced in a hug.

CHAPTER 42

THE PLACE LOOKED ENORMOUS WITHOUT THE ROWS OF BOOKSHELVES, towers of novels piled in spots, the counter used for ringing up customers, all the furniture, and Teresa's unique treasures. I released a squeal. Teresa's Bookstore was about to get bigger.

It was finally happening. The remodel.

Princess darted across the hardwood floors followed by Butterscotch. If Teresa had known how stunning the floors were under the green carpet, she would have ripped them out a long time ago. Especially seeing the cats at play. I laughed while watching their game of fun.

"Are you ready for them?" I asked Jane.

She appeared at my side holding two cat carriers. With her hair in a high ponytail, and wearing blue jeans and steel toe boots, Jane looked more than ready for our next adventure.

"I did have a cat growing up. I can handle them until the store is back in order."

I smirked, thinking these two cats might be a lot to handle. Secretly, I hoped to visit them soon.

Jane gazed at the empty store while the cat's played. "I never would have thought this place was so big."

"I know," I said, admiring the scene.

Jane retrieved the blueprint from a bag she brought. She unrolled it and held it up. We glanced between the blueprint and the store, mentally picturing what the new store would look like.

Part of the second floor would be removed to create a loft area as well as the staircase by the bargain room. I visualized the layout— me choosing a book from the kids' section, reading to them as they circled around me. The space also gave us the option to host small events, maybe start a book club. Peggy Sue would have plenty of space for kids to read to her.

After a lot of measuring and calculations, we had enough space for the conservatory framework. Jane agreed to put glass inside for customers to enjoy a sitting area and sip their coffee, without Princess making a mess. Cat's Lounge remained as it was along with a small office and bathroom. Meanwhile, downstairs would be the sales floor, but well organized and accepting only a certain number of copies per book title. And, of course, the glass for the floating books.

"I'm glad you came around to the idea," I said, as Jane rolled up the blueprint. In the previous weeks, we worked long hours to pack up everything in the storage units. I'd learned that Jane had a soft spot under her serious-shell as I called it. She loved reading historical books, and seemed just as excited about the update.

I hadn't forgotten the mess in the backseat of her car. If I wanted the store to be neat, I'd have to maintain that side of Jane.

"I had a lot of help."

I concealed an eye roll. "Yes, Leo was very helpful moving the big stuff." A few days ago, he, Austin, and Roland helped load the bookshelves onto trucks and moved them into the storage units. I still hadn't called Leo for a date. Once I got to know him better, without fearing he might turn into Drake, I'd make the call.

"I meant you, Garnet," Jane said. "You've been helpful." Then her tone turned serious. "I've been thinking. Since we are updating my aunt's store, maybe a new name is in order. New owner. New layout." Her brown eyes stared into mine, worried. "What do you think? Do you like it?"

I blinked a few times. "I've never thought about renaming the place."

"We can keep it, if you want. But if we do change the name, my aunt will always be a part of this place. I want a picture of Teresa on the wall when she first opened the store. Actually—" She paused for a moment, giving me a certain grin. I'd learned this was her guilty face, yet she wasn't really sorry. "I've already made it into a canvas. It's in my car. Can Austin hang it in the house until I hang it in here?"

"I'm sure one more thing in the house will be fine."

Jane's eyebrows narrowed. "What does that mean?"

I refrained from telling Jane that Teresa's house has become a bigger mess since she moved in. Instead, I said, "I like the idea of renaming the store. Let's do it."

Jane smiled wide. "What do you think of Bind Me Again Bookstore?"

"Bind Me Again Bookstore," I said aloud. "I love it. We have to use it."

Behind us the cowbells clanged. "*Hola*, are you *señoritas* ready to get started?" Mateo asked as he and his crew walked inside.

Jane beamed and met Mateo halfway. This was my cue to get the cats in the carriers so Jane could take them to her house. Before I grabbed Butterscotch, the easy one, my phone dinged with a new email. After my encounter with Preston, Dad emailed me at least once a day and called when he had a free moment. The air sucked out of me when I saw the subject line. I opened it and quickly read it.

"Garnet. Hey, Garnet."

I looked up and saw Megan on the other side of the window. She stood on the sidewalk, holding two pastry boxes. "What's wrong?" Megan asked me.

I played with my necklace's charm, feeling tears bubbling. I had to walk outside and tell her the news.

"Is something wrong? Is Mateo delaying the remodel?"

I shook my head, wiping away a tear. "No, everything is great." I held up my phone. "Regan wrote back."

The End

ABOUT THE AUTHOR

Jessica Brimer is a Tennessee native who spends most of her time writing and far more time browsing the bookshelves at her local library. Growing up, Jessica was fascinated with the mystery genre, which sparked her desire to write them. If she isn't spending time with her two kids and husband, you can almost always find her dabbling with essential oils while reading something mysterious.

To learn more about Jessica Brimer and discover more Next Chapter authors, visit our website at www.nextchapter.pub.

A Binding Chance
ISBN: 978-4-82414-866-7

Published by
Next Chapter
2-5-6 SANNO
SANNO BRIDGE
143-0023 Ota-Ku, Tokyo
+818035793528

25th August 2022